THE
CONFESSIONS
OF
MATTHEW STRONG

Ousmane K. Power-Greene

OTHER PRESS
NEW YORK

Production editor: Yvonne E. Cárdenas
Text designer: Jennifer Daddio / Bookmark Design & Media Inc.
This book was set in Cochin and Octin Spraypaint by
Alpha Design & Composition of Pittsfield, NH

1 3 5 7 9 10 8 6 4 2

Library of Congress Cataloging-in-Publication Data
Names: Power-Greene, Ousmane K., author.
Title: The confessions of Matthew Strong / Ousmane K. Power-Greene.
Description: New York : Other Press, [2022]
Identifiers: LCCN 2022002762 (print) | LCCN 2022002763 (ebook) |
ISBN 9781635422085 (hardcover ; acid-free paper) |
ISBN 9781635422092 (ebook)
Subjects: LCGFT: Novels.
Classification: LCC PS3616.O88336 C66 2022 (print) |
LCC PS3616.O88336 (ebook) | DDC 813/.6—dc23/eng/20220307
LC record available at https://lccn.loc.gov/2022002762
LC ebook record available at https://lccn.loc.gov/2022002763

Publisher's Note: This is a work of fiction. Names, characters,
places, and incidents either are the product of the author's
imagination or are used fictitiously, and any resemblance
to actual persons, living or dead, events,
or locales is entirely coincidental.

THE CONFESSIONS OF MATTHEW STRONG

ALSO BY OUSMANE K. POWER-GREENE

Against Wind and Tide: The African American
Struggle against the Colonization Movement

For my grandmothers,

HELEN ALLEN

and

MADELINE GREENE

And to all

THE BLACK FAMILIES

praying for the day their

MOTHERS, DAUGHTERS, SISTERS,

and

BROTHERS

come home

YET ALL THROUGH THE DARKEST PERIOD

OF THE COLORED WOMEN'S OPPRESSION IN THIS

COUNTRY HER YET UNWRITTEN HISTORY IS

FULL OF HEROIC STRUGGLE, A STRUGGLE AGAINST

FEARFUL AND OVERWHELMING ODDS, THAT OFTEN

ENDED IN A HORRIBLE DEATH, TO MAINTAIN AND

PROTECT THAT WHICH WOMAN HOLDS

DEARER THAN LIFE.

—ANNA JULIA COOPER

PROLOGUE

If you keep coming around here little girl people will begin to think you've taken a liking to Matthew Strong. I guess there are worse things than befriending an old man like me. But you don't seem like the sort of person who'd concern herself with what others say about her. Tell me something. How come you out here by yourself?

Oh, I see. These cats sure are cute. You got your eye fixed on one of them? Her? Why don't you pick her up and bring her closer so I can get a better look.

Yes, she's a pretty one indeed. I like ginger and white as well. Matter of fact, now that you got me thinking about it, I do recall seeing another cat just like her. They like to congregate out here near this abandoned shack.

I wasn't born with bad vision. In fact, I had about the best vision of any of the white or colored boys I used to play with when I was a kid. When them boys were waiting while their fathers weighed the cotton, they'd come out to where I'd be, pump gun on my shoulder, tin cans on a stump and a few dangling from a fishing line tied to a birch branch. I'd tell 'em they could borrow my pump gun if they'd give me a penny, and they'd say, "Nah." Then I'd cock the gun and shoot a pellet in one of them cans. I'd say, "Bet you can't hit none of 'em." They'd pull off their straw hats, making all sorts of bold claims. I'd laugh and bet 'em a dime they couldn't hit not one of 'em. Got 'em every time. I must've earned me ten dollars over the years.

You like stories?

Me too.

There was this old Negro who worked on my daddy's land used to always say, "Truth is buried within those tall tales old folks tell. You just gotta take the time to untangle them." But most young people these days ain't got no patience to figure out any of the stories I tell whether they're true or not.

I've learned over the years most people have a hard time accepting what's true even when it smacks them on the back of their head. But a man got no problem believing a pack of lies. Especially when he don't have the courage to make amends for his sins, and the lies he tells to justify 'em.

What's that? Time for you to go home?

You right. Bet your grandma be worried with you out here by yourself. Now, remind me again what you said your name is?

Oh, yes, Odessa, that's right. A beautiful name for a beautiful girl.

Before you go, you mind doing me a favor? Think you can help me find my brown leather book where I keep my stories? I dropped it somewhere in this shack when I was feeding them cats. My vision ain't so good no more.

You see, that leather book is where I keep those tall tales this old Negro used to tell me when I was a boy. You think you have time to listen to me read one?

Whichever one you like. Don't make a bit of difference to me. Maybe something short? It'll be dark soon. No telling what's in these woods.

BOOK I

DEATH

My God, My God, why did you abandon me?

—MATTHEW 27:46

I CANNOT SAY, WITH TRUTH, THAT THE NEWS OF MY OLD MASTER'S DEATH SOFTENED MY FEELINGS TOWARDS HIM. THERE ARE WRONGS WHICH EVEN THE GRAVE DOES NOT BURY.

—Harriet Jacobs, *Incidents in the Life of a Slave Girl*

PRESENT DAY

My name is Allegra Douglass.

I am one of the survivors.

My story may make you angry. Not necessarily at me, but about the reason things happened the way they did. Only looking back can I put the pieces together in a coherent manner, or at least in a way that makes any sense at all.

As a philosopher, I am drawn to problems. I'm fascinated by the relationship between ideas and actions; ideas behind our motivations; ideas beneath our fears. Some ideas, however, take you down paths best left unexplored; ground best left undisturbed.

Many newspapers, publishers, and magazines begged me to tell this story. But I have no desire for the media to frame my story as one of race redemption or progress from the days Klan night riders paraded openly down Sixteenth Street in Birmingham.

I refused to allow them to exploit the kidnap and torture of black girls. I wouldn't tell them what Matthew Strong confessed to me when I was trapped in that plantation home and forced to write his white supremacist mission to redeem the South. I refused to make him more well-known than men like Charles Manson or let him go down in history as some modern-day Nathan Bedford Forrest.

At least, that's what I told everyone who asked.

But what is the truth? The truth is that I feared having my name forever associated with Matthew Strong. And I feared, after people read my story, they would sympathize with his mission even if they deplored his methods.

And this was exactly what he wanted.

There are those who never believed I'd remain steadfast in my determination to withhold my story from the public. Some assumed when I finally accepted what happened I'd be ready to speak. Others shadowed my posts online, waiting like dogs for me to toss a bone, trying to anticipate when I would break my silence. One thing is for certain: all the talk in the world won't change anything.

So why have I decided to tell you this now? Maybe it's because of something my grandma used to say: "Let your faith be greater than your fear." Of course, she meant this from a Christian perspective, an entire system of beliefs I had abandoned when I entered college. I may still question the whole "Jesus died for your sins, on the third day he was resurrected, he ascended to heaven, and will come again to judge the living and the dead" thing. But now I find St. Paul's claim that "faith is the substance of things hoped for, the evidence of things not seen" to be a guiding principle. Maybe my fear has forced me to have faith that what I say will change the course of events unfolding just how Matthew Strong said they would.

Ever since I was liberated from the plantation home where Matthew Strong and his men held me and eleven other black women and girls, whenever I hear a southern accent, memories of my abduction return like mosquitoes at sunset hovering over my arm, darting through my fingers, daring me to slap so they can laugh and dash, laugh and dash.

That's how my memories come back to me. The first time after I heard a man's voice at my favorite coffee shop, another time when I came out of my apartment and stumbled into a UPS delivery man.

Then, I'm there again, feeling my legs go numb, my mind distorted by whatever they drugged me with. I hear the man who said he came to protect me ask if I feel strange—the ends of his words clipped like he was speaking into a fan. I glance at him and his concerned face melts into a cocky grin. Now he's laughing. They were all laughing, laughing, laughing.

Next, I feel them lift me through the air like a suitcase, before pushing me in the trunk. Keys click; the car engine revs. Windshield wipers slap against the glass, rapid beeping, then I black out.

When I woke, I had no idea how long we'd been driving or where we were. Had we left Alabama? Were we in Mississippi? At one point we stopped and I had to go to the bathroom badly. I tapped the trunk with my knuckles. Silence. I was desperate. I banged harder. Finally, I heard feet crunching over.

"If you keep banging, we're gonna have to give you more medicine. You wouldn't want that, now would you?"

"I have to go to the bathroom."

There was a pause.

Then I heard a beep and the trunk opened. Two masked men stood over me, one with a drawn pistol. The other held a machine gun strapped across his back. I had pulled down my blindfold, but they insisted I put it back on before they lifted me out of the trunk.

"Where are we?"

They said nothing as they walked me across gravel to the bushes.

"Go here."

"Can I at least take off my blindfold?"

I heard whispering, then I felt the barrel of a gun against my back as one untied it. I squinted, my eyes adjusting to the light. I pulled down my pants and squatted.

As I peed, I noticed a stretch of pine trees rising up a mountain range, but it was impossible for me to tell if we'd driven east to the Appalachian Mountains or south to the Oak Mountains. Think, Allie. One of them jabbed the gun against my back.

"Keep your eyes on the leaves or you'll be pissing with the blindfold on."

He surveyed the woods as if he feared someone would jump out and rescue me. Or was he trying to give me some respect? How ridiculous.

For a moment I considered running. But that'd be stupid. I had no idea where I was. They'd shoot me anyway.

I pulled up my pants and one took my arm and the other pressed his gun to my back again. I pleaded with them as the third one blindfolded me.

"Please. I'll pay you. My husband and I have money."

One of them laughed. I hated myself for begging, but I begged with all I had.

"Wait! Please!"

I shouted as they tied my hands behind my back and shoved me in the trunk.

We drove for a while and then stopped. Doors opened and closed. The trunk popped up and a flashlight shined through my blindfold.

I felt hands lift me out; then they marched me across a stretch of grass. Tears slipped from beneath my blindfold. I tried to prevent myself from sobbing. They were not tears of sadness, or even fear, although of course I was scared. They were tears of frustration. I had allowed myself to be caught off guard. I had let him outsmart me.

I heard a door squeak. They escorted me into a room. When they sat me in a chair, they untied the blindfold. I glanced up, blinking. Hazy. An arm dropped over my shoulder, pulling me close like an old friend. I didn't need to see his face to know who it was.

TWENTY-FOUR DAYS BEFORE
MY ABDUCTION

Two detectives—Detective Landers and Detective Kelley—showed up at my New York City apartment to ask about one of my only black graduate students, named Cynthia Wade. I offered tea, but they politely declined. Detective Landers put a banker box filled with books on my coffee table. He pulled a small spiral notebook from his front coat pocket and inquired about our relationship. I explained that Cynthia had left the program the previous fall, but she lived in my apartment building, so I still ran into her once in a while.

"And you two were close?" he asked, scribbling in his notebook.

I paused, wondering what this was about, wondering if they were investigating something Cynthia had done. There was a time in my life—fifteen years ago, perhaps—when I would have never let them into my apartment, let alone offered them tea. I thought about the detectives who used to show up at rallies posing as journalists, asking questions, taking down names. Then, a few days later, I'd find them sitting on the steps outside my apartment waiting to ask about someone they were looking for—a wanted activist, a former Panther, perhaps.

I crossed my arms. "Did she do something wrong?"

Detective Landers glanced over to his partner. "It seems a few weeks ago Cynthia vanished—phone's turned off, no ATM withdrawals. Roommates haven't seen her in weeks. One of them gave us this."

Detective Kelley motioned to the box they'd brought. "Some books in here have your name written inside."

I went through the stack, and noticed a copy of my latest book. I didn't remember Cynthia borrowing it from me.

"And there's that, too." Detective Kelley motioned to an envelope in the box. I noticed my name and address. There wasn't a postmark below the stamp.

"Did she collect your mail?" Detective Landers asked. His crew cut and pimpled cheeks made him look too young to be a detective.

"Sometimes. I used to have her stop by my apartment if I was away."

They looked at one another again. Detective Landers came forward, his hands in his suit pockets. "So, this letter came for you, and she picked it up?"

"I guess so."

I pulled the letter from the envelope. The investigators looked on, curiously.

Dear Dr. Douglass,

I have admired your work from afar for many years. Yet, this most recent book has misinterpreted the ideological roots of my cause. Me and others who have joined my movement are deeply concerned about how you misrepresented the noble design of men we deem true bearers of American democratic tradition. I look forward to the opportunity to speak with you in person about what you've failed to grasp despite a noble effort. It is my hope that the next time you find yourself in Alabama you will inform me and my associates so we may have the pleasure of conversing with you about these ideas and the relevance of your book for our current movement.

For the cause,
William Shields, Esq.

When I glanced up, both detectives had positioned themselves so they could read the letter over my shoulder.

"Do you know this William Shields?" Detective Kelley asked.

I laughed. "No, this has to be some prank."

"A prank? I don't follow you."

I shook my head. "You see, William Shields was a notorious white supremacist who led a reign of terror in Alabama after the Civil War."

"I apologize, professor." Detective Kelley folded her arms. "History was never my strongest subject. Rewind. You said this guy William Shields was some sort of racist terrorist in the 1870s?"

"That's correct. Okay, let me put it another way. You've heard of the Ku Klux Klan, right?"

"Of course."

"Well, scholars believe William Shields murdered more black political leaders and white sympathizers than the Klan in Alabama until the federal authorities caught him in 1873."

"What happened to him?" Detective Kelley asked.

"He was sentenced to death. But he did write a confessional, which chronicled his deeds and tried to justify his murders as an effort to 'redeem' the South after losing the Civil War."

"Really? I never heard of this guy," Detective Landers said.

"If you were from Birmingham, you would have. His father, Andrew Shields, was the wealthiest slaveholder in Alabama before the Civil War. After the war, he founded Birmingham Iron and Steel Company. Practically owned all mines in Jefferson County."

"Is that where you're from?" Landers asked.

"Alabama? Yes."

"Like Cynthia?"

"That's right." I didn't care for this guy. Did he actually think I had anything to do with her disappearance?

"Do you have any more questions? I really need to get some things done before I teach class."

"Actually, yes. One more thing. Tell me, have you ever received a letter like this before?"

"A few since my book came out."

"What's this one about?"

"The racial ideology of southern slaveholders."

"Southern slaveholders, huh? Men like William Shields, I gather?"

"Yes, that's right."

Detective Landers pulled out his cell phone. "Would you mind if I scanned that letter? You know, just in case?"

"In case of what?"

"Professor Douglass, have you ever done one of those thousand-piece puzzles? The kind that sits on the dining room table terrorizing you to complete it every time you walk past?"

"Are you suggesting this letter is a puzzle piece that'll help you figure out what happened to Cynthia?"

Detective Landers held out his open palm. I handed him the letter and he placed it on the coffee table to scan with his phone.

"I may not know where it fits"—there was a flash—"but I'm certain it's a piece."

Detective Kelley came over. "Thanks for your time and cooperation, professor. Please call us if you hear from Cynthia. Here's my card."

"Yes, of course," I said, as Detective Landers tucked his phone in his coat pocket and returned the letter.

All day the detectives and Cynthia's disappearance stayed on my mind. I thought about how often Cynthia visited my apartment after she learned I lived in her building. Sometimes she'd stop over to borrow books for a class. Once in a while, she'd stay and read on my couch. As I watched her immersed in a text, eyebrows squeezed together, feet hanging off the couch's arm pad, twirling her pen between her fingers like a baton, I thought of my graduate school days. She'd take a break and convince me to climb onto my fire escape to share a cigarette. Smoking with her made me feel youthful, rebellious. Back during graduate school, I smoked to stay awake and finish papers, or to calm my nerves before an exam. Since those days I had lost the desire to smoke. But, periodically, the urge seized me. My sister used to say desires embed in our mind, and even if we resist our urges, they remain like parasites. When Cynthia would return a book, she'd pull her sticky notes from the pages and lay them on the coffee table to scan with her phone. I asked why she did this and she explained that she had a digital folder with those notes that she could access anywhere, anytime.

Later that day I returned to my office after teaching my political violence seminar and noticed my department chair, Martin, loitering in the hallway, laughing loudly at something our secretary, Carolyn, had said. I was in no mood to chitchat, so I ducked inside and gently closed my door.

A few minutes passed and then there was a knock.

"Allie? Do you have a moment?"

I froze. Another knock. Keys rattled. The door opened.

"Oh! Professor. I'm sorry," Martin said awkwardly, as if he'd caught me changing my blouse.

"Is there a problem?" I asked.

"No problem."

He held up an envelope with my name typed across the front. He shook it like a ticket.

"I've been trying to catch you for two days now. I would've put it in your mailbox, but I wanted to leave it on your desk. It's quite something."

I slit open the envelope and read the letter:

Dear Professor Douglass,

It gives us tremendous pleasure to inform you that you've been awarded the Eli Jefferson Distinguished Chair in Philosophy…

I breathed a sigh of relief once I realized it wasn't another like the disturbing letter the detectives had brought earlier in the day signed "William Shields." I slipped the letter back in the envelope to read once he left.

"You realize," Martin said, "this is an honor not only for you but for the entire university. You're the first African American to hold a distinguished chair in the humanities—outside of Africana Studies, of course."

"Of course," I said, remembering all the times he'd questioned the rigor of my scholarship. Once he even asked sheepishly if I intended on publishing any of my articles in philosophy journals or only in African American studies ones. The nerve.

I usually ignored his condescending remarks, but once in a while I returned fire with a more recent philosophical interpretation I figured he was unfamiliar with. Martin, like my other senior colleagues, pontificated over antiquated ideas and sat atop thrones built on laurels earned back when black people had no real chance at professorships at an elite university in philosophy, or any academic discipline for that matter.

And now here I was being awarded a distinguished chair in the Philosophy Department, no doubt based on my third book on the philosophy of slaveholders in the age of the Civil War, which had been nominated for several major awards, including the Hannah Arendt Prize for best book on a topic related to genocide.

"Well," he continued, "I've already received a call from the president of the university about the event in your honor. And Sarah Jefferson, the niece, has requested we make haste in presenting you the award. She's adamant that her aunt—the widow of the late Eli Jefferson—be in attendance when the university awards you the prize. Mrs. Jefferson is in her nineties and hasn't been well lately. Your formal title as Eli Jefferson Distinguished Chair in Philosophy will be announced, of course, at commencement in May, but at least the administration hopes the family would turn over what will be a rather large financial gift soon. They'd like to include it in next year's budget. It'll be a symbolic chair, but the gift to the university and the department is real. Congratulations."

I read the first line of the letter again.

Finally.

I'd sacrificed so much on the hunt for this recognition. Yet, just as I caught hold of it, I had turned from hunter to prey.

Cynthia always hated Martin. Once she said she felt an urge to spray-paint "racist" on Martin's door after he dismissed Angela Davis as mediocre, claiming philosophers *like her* hadn't shaped the discipline. "Like her?" Cynthia had asked. "You mean black philosophers?" He scoffed at her insinuation and pointed out Davis books weren't scholarly. This only further infuriated Cynthia.

While I found Martin obnoxious, I knew he was no different from most liberal academics who clapped politely at my activist past but never regarded me as a serious scholar. It wasn't just Martin. Despite our president's liberalness, or his promises to "right the wrongs of the past" and create new initiatives to ensure all students "regardless of race, ethnicity, and gender identity" thrived, I didn't believe he had the courage to challenge our university's traditions. Even the flock of deans and associate deans of diversity had no real ability to dismantle the elitism and racism stitched into its DNA.

Cynthia and a few other graduate students had learned this firsthand when they abandoned the committee established to discuss renaming buildings named after slaveholders and decided to take more dramatic action. Last May, someone painted the Christopher Columbus statue in the middle of campus red. Rumors swirled that Cynthia was responsible. Once word got to the dean, rather than expel Cynthia and two others, he waited until the start of the fall semester to send her an email that claimed she was no longer eligible for her scholarship because of a previous incomplete. It was bullshit. I'd never heard of a graduate student losing funding for having an incomplete.

But what could I do?

Cynthia begged me to speak to the dean, hinting that if I threatened to resign, the dean would change his mind. I told her I couldn't, and she looked as if she had lost all respect for my years of activism. In fact, she stopped coming to my apartment to borrow books, although we texted back and forth occasionally. I figured eventually her anger would subside and we'd be on cordial terms. At least, that's what I hoped.

I don't regret my decision, yet I feel bad Cynthia was forced out. I mean, I warned her more than once that activists should never allow those in power to gain leverage over them. She had to excel in her coursework, especially in courses with white male professors like Martin. The first thing powerful people did was squeeze wherever they saw you were vulnerable. I should know. This was what happened to me.

When Martin left my office, I texted my husband, David, "I have news," and then my best friend, Michelle. David had gone to Philadelphia to interview a client, so I asked Michelle if she could meet for dinner last-minute. This was no night to be alone.

That evening I took a cab to a restaurant Michelle recommended near Madison Square Garden. The maître d' escorted me to a table by the window. I ordered a glass of wine and pulled out the letter and read it again. Eli Jefferson Distinguished Chair of Philosophy. Had I been someone else I would have posted a photo on social media of me holding the letter with a "told you so" grin. But I hesitated, worried someone from my former days as an activist would post a snarky comment about me "selling out" to the academy. I admit, I used to mock academics for abandoning the struggle against racial injustice for a cushy university job. Back then, I balked at Ivy League job postings Michelle and other friends forwarded to me and relished teaching adjunct in community colleges while I ran an education initiative in several area prisons.

I'd met Michelle in college. As we became close, my black friends jokingly referred to her as my "white best friend," a snide reference to the plethora of movies with white female protagonists and black "best friends" unthreatening to the hunk who remained central to the film. Of all my college friends, I always felt closest to her.

Two decades later, Michelle was my last college friend who lived in the city. Recent circumstances— which I'll get into later—led me to rent an apartment near campus. I spent the weekdays in this small one-bedroom apartment away from my house and husband in Westchester. The others had migrated to the suburbs after having kids.

Anyway, my husband, David, was much more social than me. He'd always received the invitations and made dinner plans customary for an attorney at a prestigious firm. As I approached my late thirties, I lost the energy to keep up with his insatiable desire to go out with colleagues.

Michelle never understood what I saw in David. He wasn't particularly handsome, but his confidence made up for it. He was the type of man you followed because you were curious to see if he was telling the truth or exaggerating. Maybe that's why our marriage faded. Maybe I lost my intrigue, and he lost interest in trying to captivate my attention—to lead me somewhere I'd never been.

Fifteen minutes and I was still solo, so I went ahead and ordered. But of course, the moment my food came I felt a hand on my shoulder.

"Allie?"

"I figured you weren't coming," I said.

"I'm so sorry. Jordan's soccer game went into double overtime."

The waiter approached. "May I bring you a menu?"

"No, thanks," Michelle said. "But could you bring two pieces of double-chocolate cake?"

The waiter left and Michelle leaned forward. "So, what's the big news?"

I pulled the letter from my bag. "My department chair gave me this."

She took it and read silently. When she came to the bottom of the page, she looked up, smiling.

"Wow, Allie! It's about damn time!" She leaned over and hugged me. "Does this mean you don't have to keep sucking up to your chair? What was his name?"

"Martin. Yes, I guess."

Michelle tilted her head to the side, then took my hand. "This is great news. Isn't this what you wanted?"

"It's not that. A couple detectives came by my apartment this morning."

"About what? Don't tell me they're still harassing you about Winfred."

"No, not that. I guess one of my former graduate students hasn't been seen in a while and her mother filed a missing person report."

"That's horrible."

"I know. That's not all."

I explained to Michelle about the letter someone left with Cynthia signed "William Shields," which I had interpreted as either a twisted joke or a threat. Either way, Cynthia's disappearance had me spooked. Michelle offered me her guest room for the night, but I declined. Which might have been a mistake. Yet, something inside me could not fathom some disgruntled white guy showing up at my apartment building, in

Harlem of all places, to hurt me, or kidnap Cynthia. I
told her I'd be fine.

When I returned to my apartment, I changed into
pajamas, then put on some Miles Davis to relax.
I sat on my bed, legs crossed, checking my phone to see
if Cynthia had replied to any of the text messages I sent
her after the police came.

I heard tapping on my window. I clicked on the
light. There it was again, gentle tapping.

Cynthia?

I opened the window shade, expecting to see
Cynthia on the fire escape like always, leaning against
the railing, smoking. To my disappointment, a
clothesline had snapped loose, and flailed against the
window with the breeze.

The first time I'd noticed a figure standing on
my fire escape I jumped, thinking I saw a ghost. Not
because of how she looked. You never see a ghost
in a movie represented as a thin dark-skinned black
woman with tight natural hair, lip piercings, and two
small rings dangling from her left eyebrow. She just
surprised me. When Cynthia smiled—which she did all
the time—her lips, brushed with purple, magenta, or
blue lipstick (depending on her mood), called your eyes.
If my teeth were that straight and white, I'd smile all
the time too.

Outside my window that night, Cynthia was equally surprised to see me—the only black professor in the department—living a few floors below. When I joined her, we talked until we saw the sun. Then she apologized for keeping me up all night, smiling flirtatiously as she climbed up to her place.

When I told Michelle about my encounter, she pushed me to confess I found her attractive. I denied it outright. No, she was too young, plus I wasn't like that.

"Like what," Michelle asked.

"You know what I mean. I haven't given up on my marriage yet."

"So?" Michelle said, nudging me. "Men do it all the time."

"Oh please. I'm not a man."

After a few nights without any response from Cynthia, I smoked for the first time since she and I had a cigarette on my fire escape months before. I flipped through the copy of my book the detectives had brought in the box with the letter. I noticed underlined passages in my book. I grumbled. It always annoyed me when people borrowed my books and wrote in them. Still, I was unsure why Cynthia borrowed it without asking. I would have just given her a copy. I paused at an underlined passage in a chapter about slaveholders' shift from utilizing positions to maximize physical pain, toward psychological torment as a means of discipline. By the 1850s, I had argued, this trend coincided with the emergence of pro-slavery rhetoric designed to recast slaveholders as enlightened and progressive rather than violent and reactionary. All of this was underlined.

As I continued reading, I was surprised to see she had highlighted quotes that referenced biblical prophecy. Like me, Cynthia had abandoned her Christian faith when she moved from the South and now subscribed to the Marxist view that religion functioned as a form of social control.

When I came to the end of the book, a piece of paper fell onto my lap. It had four handwritten columns with the names, death dates, and publications of slaveholder ideologues I wrote about in my book. The fourth column listed the archives I used to research their pamphlets and books. I noticed two commonalities among the slaveholders: each had completed at least one book or pamphlet that defended slavery; and each held a high-ranking position within the Confederacy. Strange that Cynthia would be so interested in all this. Then it hit me. I went to my desk and picked up the letter from whoever signed his name William Shields. I compared it to this list.

The handwriting was the same.

NINETEEN DAYS BEFORE
MY ABDUCTION

The next morning, I called Detective Landers about this discovery, and he asked me to stop by the station after I taught my 9:00 a.m. seminar on continental philosophy. On my way over to the station, I tried to relax, not overthink it and let my imagination get the best of me. I mean, after all, people didn't stalk philosophy professors, right? Why would they? As I strode up the precinct steps Detective Landers leaned against the wall in front, waiting to escort me inside. We ducked into an empty room like the ones in cop shows, with its two-way mirror taking up the back wall.

I handed him the copy of my book.

"This was the one Cynthia borrowed, right?" He flipped through and the sticky notes flapped like dragonfly wings.

"That's what I initially thought. But when I looked on my bookshelf, I noticed my two copies were still there. Then I realized the handwriting on the paper tucked in the book is the same as the writing on the letter."

He pulled his glasses from his shirt pocket, scooted up to the table. I noticed his gun tucked beneath his armpit, the black handle jutting out from the leather holster. My grandfather had guns when I grew up. He would even take me hunting once in a while. But he used to always say a handgun has only one purpose.

Detective Landers pointed to the underlined passages. "Do you have any sense why this guy would care so much about these passages?"

I shrugged my shoulders. "No, not really. I mean, beyond what I mentioned."

"Any chance this connects with your memoir about Winfred Cookman?" He smiled.

I had figured it was only a matter of time before the detective brought up my past. For decades I had been harassed for speaking publicly about police brutality. But, after an armed group in ski masks had seized a Department of Corrections van transporting black anti-apartheid activist Winfred Cookman to a pretrial hearing, the district attorney indicted me for conspiracy and murder charges, and I became the target of a concerted effort to drive me from my position at Queens Community College. Two police officers had been shot; one died. Before long, right-wing hacks used their reviews to attack my arrest record, suggesting someone like me shouldn't be permitted to teach at a state school—even a tiny community college in Queens. They wanted me exiled for "infecting" young people with my "anti-white" ideas. I knew this was just another missile deployed in the cultural wars that sought to prevent me from teaching courses on black women radicals, which they didn't think New York City taxpayers ought to fund. I was ultimately cleared of the charges, but the campaign against me continued over the next year, as I wrote a memoir about my experiences. Even though I've been told the national and international celebrity from the campaign to free me drove my preorder book sales, it also alerted my enemies in Albany to work faster to figure out a way to have me fired.

In my early drafts I situated my activism to free Winfred within the context of other former black radicals who had been hunted and jailed under Ronald Reagan's supposed war on drugs. This, I explained, had really been a war on people of color, which, for me, illustrated the centrality of racial ideology as a means to fuel the US Empire. Yet my editor prodded me to focus on my own story about what it meant to come of age in Alabama a decade after the fire hoses and police dogs made the city into a global representation of white supremacist rule. Most importantly, she wanted me to write about my mother, who disappeared when I was young, and how this shaped my activism. So, I relented. I wrote about my father abandoning me and my sister, Janice, and how, despite the civil rights movement, nothing had really changed in Birmingham or the South. Black people remained trapped in a racist and capitalist system, praying to God for salvation rather than continuing the fight for racial justice.

I still stand behind all I wrote, yet I confess my bruised ego played into my decision to write so critically about Alabama. There are those who believe the charges I leveled against civil rights activists in Alabama who ceased challenging systemic racism and settled for token political appointments should have been a part of a broader academic study. At the time, I talked myself into believing my commercial success would serve the "greater good." You know, the whole speaking truth to power. But deep down I knew I fell under the spell of the limelight. Another academic book about racism or political corruption would never reach a broad audience.

When my grandmother read my memoir, she was hurt. She asked why I spoke with such condescension about those like her and my grandfather who fought so hard against Jim Crow to make things better for me. She said I spent too much time with my head in the clouds to see that the grassroots struggle today faced new obstacles—ones she and others continued to struggle to remove. For years after its publication, I didn't communicate with them much, or even visit Birmingham. I felt as if I had been cast out into the sea, and I was too prideful to swim back toward the shore.

Few of the reviewers cared much about my critique of the South. Instead, they sensationalized my relationship with Winfred, focusing more on scandal than on my ideas. Regardless of the political attacks against me, my memoir afforded me ten minutes of fame. For a season, I was the light of the literary establishment; until the next "compelling" work by a black author dashed out my flame. However, not all was lost. As it turned out, Ivy League universities care more about hiring black intellectuals who, even if so briefly, gained the public eye than those who have published cutting-edge scholarship. Shortly after I was fired from my job at Queens Community College, I received a call from the dean of humanities at Faneuil University. He offered me a tenured position in the African American Studies Department, but I told him I had no interest in living in Boston. He said the university would pay for me to commute there each week from Harlem.

Although I said I needed time to think it over, after I hung up, I phoned my friend Andrea, who lived next to a philosophy professor who taught at Christopher Columbus University. I asked if she would see if the Philosophy Department might consider me for a

position, given Faneuil University's offer. Within the
hour, the humanities dean at Christopher Columbus
University countered. Like that, I went from being an
unemployed community college professor to a tenured
one at an elite university. Only in America, Andrea
joked at my book release party a few months later.

leaned forward onto my elbows. "Don't tell me you're
going to harass me about that."

"No, professor. Let bygones be bygones."

"Why'd you read it?"

"I thought maybe it would provide me with some
insight into the type of person who might send you a
letter signed 'William Shields.'"

"Any puzzle pieces?"

"Actually, yes. A few. Like, for example, you and
Cynthia are both from Alabama. And both of you have
your share of arrests for disturbing the peace and other
charges from activism."

"So her activism provoked someone to kidnap her?"

Detective Landers intertwined his fingers under
his chin. "Look, Professor Douglass, I think we've
gotten off on the wrong foot. I'm not interested in your
political views or your past. I'm just trying to see how
all of this comes together. But tell me something. Have
you had any threats against you recently?"

"I don't know. Last month? I gave a talk in Warrior, Alabama, and someone seemed a bit annoyed about my argument that American slaveholder ideology influenced the Nazis."

"Fascinating. Mind if I hold on to this copy of your book?"

"Of course not."

"Given the book and the letter were found in Cynthia's apartment, she might have run into this person who wrote the letter, and he gave them to her for you. Here's what I'm going to do. I'll continue checking on any leads. And if she contacts you, please let me know."

"Well, she hasn't replied to any of my text messages. But, yes, of course."

"Great. Often people assume we know when a person reported missing has been found. But half the time the mother—it's usually the mother—doesn't bother letting us know."

The problem with writing a book about nineteenth-century slaveholders isn't wading through reams of paper devoted to biblical justifications for holding human beings in chains. It's exposing myself to internet trolls who sit in their boxer shorts and post comments that demonstrate no real desire to think critically about my ideas. A cursory look at my recent Amazon reviews attests to this.

Over the past few months, I had given nearly a half dozen lectures at historical societies in the South to speak directly to those interested in my interpretations. I admit my book likely benefited from recent controversies over Confederate flags and memorials. I just hoped that with my scholarship it would, perhaps, push Rebel flag–waving men to think beyond slogans or hero worship.

While most academic books include the author's photo, I declined because I wanted potential readers to focus on my ideas rather than the person who came up with them. My editor wasn't thrilled about this decision, given my previous notoriety. Most academic books barely sell enough to cover their expenses, and my editor thought without the photo of a black woman in the back, potential readers might assume my book defends slaveholder ideology rather than critiquing it. You'd be surprised how many neo-Confederates publish books with academic-sounding titles that defend the South, as well as slavery. But, without my photo on the back flap, those who invited me to speak assumed I was white. After I introduced myself, they'd always smile, as if I had told them a joke, then wait for me to introduce the real "Allegra Douglass." But one thing about southerners, they're polite even when caught off guard. They know how to make a person feel comfortable even when they don't.

My book resonated with the progressive southern women who asked me to give book talks at these underfunded institutes of southern heritage—basically worn-down ranch houses run by passionate people eager to understand the cause of our nation's rupture. More often than not, they'd ask if I could tell them about their own families, or some military monument in their local community. I'd remind them I wasn't a historian. I studied the ideas, not the men.

I always made it a point to end these book talks by telling the audience that we must treat all ideas critically and objectively; listen to all ideas, even those we find reprehensible. Then I made certain to read aloud at least one especially racist or sexist (often both) email to show that I too take all ideas seriously, even the offensive ones. Remember, I'd say, free thought and curiosity are always the first casualties of a fascist state.

Later that day, I was working on a long-overdue book review when I heard a knock and Martin's voice.

"Allie? Can I have a word?"

I opened the door and there Martin stood, arms clasped behind his back.

"What is it, Martin?"

He looked past me, as if waiting for me to invite him in. I motioned for him to come in, then returned to my desk.

"It appears that Eli Jefferson's family has requested we arrange a closed event in your honor Saturday."

"This Saturday?"

"I know, it's last-minute. But the late Eli Jefferson's widow has a medical procedure that requires her to leave for Europe sooner than later, and her niece requested the department organize a dinner as soon as possible."

It didn't bother me. In fact, I much preferred a more intimate gathering rather than something big.

"That's fine."

"One other thing. It's about your former graduate student Cynthia Wade? An investigator called. Has she been in some trouble?"

"No, she hasn't been seen by her roommates or contacted her mother in a couple weeks. I've been in touch with the investigator."

"Alright. The last thing we need is some political issue right now. I mean, given the trouble we've had over this donation from the Jeffersons."

No doubt. "Is that all?" I said, typing away.

"Ah, yes. That's all."

When he shut the door, I sighed. *Shit.*

My grandma always said two things you never chase—dreams and men. Both are bound to disappoint. It wasn't that my grandma didn't believe in dreams, or didn't expect us to find a decent man. She just found in her life that ambition drove young people to make poor decisions—decisions that had long-term ramifications. She'd remind me and my sister that the flame within our hearts could warm us, or consume us. It could drive us to achieve death-defying feats, or sear in our soul-crippling disappointment. She'd watched two of her brothers flame out, returning to Alabama after living in Detroit and Chicago, mired in self-defeat, pity. Soon, they took to drinking to soothe the pain.

Some in my family figured the first time my mother left home was to chase a man—perhaps my father. I never knew if my grandmother believed it, but she was damn sure it wouldn't happen to me and my sister.

No one ever talked about my father. In fact, I don't think my mother ever told my grandmother who he was. I heard from my aunt Elaine that my mother convinced my grandmother to allow her to enroll in nursing school in Montgomery. My grandmother didn't buy it. She figured it was a front so she could live with some man who'd poisoned her mind with dreams he had no ability to realize. Promises he couldn't keep. We had relatives in Montgomery who kept an eye on my mom, sharing with my grandmother how frequently they saw her with a man—high yellow, as they'd say, who drove an Oldsmobile and went around to the other side to help her out of the car.

My grandfather wanted to go immediately to
get her, but my grandma said to wait. But when my
mom didn't visit for Thanksgiving or Christmas, my
grandfather couldn't be held at bay any longer. He and
my grandma went to Montgomery to confront my mom.
They met her as she came out of an apartment building
where she must have lived with the man rather than the
dorm. Grandma demanded she return home, but she
refused. My grandmother never told my aunt what was
said between them. She shook her head and said: she'll
reap what she's sown. That was it.

Until that May, when my mom climbed out of the
bus with my sister in her arms, and a bruise under her
eye.

This wasn't the last time my mother left abruptly.
But the next time, my grandmother didn't chase. When
weeks turned into months, months became years, my
grandmother regretted choosing to wait so long before
she filed a report. I don't think she ever forgave herself
for that.

FOURTEEN DAYS BEFORE
MY ABDUCTION

Martin had always taken credit for convincing the dean to hire me. Yet, at the dinner in my honor, I learned this was not completely true. Yes, Martin had been the head of the department at the time, but Professor Eli Jefferson, for whom I had been awarded a chair, had convinced the dean my previous writings warranted my hire. With only one other continental philosopher, my work on Kantian notions of "empirical self-consciousness" in nineteenth-century female slave narratives complemented the other philosophers in the department.

This revelation, while important to my story, is less relevant than what transpired right after the ceremony. I'll come to that in a moment, but first, I should provide a crucial piece of context. The day before the award dinner, my sister, Janice, called to tell me our grandmother had had a heart attack. She was stable, but Janice implored me to come home immediately.

I left a message for Martin explaining the situation and that we needed to postpone the award dinner. Ten minutes later he called back, sounding desperate. He told me if we canceled, we would have to wait until fall, and this jeopardized the donation. Apparently, the man who donated the money had been a former student of Eli Jefferson. When this donor learned the department and Jefferson's widow decided to award me the chair, he had threatened to pull the funding. However, cooler heads prevailed and he relented. The bottom line, Martin explained, was that the situation was too fragile to delay. And what was a day? My grandmother was stable, right?

Despite my reluctance, I agreed to catch a flight to Alabama the morning after the event. I admit my ego once again got the better of me. I couldn't have cared less about Martin or the university's budget. It was the notion that some guy who donated money in honor of Eli Jefferson changed his mind and threatened to pull the funding when he learned a black woman had been given the award. This was disgraceful.

———

arrived at the University Club that night. I hadn't even found the drinks table before the president draped his arm over my shoulder, demanding a photo from one of the swarm of young women from the alumni office. Martin approached us, eyes wide, stupid smile, red face. Had this been a costume party, he could be mistaken for the devil. His breath smelled like he'd already found the bar. Several times.

"Allie—finally!" He pulled me over. "I am so honored to introduce you to Mrs. Jefferson."

Eli Jefferson's widow, Martha Jefferson, sat in a wheelchair with pearl earrings and matching necklace. Her blue suit coat and white skirt seemed too large. I assumed she must have lost weight given her illness. Her personal nurse bent down and locked the wheels in place and flipped up the footrest so Mrs. Jefferson could stand.

Mrs. Jefferson took my hand, her head cocked to the side, smiling. "How wonderful to meet you. And please, call me Martha."

"It's wonderful to finally meet you, Martha," I said, shaking her frail hand.

"This is my niece, Sarah," Martha said, motioning to a young woman standing beside the nurse.

Sarah beamed. "Professor Douglass, this is a true honor. I read your memoir as an undergraduate. It's so beautifully written. I must say, your photo on the university website was quite intimidating. It certainly doesn't do you any justice."

I shrugged my shoulders. "Well, I'm not the most photogenic person. Not to mention, I've always found digital photos make me look two shades darker."

"Well, I always look pale as a whale's belly. But you, professor, look like a younger version of Angela Davis—a brilliant beauty," Mrs. Jefferson said.

"Now you're just exaggerating," I replied, smiling.

A thin man in a gray suit with wire glasses stepped forward. He eyed me up and down.

"I'm Wallace. Mrs. Jefferson's nephew."

I nodded. "Nice to meet you."

"I'm looking forward to hearing you speak tonight."

"Oh, Wallace. She's not here to give a lecture," Mrs. Jefferson said.

"Of course not. Though it'd be delightful if you'd share a little snippet from your award-winning book. What's the title again?"

"*Prophets of Fire: Slaveholder Ideology in the Age of the Civil War.*" I scanned the room more desperately for a glass of wine.

"Sounds titillating to say the least. Any copies available for purchase?"

I caught Mrs. Jefferson rolling her eyes. Sarah held up her glass.

"Seems to me, Wallace, my glass is empty. Would you mind?"

"Yes, certainly." He took her glass. "Wonderful to meet you, Professor Douglass." He nodded, then slid through the crowd.

"Please don't pay him any mind. He is not as enlightened as some of us," Mrs. Jefferson said.

"He's fine."

"Come dear, let's sit for a while." Mrs. Jefferson led me to a table as she chatted about her late husband. She told me Professor Jefferson had been a great admirer of my work. He had also grown up in Alabama, and despite having taught at Christopher Columbus University for over half a century, he returned each summer to his boyhood home in Jefferson County.

What a coincidence, I said, explaining that I grew up in Jefferson County. Just outside Birmingham in Elysian. This prompted an invitation to her estate when she returned from Europe. When she mentioned "estate" I couldn't help imagining the absurdity of me—Allie Douglass, a once jailed black activist turned philosopher of slaveholders—sitting on this elderly white woman's veranda, sipping mint juleps, speaking casually about the struggle to halt the white supremacist insurgency in Alabama. Don't get me wrong. I appreciated the award. But you will never find me lounging on her plantation porch trying to flatter her into donating money to the university, even though I knew our university president forced faculty to swallow their pride and manipulate wealthy potential donors to support a capital campaign. Not to mention, my grandmother would kill me if I visited this white woman while almost never finding time to visit her.

After a bit more small talk, Mrs. Jefferson asked how I became interested in untangling the ideas of slaveholders. I explained my graduate research on the German concept of *Bildung*—honor, loyalty, and education as means to lift the fog from the minds of people who, as some argued, had been trapped in darkness and fear. On the heels of the Civil War, the sons of slaveholders drew inspiration from this concept as they organized their terrorist campaign to redeem the South from the Northern army that continued to occupy the region for nearly a decade after.

She listened, nodding occasionally. I couldn't tell if she was impressed by my analysis or that I—a black woman from Alabama, a daughter of the same dust— was giving her a philosophy lesson.

When I finished, Mrs. Jefferson said her husband never explained things in such a clear manner. She thanked me, then said, as southern women, we had an obligation to guide our people toward racial tolerance and away from the ignorance that fueled inequality, which continued to plague Alabama.

Fact was, Mrs. Jefferson said, her life had been dedicated to helping whites like herself embrace the changes brought on by the civil rights struggle of the sixties. Yet, she'd grown pessimistic over the past decade. Seemed racial hostility had grown— particularly in Birmingham.

Mrs. Jefferson rested her hand on my leg. "Professor, your work could potentially expose the false ideas that seem to be poisoning the minds of young white men who glorify the Confederacy. This must begin with new interpretations rather than old ones from white men like my dear Eli: God rest his soul."

She shut her eyes, her bottom lip quivering. Her niece placed a hand on her shoulder, gently patting for a moment. When it passed, she took a deep breath, dabbed her eyes with her handkerchief, then raised her glass, and everyone around followed suit: "To a new beginning," she said, then we clinked glasses.

Soon I was called onstage for the formal part of the evening. I hadn't realized how many people were there. I looked out at the crowd, noticing several of my black colleagues gulping scotch, sipping wine, fingers finding the waists of graduate students, whispering introductions to interdisciplinary faculty. Given my absence at so many of their events, I assumed they were here out of ethnic obligation or racial politics, or they were attracted to "black firsts."

In fact, I was not only the first black professor awarded a distinguished chair in the Philosophy

Department, but also the first woman. This was part of the reason the dean seemed so keen on using my award to show the success of recent diversity initiatives. Even if other black faculty affiliated with the Center for the Study of Race, Gender, and Ethnicity criticized me for rarely finding time to attend their events at the Umoja House, they appeared delighted to witness a black woman climb to the top of the ivory tower without slipping. Or so it seemed.

I did feel bad about avoiding black students' raucous demonstrations or the blaring of music from four-foot speakers into the quad nearly every other day. But over time, I grew exhausted from feeling that every interaction I had with black students congregated on the steps of the Umoja House was a test of my racial solidarity.

Our president took to the podium, reminding those gathered about the capital campaign for a new business school, as well as a tech center and a solar-powered dormitory—the first of its kind in the city.

Martin went next, reading passages from notes sent by retired faculty and alums who recalled the optimism of the late Eli Jefferson during the changes wrought by the 1960s. As one of the few southern faculty members, Martin explained, Professor Jefferson found himself translating the events in his home state of Alabama for a university community who rarely ventured much farther south than D.C. Yes, he continued, Professor

Jefferson was a true southern gentleman who showed by example how to live a dignified life.

Martin introduced me next, his face lighting up as he recounted the story of how he'd "rescued me from Faneuil." Mrs. Jefferson leaned toward me, her left palm cuffed over her mouth:

"Aren't men full of it. Always finding a way to take credit."

I smiled. I liked this woman.

When it came my turn to speak, I kept my comments brief, thanking my grandmother, who inspired me, despite her desire for me to become the kind of doctor who saves lives rather than changes minds—and, of course, find a decent man (in her eyes I did one of the two). The audience laughed. I also thanked those colleagues who supported my work. And most of all, I thanked the Jefferson family for having the foresight to see our futures intertwined.

Looking back, I can't believe the irony of that statement.

After I spoke, I was called over to pose for photos with the Jefferson family. Then, I gathered my sweater from the spine of my seat and started for the coatroom just as Martin came over, took my hand, and held it delicately, eyes misty like I'd saved his daughter from drowning or something.

"Allie, you have no idea how much this means to the department. And, of course, your career. University chair before your fifties. Your book nominated for the prestigious David Hume Award in American Political Thought? You're on fire!"

"Thanks," I said with a quick smile, then pushed past him to the coatroom.

I found my jacket and checked my phone. I had five messages and a text from my sister to call. I tried calling back, but the reception was poor. I accidently dropped my phone as I put on my coat. When I bent over to pick it up, I bumped into a man pulling his arm through his coat's sleeve.

"Pardon me, Dr. Douglass."

It was Wallace, the man Mrs. Jefferson introduced to me earlier.

"I want to thank you for making my aunt Martha so pleased," he said, buttoning his coat.

At this point, I had had enough small talk with rich white people for the evening. I was tired. My feet ached. I nodded, trying to avoid conversation. He stepped in my path.

"To tell you the God's honest truth, I was appalled when I learned my aunt chose to honor you with a distinguished chair. Fact is, I fought it tooth and nail. But I'm a good sport about such things. If that's her wish, so be it."

He held his face stern, one eyebrow raised.

Now I understood why Mrs. Jefferson and her niece were so quick to send him away. My phone vibrated and I glanced down. "I should take this."

"You go on now. I'm certain you have much more important business to attend to than listening to me. I'll probably see you again. But be careful, there are some in our family who are less gracious than I. Some who'd die before they see you honored by an award named after a member of our family."

Wallace stepped aside, allowing me to escape from the coatroom.

What an asshole. I took a deep breath to calm my nerves as I tried to understand my sister's message over her choked sobs. I stepped into the elevator and before the doors closed a man in a blue suit with a gray beard slipped in. I kept texting my sister, hoping the man would ignore me—maybe think I was one of the waitstaff.

I had come off the elevator when the man called out.

"Professor Douglass? Good gracious, is that you? I've been so caught up in my own head that I nearly missed an opportunity to meet a lady I've come to admire so."

I held up my phone. "Listen, I don't mean to be rude, but I have an emergency call to make."

"Oh no please, I completely understand. No need to apologize. I just wanted to let you know that I am a big admirer of your work. This recent book, especially."

I hadn't noticed him carrying a copy of my book. He tapped the cover.

"Would you mind signing this?"

"Sure," I said, sliding my phone into my pocket. "Who should I make it out to?"

"Matthew Strong."

I signed quickly and thanked him.

"Pleasure's mine. In fact, it's an honor to meet the smartest one of your kind."

My kind? I thought, nodding awkwardly as I walked away.

My sister returned my call just as I arrived in front of my apartment.

"Janice? What's going on?"

"Allie..." she paused. I heard her sniffling. "Grandma's passed."

"Wait, what? What do you mean?"

"She died this evening. We need to get things in order—when are you coming?"

"Janice, oh my God." I took a deep breath and began to weep.

"I'm sorry, Allie," she said, her voice choked up.

"I just...I was just on my way down. My flight's in the morning. How is this possible?"

"Listen, I need to speak with the nurse. Here's Robert." My sister handed the phone to her husband.

"Allie?"

"Hi, Robert." I felt a ball in my throat.

"It's awful. Really. I'm so sorry," he said.

"What happened?"

"Just today she was talking fine. Things seemed to be getting better. Then, we get a call around suppertime from the Home Health Aide woman we hired that she passed."

"I'll be down as soon as possible."

"Okay. Let us know the details and we'll pick you up."

Janice blamed me. I could tell. Not by what she said, but by her tone and how quickly she passed the phone to Robert. I felt defensive. How could I know my grandmother would die the night before I got there? This, of course, wouldn't matter. My sister was sad and angry. I was the scapegoat. This was the family dynamic. I'm the selfish one.

I hadn't seen her or my grandmother since they visited me in the hospital after my mastectomy a few years before. And I couldn't even remember how many years it had been since I visited my family in Alabama—even when I gave lectures there. Whenever my grandmother called with some "news" about a family event, I came up with something I thought would justify my absence. Whether it was a lecture, or a deadline, I came up with an excuse that seemed reasonable to me. Of course, none of these reasons mattered to Grandma. Once my sister told me she found our grandmother crying when she got off the phone with me. As Janice comforted her, Grandma asked God how she could have raised a child who wouldn't find time for her people.

The truth was, over time, I had become disconnected from my family and increasingly disinterested in my sister's talk about her job, God, and the new car she'd bought. I remember she once accused me of becoming one of those absentminded professors who always appeared lost in thought. After my first book, I remember my sister questioning why I wrote about the ideas of racist dead white men who most people wanted to forget. Couldn't I write more about black women, like Sojourner Truth? Maybe focus on ideas to help our people combat racism? When I told her that I studied them to contextualize the racist teleology they used to persuade others to their cause, she just shook her head and mumbled under her breath, "Teleology."

My sister said she never understood half the words I said, nor my "obsession" with proving myself to white folk rather than having kids or, most importantly, visiting her when I was in Alabama doing research or presenting my work at conferences. None of it made any sense to her. She blamed my ambition for my absence, not only the night my grandmother died, but over the previous twenty years. She blamed me for Grandma's constant worrying. Adding that Grandma never understood how I could go on and disappear from her life after our mom did the same thing.

I took Metro-North to my house in Westchester to grab clothes before my flight to Birmingham the next day. I was emotionally drained by the news of my grandmother's death and frustrated by Janice's reaction.

When I arrived home, I went right to the attic to find clothes appropriate for Alabama in March. As I searched for the bin with summer clothes, I came across a framed photo of me on my mother's lap, her eyes cast down at me, beaming. My sister knelt beside her, all teeth and two thick braids that flopped on each side of her head like rabbit ears. I must have been four, she seven. Mom had an Afro, tight maroon bell-bottom slacks, and a flowery shirt. I smiled, thinking of all the dorm rooms and apartments where this framed photo waited on a wall or countertop to greet me. When I moved into this house, though, I never unpacked it. Perhaps I abandoned hope that one day my mom would return and tell me what she'd been smiling about.

I hated that I'd forgotten what her voice sounded like. I must have been eleven when it vanished from my mind. Kind of like a foreign language you learned as a child but stopped speaking before you became an adult. By my twenties my memories of Mom were like a movie trailer: her shaking her head at something silly I'd done; her pulling me out of the creek after I'd fallen in.

My mother vanished like hundreds of other women each year destined to become one more thin manila file with no witness statements, no forensic evidence, no puzzle pieces to fit into a discernable pattern. The problem with vanishing is that your loved ones can't bury you. Instead they wait, praying one day you'll come back just as suddenly as you disappeared. And they never stop looking for you at the corner store, at the park, in the faces of women crossing the street.

As a child, I'd ask my grandma if my mother was coming back, and she'd make some general statement like "When the Lord calls her home." It's not that my grandma wouldn't ever talk about her. I remember my grandma telling me about a day she searched the woods for my mom for three hours. My mom had lost track of time looking for fairies and other mythical creatures. Grandma always said my mom loved walking the old dirt paths in woods that once mattered to men who ruled these lands a century prior. When Grandma finally found her, my mother said the trees whispered stories about treasure buried in the woods and ghosts protecting it. My grandma didn't pay her stories any mind until she disappeared. Years after the police dogs scoured those woods, my grandmother continued up and down the dirt path spitting Bible verses between sobs.

I heard creaking on the wooden pull-down ladder.

"Need some help?" David said, his head poking in.

I held up an album labeled "Honeymoon."

"Do you remember what it was like back then?" I pulled out a photo of us holding each other in front of a castle in Nantes, France. I turned it for him to see.

"You're as beautiful now as you were then."

I shook my head. "Yeah, right."

"What time does your flight leave?"

"Nine thirty."

"I fixed some dinner. I'll warm it up."

"Thanks. I'm not hungry, though."

"Yeah, that's what you always say." He crept back down.

I searched bins for summer clothes and found shorts and a few nice blouses.

By the time I went downstairs David had set the table, put a piece of fish and broccoli on my plate.

"How'd the ceremony go?" he asked.

"Fine."

He sipped his wine. "Just fine? What about the family of this guy—Eli Jefferson? From Alabama, right?"

"Yeah, actually not far from where I grew up."

"And?"

"And, what? Like I said. It was nice."

I felt his eyes pressing me, trying to interpret my response. Our relationship had been strained during the past year because I thought David was having an affair. I never asked him the truth. Instead, I rented an apartment in the city and told him we needed space. When he didn't argue with me about this decision, I felt like his silence confirmed my suspicion.

David leaned back in his chair, arms folded. "Are you going to be alright going down by yourself? I can cancel this deposition tomorrow and go with you."

"I'll be alright." I took a bite of corn bread.

"I'm really worried about you, Allie."

"About what?"

"You haven't spoken with your sister in what, a year?"

"I'll be fine. I need to finish packing." I took my plate to the sink and wiped tears from the corners of my eyes.

I knew it was selfish of me to push him away. All the emotions I held in about my grandma's death paralyzed me. But it wasn't just that. Returning to Alabama meant I might have to listen to my sister, Janice, go on and on about women who dedicate more time to their career than their marriage. I wanted to deal with my grief without her judgment.

When I started up the steps, David called me back.

"By the way, there's a package for you."

"What?"

"Over there." He motioned with his fork. "It was tucked in the screen door."

On the desk in our study there was a package. No return address. I took out an envelope inside that looked similar to the one I'd seen before:

Dear Professor Douglass:

I must apologize for the tone of my last correspondence. As you know, I have a different interpretation than you about those whom you write about. I must confess that you seem to have identified connections between slaveholder ideology and European theory I find intriguing. Yet, you fail to grasp the true important role slavery played in our modern world.

Given our mutual interest in truth, I'd like to extend a friendly invitation to you for an event we're sponsoring over at the Jefferson Historical Society that reinterprets some of the ideas you write about in your book within the context of our current crisis over the Confederate memorial in Birmingham.

Seeing how well your book has been received, I contacted the organizers and requested they fund your participation. I'm delighted to be able to offer you a $5,000 honorarium if you can find time. I realize this modest amount does not fully reflect your worth. I'm sure some pay a pretty penny for one of your kind.

I know this is coming at the last minute, and

you have a lot on your mind right now given your grandmother's passing, but I figured it wouldn't hurt to ask, seeing you will be down in Alabama anyway. I look forward to meeting you again. This time for a bit longer.

For the cause,
William Shields, Esq.

Down in Alabama? I reread the last few lines and tried to keep my cool. I went back into the kitchen, where David was rinsing the dishes and loading the dishwasher.

"This was in the door? Just now?" I asked.

"Huh?" He shut off the faucet.

"This?" I held up the package.

"Yeah, that's right. It was tucked into the screen door when I came in."

"Did you see anyone leave it?"

"No, why?" His eyebrows raised.

"It's just...there's no postage on the package." I handed him the letter, recalling the previous one at my apartment. My face felt flushed.

He looked it over. "What's this about?" I leaned into him, tears falling freely now. I told him about the other letter and Cynthia's disappearance. I mentioned the interaction with Wallace Jefferson, who practically threatened me in the coatroom. At the time I had no sense of how all of these events connected, but they were puzzle pieces just like the detective said.

David whispered in my ear, "Please. Let me come with you. I'll cancel my pretrial hearing tomorrow."

"No, it's okay. I'll be fine. You've been working on this case for months, and the funeral isn't for a couple days. I'll be busy helping my sister, anyway. I'll see you at the funeral."

BOOK II

RESURRECTION

Who will roll away the stone for us...

MARK 16:3

EACH SOCIETY HAS ITS REGIME OF TRUTH, ITS "GENERAL POLITICS" OF TRUTH: THAT IS, THE TYPES OF DISCOURSES WHICH IT ACCEPTS AND MAKES FUNCTION AS TRUE...

—Michel Foucault

THIRTEEN DAYS BEFORE

The next day I called Detective Landers about the letter left at my house in Westchester, as well as my trip to Alabama. I arrived at the airport in the early evening to avoid the rush-hour traffic and be sure I didn't miss my flight. I couldn't imagine telling my sister I neglected to give myself enough time, given I felt she blamed me for not being there. As I waited, I scrolled down my inbox, glancing at the sweet sympathy notes from colleagues and friends. I moved on to Instagram and checked my sister's page. She had photos of my nephew, Davon, and my niece, Naquasia, with Grandma, #tbt shots of me and her as kids blowing out candles at a birthday party. I felt a lump in my throat as I watched how Janice cataloged her love for Grandma. The only recent photos of me and Grandma were when Janice brought her to visit me in the hospital after my mastectomy.

Just as I boarded, my phone vibrated. It was my friend Michelle. We hadn't spoken since the night I told her about my award and Cynthia's disappearance.

"Are you holding up okay?"

"Yeah, I just feel like shit for not going home more."

"How long has it been?"

"God, I haven't stayed down there since Janice's daughter, Naquasia, was born. She's ten."

"Don't be so hard on yourself, Allie. Appreciate reconnecting with family and friends."

"You're right. Thanks for reminding me, Michelle."

"No problem. Anything I can do here?"

"Actually, yeah. Can you check on my plants?"

She sighed. "Plants? Not again."

"They were a gift from Mrs. May in 24B. What was I going to do?"

"Tell her the truth. You're a black widow of vegetation. Kinda like agent orange."

"That's cruel."

She laughed. "Nobody's perfect, Allie. Not even you."

"Well, can you at least water them?"

"Fine. I'll go over tomorrow."

"I appreciate it."

"I'm so sorry about your grandma, Allie. Really."

After the plane lifted off, I pushed my nose against the cold plastic window, glancing down below at the city's lights dotting the ground like glass marbles scattered in darkness. I shut my eyes, and I was twelve again, imagining my arms outstretched flying beside the plane, the wind on my cheeks, my fingertips tingling, my dreadlocks flapping.

When I opened my eyes, I gazed at the vast Atlantic Ocean stretching from Long Island Sound to Cape Coast. I felt like a ghost returning to my place of birth, riding the clouds like waves soon to crash against rocky shores of my past.

I was seventeen when I told my grandma I wanted to go to college in New York City. I tried desperately to convince her that this didn't mean disowning the family or my heritage, or that I had lost faith in Jesus. She rattled off the names of other women who had gone to New York only to return six months later with big bellies. When I was a kid, I remember asking her if you go to the city to get a baby. But as a teen those stories no longer deterred me. She said I was foolish for searching for something there when all I needed was down here. Not to mention she wanted me to be the first in our family to attend Birmingham University. Given the scholarship they offered, she didn't think it made any sense to enroll anywhere else.

After I completed my undergraduate degree, I moved to Germany to pursue a doctorate in philosophy. This made my grandma furious. She couldn't understand why I'd spend my prime years trying to understand the ideas of white men in Europe when there were plenty in Alabama who didn't make a bit of sense to her.

The Sunday before I left for college, my grandfather gave one of his sermons about the sacrifices made during the movement so we might live free from the pervasive fear black people felt in the past. He spoke of lives lost and people kicked off their land for us to one day enjoy the opportunity to do what the good Lord set out for us to do.

After church my grandma had our entire family over. She repeated parts of my grandfather's sermon that she said seemed pertinent. I'd tried to prevent my eyes from rolling, knowing if she caught me she'd give me one of her stares that'd stop a steer dead in its tracks.

When we were washing dishes, I asked why she wasn't proud that I'd been accepted to a prestigious university in New York, especially when they offered me a full scholarship just like Birmingham University. She told me once I left I'd never come back. She said she couldn't see me living in one of those godforsaken cities where buildings blocked the sun (and God's grace as well).

I wondered if she had ever looked.

When my flight landed, I saw several text messages from my brother-in-law, Robert, asking me to wait near the long-term parking sign.

Once I gathered my bags, I met Robert outside, leaning on his car. I searched the passenger seat, expecting Janice, but Robert said she'd fallen asleep on the couch.

Robert had met my sister in college at Alabama A&T. I always appreciated his humor and his passion for all things related to weather—how hot, or cold, it was outside in comparison to the year before. He was the first to text if he read a snowstorm was about to hit New York.

On the drive home, Robert congratulated me for finishing my book project and being awarded the Eli Jefferson Chair, adding that David seemed elated that maybe now the two of us would have more time together. I smiled, reminding Robert that David worked longer hours than I did. He gave me the update about how Janice and the kids were holding up since my grandmother passed. I learned that Naquasia was heading to middle school next year. Davon was finishing his junior year at the Oak Mountain Christian Academy, one of the most prestigious schools in the state.

As we approached downtown Birmingham, Robert exited in order to bypass traffic on the highway. I realized I hadn't been downtown since my grandfather's funeral fifteen years before. I still missed the way my grandfather would support every crazy idea I had, every whimsical decision I made. He was a minister at the AME church in Birmingham, so he always found a biblical precedent for my inklings. But, right when I became confident enough to follow through with some wild idea, he'd pull me aside and say, "There may be another way of thinkin' 'bout it." Even though he was right nearly every time, he never made me feel ridiculous. He'd just nod and remind me, "The Lord always offers a path. You just gotta be willing to follow regardless of your uncertainty."

Passing Sweeties candy shop, I recalled how fast I and my sister would sprint there and back to church before our grandmother realized we were gone.

Although I'd been invited to give talks in Montgomery and at several smaller historical societies around the state, my work on slaveholders didn't resonate with those at the Birmingham Civil Rights Institute or Birmingham's Historical Society. I didn't mind because I knew a return to Birmingham would require me to visit aunts, uncles, and cousins with whom I felt disconnected. Over the years, I'd grown tired of defending my choice to live in New York. My sister resented my absence and she said people thought I had become "uppity."

When Robert drove past Linn Park, I noticed black plastic covering a statue.

"What's up with the plastic?"

"Oh, it's a long story. The short version is that the city council voted to remove all the Confederate monuments, but the governor vetoed that decision."

"Why?"

"I guess it stirred up too much controversy. Besides, it appears to have provoked racists from surrounding towns. There are even people from other states who joined the protest against removing them."

"I actually was invited to a panel in Warrior organized by some of the same people."

"I don't advise that."

"Trust me, I have no intention of going."

"Hey, are you hungry?" Robert said, motioning to an all-night beer and burger joint with the word "fresh" flashing.

"Thanks, but I'm fine."

As we continued through downtown Birmingham, I gazed out the window, catching a glimpse of statues that served as physical representations of civil rights activists frozen in defiance for residents to witness, again and again. We passed Kelly Ingram Park and my eyes came upon a huge tree with its roots raised from the earth and its trunk bent over feebly, as if a hard gust of wind would send it toppling onto Sixteenth Street.

Robert told me the tree's bark had been infected by some disease, and a controversy brewed when the city scheduled to cut it down before it killed some child playing in the park. I said I didn't understand the big deal about cutting it down.

"Naquasia's teacher told her it was a gift to the city. It's the same type Anne Frank drew inspiration from outside her window."

"Really? I never knew that."

"Most folks don't. Just enjoy sitting under its shade eating lunch, not thinking much about it."

By the time we arrived at their house it was late. Robert showed me to the guest room that doubled as his office, with a futon set up as a bed.

I struggled to fall asleep. I couldn't push out of my mind the letters signed "William Shields," or the cryptic notes in my book. It had been a week since Cynthia had been reported missing, and I had no idea how they fit together. But I had a horrible feeling she'd been kidnapped by this person sending me letters. Too much coincidence otherwise.

I checked my cell phone: 2:30 a.m. I clicked on the light and searched Facebook for William Shields, but nothing popped up there, or on any other social media sites. Eventually, my eyelids became heavy and I put my laptop on the floor.

I woke a few hours later and followed the sound of someone crying in the kitchen, where I found Janice. I hesitated in the hallway, remembering her tone when we spoke over the phone, feeling guilty for not flying down immediately after she called. I took a deep breath before I walked over and put my arm around her.

"Hey, you okay?" I whispered.

She dabbed her cheeks with a tissue.

"I didn't mean to wake you."

I sat on a stool beside her.

Janice shook her head, gently. "Grandma's certainly smiling down on us. Guess she got you down here after all."

"I'm sorry. Really. I feel terrible."

"'Bout what? You didn't do anything to cause this."

"No, Janice. You were right. I should have come right after you called. To be beside y'all."

She shrugged. "Would've been nice. But it is what it is. Can't change anything now."

"I still don't understand what happened?"

"Nothing out of the ordinary, really. They dismissed her from the hospital after running some tests. Seems they thought she had been suffering from a panic attack. Nowadays, they want you out of the hospital as soon as possible. In the morning, Maggie—a woman we hired from Home Health Aide—dropped over to check on her, and when Grandma didn't answer, Maggie went around back to the sliding glass door and saw Grandma on the kitchen floor. By the time the ambulance arrived, Grandma had passed. We were all surprised. Just a few hours before, she seemed fine."

I felt ill as I imagined my grandmother facedown on the kitchen floor. All alone.

"It seemed so quick," I said.

"When it's time it's time."

The casual way Janice said this felt dismissive. It was as if she was trying to prevent me from overanalyzing the death. Let it go. I held my tongue, choosing silence over arguing with Janice so soon. Instead, I asked about the funeral.

"Nearly everything's in place as she wanted. One thing folks around here know how to organize is a funeral. Got a meeting with Reverend Cary tomorrow to go over the final program. Grandma had money tucked away to cover all the expenses. Her plot's beside Granddad over at Brewer Cemetery. The aunts are taking care of the reception. Only thing we have to deal with is the lawyer and the will."

"The will?"

"Not much in it, really. She left the land and house to us. It listed some items to be donated to the women's shelter on Tenth Street."

"Thanks for getting all this together. I wish I could have been more of a help."

"You fine. It's just good to see you."

TWELVE DAYS BEFORE

A line stretched beyond the church doors as crowds
waited to tell our family how much Grandma
meant to them; that she had finally put down her
earthly burdens; that she's in a better place. Janice and
Robert shook hands with cousins, uncles, and aunts,
as well as elderly folk who had attended our church
in Birmingham for decades. Janice appeared relaxed
as more and more people arrived, some of whom we
hadn't seen since we were kids. Davon handed out
programs near the front of the church, and Naquasia
read picture books to a group of young cousins decked
out in miniature suits and fancy dresses in the back.
For the first time, I actually felt comfortable among
my family and friends. They were all so glad to see me.
And proud, too. Of everything. My awards, my books,

and even succeeding in New York. I realized my fears of family resentment were unfounded.

I gazed at Grandma in the casket with her fingers intertwined across her chest. My grandmother didn't look peacefully asleep, as some said. She looked dead. Even though over the previous two days family and friends spoke lovingly about eternal life and how she's in a better place, sitting there in front of her coffin I couldn't see beyond this cold, simple fact.

I felt a hand on my shoulder. David. He leaned down, kissed my forehead, then slid beside me in the pew. He dropped his arm over me like a blanket, and I leaned into his shoulder, eyes shut. For the first time since my arrival I wept openly.

During the service, I was so overwhelmed I went to the bathroom, latched the lock, collapsed on the tiles, and sat against the door and wept. Over the past few years I'd been so consumed with my own struggle with death after my fight with cancer that I hadn't considered anyone else's death. She had always been there for me regardless of how often I disappointed her. Now I was caught off guard by how lost I felt. I must have been sprawled on the floor for several minutes before I heard a soft, cautious knock, then David's voice.

"Allie? You okay?"

I went to the mirror and fixed my makeup.

There was another knock.

"Allie?"

"I'll be right out."

After the church service our family climbed in black stretch limousines and a Lincoln Town Car to lead the procession to Brewer Cemetery. My sister told me our grandmother brought Naquasia over here weekly to pull up weeds, replace flowers, and brush off tombstones.

David, Robert, and my cousins carried my grandmother's coffin. Fans flapped, flies buzzed, as the sun gleamed off the minister's forehead, the heat calling her handkerchief, hanging damply from her fingers as she read from the Bible.

"Brothers and sisters, let us remember death is not the end, but the beginning of a new phase of our existence. While our dear sister Mrs. Maddie Douglass has been called home to the Lord, she joins her beloved family, who sit beside Christ, who lives and reigns in us here and in heaven. Oh Christ, our redeemer, who died for our sins, was resurrected, and ascended into heaven, be our guide during this moment. And let our dear sister's life laboring on behalf of our community inspire us and guide us in our search for answers. Amen."

The crowd murmured, "Amen."

After they lowered the coffin in the ground, Reverend Cary said one final prayer. Each member of our immediate family dropped a handful of earth onto the casket. We embraced Reverend Cary and stood beside her as others followed suit, dropping earth, and giving their condolences to me and my family before proceeding to their cars.

As I walked back, I noticed the obnoxiously large tomb up the hill in another section of the cemetery where the white family who had owned the plantation around here buried their kin. I remembered my grandfather once saying that even in death they wanted to stand above us.

By the time I returned to church for the repast, people had already queued in line, clenching paper plates as women unfolded foil table pans on wire racks, steam hovering. Blue flames warmed trays of collard greens, black-eyed peas, chicken, yams, and rice. In New York, I rarely ate these foods from my childhood, but now I realized how comforting those smells were.

My sister came to my side.

"Allie, you remember Tommy?"

Standing beside her was a tall black man I didn't recognize. Dark suit, green and blue tie, clean shaven, bald head. His eyes somber, his lashes long.

"It's been decades, but you look nearly identical to the last time I saw you," the man said.

I nodded, struggling to recall him. My sister nudged me. "Tommy used to live over on Evergreen Grove. Remember?"

"Oh right." I faintly recalled his smile from when we were kids.

"Tommy is now the mayor of Birmingham." My sister grinned. "God willing, he'll soon be Alabama's first black governor."

"Really?"

"Perhaps," he said, playing it off. "Your grandmother was a wonderful woman. No question that she's sitting at the right hand of the Lord. You and your family are in my prayers."

"Thanks," I said, squeezing out a smile. I turned toward the window and watched Naquasia getting chased by her cousins and a couple of other kids.

Tommy pointed out the window at one of the girls running around. "That girl's my daughter, Odessa."

She looked about nine, cute, with a wide smile like her father. I watched Naquasia show Odessa how to juggle a soccer ball. Each time Odessa bounced the ball off her knee she missed it with her foot. Her little dress tangling up.

"Seems Naquasia and your daughter get along well."

"Sure do. They've grown close over the past couple years since we moved back from Kansas. When we visit with my mother here in Elysian, Odessa often goes over to play with Naquasia. In fact, Odessa's staying with my mother for spring break. It's good for her to reconnect with her roots, you know?"

"How's that going?"

"Fine." He chuckled. "Her mother is more adamant than me that she not lose sight of her 'black-side,' as she likes to call it."

Tommy's wife was not the only white woman at the funeral, of course. Yet her blond hair certainly stood out as she talked among the mostly gray-haired elderly women whom Grandma had known for fifty years as a social worker.

"Progressive wife. Let's just hope your daughter doesn't pick up waving at strangers like rural folk do."

"Why is that bad?"

"Maybe it's okay in Birmingham. But in New York, it's a good way to get yourself robbed, or worse."

"Have your own children abandoned that 'bad habit'?" He used air quotes.

"No kids, so I haven't had to worry about it."

"Really? You seem like you'd be a great parent. But it isn't easy saving for both college and a Christian-based private high school."

"Yeah, my sister said Davon's tuition at the Oak Mountain Christian Academy is expensive."

"You know I graduated from there, right?"

"No, I didn't."

"Class of '81. Among the first black graduates."

"I'm sure the headmaster has you on speed dial. Mayor soon to be governor?"

He nodded, crossing his arms. "Yes, of course."

Tommy's wife came over with Janice, laughing, shaking their heads at something Tommy's wife had said. She wore a black dress with a tie belt and short sleeves. Her blond hair was held in place by sunglasses resting on her head. She slipped her arm around Tommy's waist.

"Allie, this is my wife, Susan."

"Nice to meet you."

"Pleasure's mine, Professor Douglass. I'm sure you've had a hundred people tell you how special your grandmother was, but let me be one hundred and one."

"Thanks."

"When I first met your grandmother, I knew immediately why she inspired so many people."

I smiled.

Janice put her arm around me. "Tommy, I just mentioned to Susan that we'd love to have your daughter come to Naquasia's birthday party. Since she'll be here for Easter break."

Tommy looked at his wife, then back at Janice. "Oh, I'm sure she'd love that."

I used this shift in conversation to find David in the front room, flipping through one of my grandma's photo albums. I rested my head on his shoulder and he kissed my forehead. He pointed to a photo I had mailed my grandmother of him and me camping in the Appalachian Mountains. I remember David joking we could walk all the way from New York to Alabama.

We stood at the top of a huge summit, posing in front of the sun half buried in the horizon. I wore a purple bandana, my dreadlocks falling to either side. His Red Sox cap was turned backward, and his gray shirt was drenched with sweat.

"Dr. Douglass?"

A woman who looked around my grandmother's age reached for my hand.

"My name's Marzi Davis. I was a friend of your grandmother's."

"It's a pleasure to meet you, Mrs. Davis."

"She used to talk about you so much."

"Is that so?" I said, feeling suddenly shy.

"Oh, sure. Told me all about you being this big-time New York professor. But it didn't surprise me. Seeing how brilliant she was, God rest her soul."

"She certainly was," I said.

"I know you have a lot of people to speak to, but I just wanted to come on over here, introduce myself, and give my condolences."

"I appreciate that."

"And," she leaned close, "I was hoping that you would be able to come to one of our mothers' group meetings?"

"Mothers' group?"

"That's right. Your grandmother told you about us, right?"

"No, actually she didn't."

"I'm surprised, seeing how active we've been lately."

"I'm sorry, what do you mean?"

"Been about five weeks since we first met. Seems like a week don't go by without a letter arriving from some poor mother concerned about her missing daughter. Mrs. Maddie took their calls and invited them to our group. She taught them how to file missing person forms and police paperwork."

"So, y'all are a support group?"

"Kind of. We spend part of our meetings letting the new ones talk about their daughters. Your grandmother helped them with the anger and grief that came with such a horrible experience. But she also took it upon herself to look into each one of their cases. Like she used to do in the sixties? With the NAACP?"

I knew about her work with the local NAACP when I was a kid, but I didn't realize she continued to be involved.

"You said that she looked into these cases?"

"That's right. Research. She was serious, too. She even gave us homework."

"Did you come up with anything? I mean, did you ever find any of the girls?"

"Well, your grandmother had some theories. In fact, right before her heart attack she found some new leads she planned to bring to Sheriff Morgan."

Mrs. Davis went on to explain that the sheriff had investigated some of these disappearances but hadn't yet found any evidence connecting them.

"But your grandmother wasn't waiting around for him to figure it out. To tell you the truth, I don't think she had much confidence he was doing everything he could about it. Even though she had known Sheriff Morgan for decades."

"You'd think they'd be working harder to help."

"Around here, if you call the police they're just as quick to assume you were involved as they are to try to find out what happened. Asking a bunch of questions with an accusatory tone."

I did recall my grandma complaining about how little the police had done after my mother disappeared.

"That's really terrible."

"Sure is. But you know black folk down here is used to finding solutions to our own problems. Self-reliance is in our DNA. You black in Jefferson County, Alabama, you got no choice but to figure stuff out on your own."

"Do you have notes?"

"Some. But your grandmother had all the files at her house. That's where we held our weekly meetings."

"You all met once a week?"

"Twice last week. Now, me and other mothers are planning to continue where she left off. Seeing how we almost put it all together."

Janice came over and embraced Mrs. Davis. As they talked for a few minutes, my mind returned to Cynthia and the letters. Before she left, Mrs. Davis asked if my sister and I would hold a meeting at Grandma's house with the sheriff to push him to investigate further some connections they had made.

I felt a strange dark feeling, wondering if my grandmother's work might provide some insights I could pass on to Detective Landers.

A few weeks prior, my grandmother had introduced Mrs. Davis to Janice. Yet, Janice was surprised to hear our grandmother had been so involved in these recent kidnappings, and that she had established a mothers' group. Janice hadn't even heard of this spate of disappearances; there'd been no news coverage. She admitted she'd been so focused on managing her son Davon's schoolwork, her temporary job at an accounting firm, and volunteering at church that most of her interactions with our grandmother had been picking something up or dropping something off. Naquasia, usually. We agreed to have Mrs. Davis over to my grandmother's house to go through the files in a few days.

When the last family left the church, I went outside and found David talking with a young black man, thin tie, horn-rimmed glasses. I looked closely, trying like hell to remember him. Nothing came.

"Allie, you remember Daryl? Your cousin?"

"Hi, Daryl. I barely recognize you."

"I was like real little last time you saw me."

"How are you?"

"I can't complain. Got a job over at the university. Things are good."

David motioned to Daryl. "Daryl was just telling me that he and Mrs. Maddie sometimes hiked in Oak Mountain Park. At her age?" David shook his head in disbelief.

I rolled my eyes. "Ah yes. You see, Daryl, David's got respect for a good hike. Let me guess, he told you he's an Eagle Scout?"

"He was just getting to that."

As a kid, David took to heart the meaning of his African name, Oyono ("to cross a difficult river"). He rose from Cub Scout to Webelos and became an Eagle Scout as a teen. I told Daryl our last hiking and camping trip was in Spackenkill—an isolated upstate town with more black bears than black people, and no cell phone service. David seemed to always choose towns with creepy names like Spackenkill or Fishkill. Once we camped in Plattekill. He insisted we only bring necessities—a flashlight was okay, but no lighter fluid (which I thought was a brilliant purchase when we stopped for gas). This time, he insisted I learn how to read a compass. Before we set out on the trail, he tried to teach me. When I acted bored, he said, dead seriously and a bit agitated, that I should pay attention; I'd never know when I'd need it. I asked if it was prep for the zombie apocalypse (I mean honestly), but he didn't get the joke.

We spoke with Daryl for a little while longer and he told us that our grandmother had become Miss Popular around town. She was everywhere. Apparently, her popularity helped him get his job at the university library after college. Daryl explained how she used to brag to the faculty about my recent book, which he put on the display table when you first walked in with other "Local Authors." I asked about the criteria for "local." He smiled.

Daryl also said that Grandma had a box of items she'd been collecting. Genealogical information about our family, maps, and research about kidnapping cases from all over the South that she'd been looking into. I agreed to come over and take a look at it all.

My sister came out of the church with two trays of leftovers to bring back to her house. Davon followed behind with flowers and other items, and Naquasia carried a box with cards from various family members and friends.

As we put stuff in Robert's trunk, Daryl offered to take David to catch his flight back to New York.

"You know I feel terrible for leaving like this. But...the judge postponed the pretrial hearing for tomorrow," David said.

"No, I understand. I hope it goes well."

"Call me later, okay?"

David blew a kiss as they pulled off.

Around the time I began to suspect David was having an affair, he complained regularly about me being distant, and even more rigid than I suppose I may typically come across. I'd been so thoroughly engrossed in discerning the Christian theological and Enlightenment roots of slaveholder ideology that I hadn't realized this. I'd disconnected. Frustrated, David stopped trying to figure out what was wrong with me, or why I was so aloof.

But when I told him I had decided to rent an apartment in the city, he began to change. My methodical ways no longer roused his annoyance. Recently, David had begun to express his love publicly, often childishly. Blowing me kisses, as he just had done; rushing into the shower right ahead of me; hiding a novel I was reading each night before bed. He insisted that embracing chaos would help me find inner peace. I had my doubts. Yet, despite myself I must admit that I enjoyed his attention. Maybe it wasn't too late for us.

ELEVEN DAYS BEFORE

The morning after the funeral Janice set a shoebox on the coffee table with bereavement cards. I pulled out stacks and stacks of them, surprised.

"This many? Just from the last few days?"

"You know people around here loved Grandma. And after devoting fifty years to being a social worker with the Board of Health, inspecting nursing homes and children's detention centers all over the state, she had many admirers. She really served her community, Allie."

"What on earth are we going to do with all these?"

"I figured since you're the writer you could come up with something simple and sweet."

"To all of these people? Can't we send them an email?"

"Where do you think we are? Anyway, Grandma would roll over in her grave if she knew we sent emails to folk. But I don't think we need to write anything personal to most of them. A polite acknowledgment will be plenty."

"Fine," I said, reaching for a few.

"We'll organize them by date, distance. Put the family ones on this side and the friends on this side. I figure the family who live near us can wait."

We waded through the piles of cards, pulling some, glancing at the names. There we sat for about a half hour organizing them according to Janice's system. Then, we moved on to writing replies. Janice read a card, then passed it to me to write a little note. We worked together in a way we'd never done before. It had always seemed like I was going one way, she another way—usually chasing balls in a field or boys at school. She was more outgoing than me, the pretty one, the athlete. I was more comfortable reading, or cheering from the stands. It was nice to do something as a team like this.

Our conversation shifted to Davon and his budding activism, and the trouble she feared awaited his involvement with demonstrations downtown at the Andrew Shields monument in Linn Park. There had been several spray-painting incidents, and rumors

swirled among the parents at his school that students
had been involved—specifically, the Students of Color
Association, which Davon had joined recently. Janice
said Davon needed to worry more about his grades
than getting into some controversy over removing a
monument.

My mind drifted back to the letters I'd received
from "William Shields," and I thought about the real
William Shields in history. While his father, Andrew
Shields, had been venerated for his role building
Birmingham into the poster child of the "New South,"
William's violent campaign sought to undermine that
progress.

"I told him," Janice handed me the last card in a
stack, "this isn't like how it was back in the sixties or
seventies when we were kids. Don't forget who you are.
These white kids can do all sorts of stuff and get away
with it."

When my sister and I finished with the cards,
Janice suggested we drive over to my grandmother's
house after her fundraiser meeting for Thomas Turner's
campaign. I still hadn't been back there, to that house.
The day before the funeral Janice asked me to ride over
there to gather photos, but I made up some excuse. I felt
a sense of dread, as if a gator waited beneath her porch.

Janice left for the meeting at the Oak Mountain
Christian Academy, and I took a shower. When I came
downstairs I found Davon at the kitchen table, laptop

in front of him and black headphones covering his ears. He wore a New Orleans Saints jersey with cut-off sleeves, and flakes of white deodorant circled his armpits.

I rested my hand on his shoulder, smiling. "Hey there. You okay?"

Davon pulled off his headphones. I noticed tears in his eyes. "Yeah, I'm alright."

I could tell he didn't want to have a conversation about feelings. This was the first time we had a chance to hang out one-on-one. I sat beside him.

"What's that you're watching?"

"Nothing. Just jotting some notes. Random thoughts, really. But I was going to catch up on this YouTube show where these guys review movies... They're funny."

"Can I take a look?"

Davon's eyebrows rose. "I'm not sure you'll like it." He glanced around as if it was something his mother, probably, didn't want him watching.

"We're the only ones here."

He shrugged his shoulders and clicked the link. The host recounted his top ten horror movies, adding snarky comments, mocking the men in masks with axes or other blades.

My husband, David, loved horror movies, but I hated them. I think he put them on because he liked seeing me squirm, shout, then hide my eyes in his arm.

He'd glance at me and grin. If I screamed during a gruesome scene, David would explode into laughter, jerking up and down in hysterics.

I never understood the point of trying to survive in a world where zombies stalked you at night. Forget rationing bullets. All I needed was one. My plan was to lock myself inside our house and climb into the attic with matches, gasoline, and a gun. If the zombies broke into the house and figured out where I hid, I would pour gas around me, toss a lit match, and then shoot myself in the head.

David said I was disturbed.

I was surprised that watching gore lifted Davon's spirits. Even if I had to shut my eyes during some gross clips, it felt good to be invited into his world.

Half an hour or so later, Davon's phone flashed on the table. He checked the message, then tucked it in his front pocket.

"I got to go."

"Anywhere interesting?"

"Just meeting up with friends."

He slipped his laptop in his backpack.

"Is this like a study group?"

"Not exactly. You probably heard about what's been going on with the protests over the Confederate statue in Linn Park?"

"Your mom mentioned it, but she didn't give me details."

"A few of us have been looking into it. You know, the real history? We even made a web page."

"Really?"

"Yeah, I mean, there's a whole bunch of students from all over on Twitter commenting about these statues. It's like everywhere you turn, one of these racist statues is coming down."

I was impressed. "Hey, I look forward to hearing more about all of this."

"Yeah, right," he said, sarcastically.

"What do you mean?"

"Most teachers hate what we're doing. And my mom and dad? Shoot."

"Come on, there have to be some adults on your side."

"There used to be one. A teacher my freshman year. But she got fired."

"For this?"

"That's what I heard."

A car pulled into the driveway and his phone vibrated again. Davon excused himself, and I watched him through the front window as he gave his backpack to someone inside the car and returned to the garage. It seemed suspicious. By the time I opened the door from the house to the garage, Davon had returned to the car carrying a crate covered with a towel.

As they drove off, I thought about Cynthia, who'd once proposed to the president of Christopher

Columbus that the university change its name back to King George's College. Of course, the president said that was out of the question.

Alone finally, I pulled a pack of cigarettes from my luggage and went for a walk on the trails behind my sister's house. All of the stress had me returning to my bad habit. I knew Janice would kill me if she found out I smoked, but I couldn't resist the urge. In fact, if it hadn't been for Cynthia showing up on my fire escape with cigarettes, I probably wouldn't have started again.

I continued down a dirt trail in the woods behind Janice's house, smoking. It was chillier than I expected, given that the sun soaked the trees. As kids, my sister and I rode dirt bikes down these trails. We'd hop off our bikes near a stream and catch frogs, or toss sticks at water snakes circling turtles. After one final drag, I put out the cigarette against a boulder and turned back.

As I approached the back porch, my phone vibrated. Michelle was calling.

"What's up, Michelle?" I said, sitting on the porch steps.

"I'm standing outside your apartment," she whispered. "The door's partially open."

"What? Did you go in?"

"Of course not. Who knows who's in there."

"Okay, just hold tight. I'll call Detective Landers."

"I didn't have this in mind when I agreed to save your plants from dying."

I dialed Landers and waited on hold for a little while before he picked up.

"Detective Landers."

"It's Allie Douglass."

"Yes, I got your message about the second letter, and I've been meaning to get back to you."

"No, this isn't about that. Or...maybe it could be. It seems someone broke into my apartment. My friend Michelle is there now. The door's open."

"I'll have a unit dispatched over right away. Are you near?"

"Actually, my grandmother just passed away. I'm in Alabama for a few more days."

"I'm sorry to hear that. We'll take a look around. See if we can find anything."

"Maybe my husband could meet you?"

"Your husband?"

"He works in Midtown. Barone, Sawyer, and Johnson? He's an attorney."

"I didn't realize you were married. Is there a number I can reach him at?"

"Let me call first. I don't want him to freak out. And I'm guessing you still haven't heard from Cynthia?"

"No. At this point we've interviewed her former roommates and her girlfriend. None of her social media sites have new posts, and her mother checked with the bank. Nothing."

I closed my eyes and took a deep breath. This was
bad.

"This has officially been deemed a missing person
case. We'll continue to look for leads, but in all honesty,
until something pops up, we're in the dark."

"I was thinking about driving to a town near me
here in Alabama, you know, to speak with Cynthia's
mother."

"I don't think that's a good idea."

"Oh, I just figured..."

"Let me reach out to the detective in Alabama
again. We've been in touch. But for now, you just enjoy
spending time with your family. When you're back in
New York, we can discuss Cynthia's case. And I'll give
you a call when we reach your apartment."

"Thanks, Detective."

I dialed David, but he didn't pick up. I texted and
he replied, *with a client.*

I sent a text back: *it's urgent.* A moment later my
phone rang.

"What's happening, Allie?" David sounded worried.

"Someone broke into my apartment. I just got a call
from Michelle."

"Really? My God. Is anything missing?"

"I don't really know at this point—they still have
to investigate. I can't imagine what value a burglar
would find. I don't have anything much, besides a

bunch of books, an IKEA couch, and a fridge full of takeout."

"Thank the Lord you're down there."

"I know. So, this detective, his name is Landers, is on his way to my apartment. Can you meet him?"

"Ah," he hesitated. "What time was he thinking?"

"I don't know. Call him? I'll text you the number."

"Okay, that's fine. And Allie. I really miss you. You know that, right?"

"Of course. Me too."

Things were getting even more disturbing. Cynthia vanished, strange letters appeared from someone who called himself William Shields, and my grandmother's sudden death after investigating nearly a dozen missing girls in Alabama. Now, someone had broken into my apartment. I remember thinking how fortunate I was being down in Alabama. How absurd.

I remember the same false sense of relief one time in college while walking home from the library late at night. I was a few blocks from my apartment when I had a feeling someone was following me. But every time I turned around I didn't see anyone. *You're just being paranoid*, I thought, feeling fortunate I lived in a safe Upper West Side neighborhood. I had almost made it to the door when a shadow appeared beside me. I felt a knife against my lower back. Afterward, I swore never to allow myself to be caught off guard. Now, here I was twenty years later. Caught off guard. Again.

I turned to go back in the house when I heard Naquasia call me from the side door. I tucked my phone in my pocket and tried to shake off my nerves as I approached her.

Naquasia took my hand. "You wanna see something?"

"Like what?"

"Come on. I'll show you."

As we walked, Naquasia told me that her cat, Athena, had disappeared a few weeks before, and she'd often search down this trail. Besides searching, she also had stapled missing cat posters on telephone poles near her house. But no one ever called.

On our walk I told her a story of how, years ago, Janice and the other older kids in our neighborhood swore if we listened closely with our eyes shut, we could hear ghosts of soldiers who'd been killed in the woods behind Grandma's house a long time ago. I shut my eyes and listened closely for horse hooves, cannon blasts, the swoosh of swords. Hidden in the trees, some older boys would groan and scream, trying to scare us. Naquasia grinned, shaking her head.

"I don't believe in ghosts."

As we continued down the trail Naquasia told me about school and her friends. She had been selected to attend a summer academy for gifted children. A few of those selected would be at her birthday party.

"I'll introduce you."

"When's your birthday?" I felt like an idiot for forgetting. "I'm sorry I don't remember."

"This Saturday. You're staying, right?"

"I'll try."

Naquasia frowned. "Whenever my mom says 'I'll try' it always means no."

She had me. What was a few more days, I thought. Besides, I wanted to reconnect, and this was a perfect opportunity.

"I'd be delighted to come to your party."

"Promise?"

"Yes, I promise."

"Pinky swear?" She laughed, holding out her pinky.

"You sure know how to get what you want, don't you?"

I gripped her pinky with mine.

Naquasia took me down a path to a shack that reminded me of something from a Brothers Grimm fairy tale. It seemed abandoned.

"Where are we?" I pointed to the shack. "I don't remember that from when I was a kid."

Naquasia shrugged. "I was always too scared to search down this way for Athena."

"So that's why you asked me to come?"

She smiled.

"Fine. Let's check it out."

When we approached, a cat bolted into the bushes. Then, I noticed a white man in overalls with a backward baseball cap wielding a long pole with a noose dangling from the end. I pulled Naquasia behind a tree. "Shhh," I said, with my finger in front of my lips. The man looped the noose around the cat's neck, yanking it up and pinning it against the shack wall. The cat screeched as he wrestled it into a cage.

"'Scuse me? Miss?"

I turned and there was a police officer with a shotgun resting on his shoulder.

"This here area is off limits."

I squeezed Naquasia's hand.

"Oh, I'm sorry, we just went for a walk and found this place." I heard twigs snapping and looked over. The man who had the pole-lance walked toward us carrying the two cages with a blanket over top. I heard the cats hissing and scratching.

The officer motioned his head to the man with the cages.

"We've been having some problems out here. Until we get it resolved it's best that folk stay clear."

I laughed, nervously. "I see what you mean. There sure are a lot of cats."

"The problem ain't the cats," the officer said; "it's that the cougars come down from out yonder and prowl these woods. It's dangerous."

"Cougars?" I said, glancing at Naquasia, mouthing *"Let's go"* as the officer continued talking, oblivious.

"Indeed. Folk have been reporting spotting them out here over the past year or two. 'Bout time we do something. One of them caught some little girl in Madison County playing in the sandbox a few months back and pulled her off in the woods. They go right for the jugular. Like tigers, really. Yes, indeed. It ain't pretty."

He pulled off his hat, wiped his brow with his sleeve.

"Well, thanks for letting us know," I said, turning back down the path to the house.

"Miss?"

I looked over my shoulder. The officer held up my pack of cigarettes.

"Think you dropped these?"

Shit. I had tucked them in my sock but they must have fallen out. Naquasia smiled, slyly.

"So, y'all the Douglass family, is that right?"

This was exactly what I wanted to avoid. Small talk in the woods with the sun about to set.

"Yes, that's right."

"Sorry to hear about the passing of your grandmother. Your granddaddy and me used to get on pretty well, considering the circumstances. 'Course, that was some time ago."

"Thanks," I said, noticing he continued behind us.

"You two want a ride? My squad car's just up the way. Be dark before you know it. Wouldn't want to see such a precious little girl frightened."

"No, we're fine. Thank you."

"Alright, then. You see any of them cougars, go on and holler. They don't like the sound of a shotgun cock. Usually run them off."

"Thanks for the advice."

I hurried a bit now, realizing the sun was lowering fast. I knew it'd be difficult to follow the trail at dusk.

"Have you ever come this far before?" I asked Naquasia.

"No."

"Are you telling the truth?"

She looked up at me. "Maybe once."

"This is pretty far from Grandma's. Probably not such a good idea, right?"

"Yeah, you right."

"Don't go this far without an adult, okay?"

She smiled. "Alright. You know smoking bad for you?"

"So is wandering in the woods."

When we returned home, Naquasia asked me not to mention our search for Athena, before racing in the side door. I agreed, but I saw Robert in the driveway and figured I should give him a heads-up. Just as I began to walk toward him, Detective Landers called and explained that my apartment hadn't been robbed, but the bookshelf was turned over. My desk drawer had been rustled through, so it appeared whoever broke in had been searching for something specific. I told Landers I had no idea what anyone could have possibly sought, but if I thought of something I'd call him immediately.

I approached Robert near the side door. He was bent on one knee, yellow rubber glove to his mid-forearm, with a dustpan and small sweeper. He noticed me walking toward him. He scooped up a dead bird and tossed it in a trash bin.

"Sorry about this. Let me get out of your way."

"Oh, no, you're fine."

"Yeah, these stray cats like to rip up the guts from these poor critters and leave them here on the porch. Like a tribute to the dominant species."

There was blood streaked on the stone steps and feathers strewn all around.

"I don't envy you, having to clean it up."

"It's not so bad. Just sad, sometimes. Once there was this blue jay with its legs ripped off, eyes blinking, wings fluttering a bit. Sad."

"I heard you lost your cat," I said.

"Yeah, Athena. She was a good cat. Searched all around for her. Put up flyers. No luck."

"I went with Naquasia for a walk behind the house. Found this shack in the woods with cats everywhere."

"Those cats, however, are probably mostly feral. Not too friendly, to say the least."

"There was a police officer out there with someone from animal control gathering them to take to the shelter. Said something about attracting cougars or coyotes."

"Matter of fact, I did hear a story on the news. There was a cougar spotted up north. Close to Warrior. Something about them losing their natural fear of humans."

"I had a talk with Naquasia about walking that trail alone. You never know."

"Well, all the kids in the neighborhood play out in what's left of those woods. Soon, there won't even be any trees or paths left to ride bikes. They're building a mall on one side, upscale homes on the other. Yeah, I give it a few years before the woods disappear altogether."

"Really? That's too bad. We had fun in those woods as kids."

"Yeah, your sister mentioned that. I guess change is inevitable."

TEN DAYS BEFORE

had planned on staying for a few days after the
funeral to help Janice organize my grandmother's
things and figure out what to do about the house.
I was also curious about this mothers' group and
what Mrs. Davis described as an alarming number of
missing young women, which she and my grandmother
had been investigating.

The next day, Janice and I prepared to return to
my grandmother's house for our meeting with Mrs.
Davis and the other mothers. While I waited for Janice
to dress, I checked my email. Four in a row were from
my department chair, Martin. The first requested
that I call him about a matter of concern. The second
explained that we needed to discuss this ASAP. The

third asked when exactly I would be returning. The fourth demanded I call immediately.

I rang the department secretary and she transferred my call to his office. Martin's voice sounded like he'd just witnessed a student jump from Central dorm.

"Allie, thank God. Where are you?"

"Still here in Alabama, Martin. What's going on?"

"Have you checked your email?"

"I'm doing that now."

"Well, I've forwarded you one from the Jefferson family. This nephew, Wallace I guess his name is, has made some audacious claims."

I clicked on the tab.

Dear Dr. Martin Hamilton:

It seems that my concerns about my aunt's choice for the Eli Jefferson Chair were founded. A top scholar whom I happen to know quite well has discovered several plagiarized passages in Dr. Douglass's recent book (see attached). Evidently my instincts about that woman holding a distinguished chair named after a member of my family were correct. Let's schedule a meeting to discuss how best to proceed. If we handle this matter swiftly and prevent alerting my aging aunt, there is a chance this will go away without destroying the university's relationship with my family or its credibility in general. I've left the

*number for my assistant. Call and arrange a time to
speak.*

Sincerely,
Wallace Jefferson, Esq.

This was absurd.

"What are you suggesting, Martin? That this is true?"

"Allie, calm down. I don't believe these accusations. Your work is authentic. Not to mention, his evidence isn't very convincing. However, I feel it's important, as your department chair and colleague, to discuss our response. That's all."

"Our response? Isn't this about me?"

"Oh, cut it out, Allie. This isn't me against you."

"Then what, Martin? Your reputation? Our department?"

"No point casting stones. Let's focus on finding a solution."

I sighed. "What do you want me to do?"

"We need to meet. Discuss the potential fallout."

"Meet?"

"With the university president."

"Oh, Lord. This is about the money, isn't it?" I laughed.

"What else could it be about, Allie? I was up front with you from the start. This donation means a lot to our department."

"Fine. I'll meet."

"Tomorrow?"

"Are you kidding? I can't just leave now."

"I can hold them off, but not for long. So, when?"

"Next Tuesday?"

"I'll arrange it."

I was furious. Here I was at the pinnacle of my career, and I could lose my promotion to full professor and the Jefferson Chair because of an accusation? My book had glowing reviews in the *Journal of Philosophy* and the *Philosophical Review*. Praise from distinguished philosophers, incapable of flattery, adorned the book's jacket. Including a blurb from Martin.

I was on the verge of becoming untouchable. That meant I no longer had to kiss up to department colleagues who never took my work seriously; no more laughing at sexist jokes at the president's annual Christmas party. And most importantly, no more having to prove I was one of the top minds in my discipline.

My sister suggested we go over an hour early to gather whatever documents and research we could find. On our drive to Grandma's house, I didn't mention Wallace's allegation to Janice. I felt completely humiliated by his accusation. I was anxious enough as it was, and in no mood to defend my scholarship to her, given she found my work superfluous at best.

My grandmother had still lived in the house in Elysian where me and Janice grew up—about ten minutes outside Birmingham. On our drive over, Janice pointed out how many houses had real estate lawn signs with the word SOLD. Apparently, over the past year developers had approached Grandma and other old-timers in her neighborhood about selling their homes. Most older residents relented to pressure from their children and grandchildren once they learned how much had been offered. Grandma had refused, and my sister wanted to keep the house. I supported her decision, but I confess it seemed more logical to sell. Unless, of course, Janice thought my cousin Daryl or someone else in our family would move there. Why pay taxes on a house no one lived in?

I mean, I understood Janice's nostalgia for this place where we were raised. Grandma's was a single-floor ranch with bowed steps and white paint flaked on the weathered boards, exposing them to air and rain, causing mildew stains. The peeling wraparound porch led up to a steel screen door that'd snap back hard, chasing you into the house. This paled in comparison to my sister and cousins' four-bedroom open concept homes with spacious living rooms, high ceilings, and two-car garages, but it felt like home.

Our property had been in the family for over a hundred years. As the story goes, my great-great-grandfather and other freedmen purchased this land from Andrew Shields and other former slaveholders in Jefferson County who, after the Civil War, abandoned growing cotton and built Birmingham into an industrial hub.

When I went inside the house I noticed bedsheets strewn over top of torn cushions with springs poked through. Staples that once held the fabric over top of the cushions were exposed like shark's teeth waiting for an unsuspecting finger to rip through. My grandma's decor was stuck in the 1960s. She'd had a radio, no TV, and certainly no internet. She took pride in living simply; living, she'd said, like her mother had lived.

My sister focused on the boxes she brought onto the dining room table, while I agreed to search other parts of the house. I paused at the doorway of our old bedroom, which looked just as it did when I left decades ago. Two twin beds where Janice and I slept, a dresser with Janice's trophies, and a bookshelf where my prized possessions—all books—remained. I went inside to the shelf and took down *The Strange Case of Dr. Jekyll and Mr. Hyde*, recalling my cousin Veronica reading it aloud when she'd babysit. I'd treasured Veronica's attention more than anyone in our family. She whispered the scary scenes as if uttering the words aloud would summon Mr. Hyde. I'd cover my head with a pillow when Janice convinced Veronica to act out the characters. Veronica's eyes widened, or narrowed; her voice became high pitched or deep depending on the story. She would crawl around the room on her hands and knees like a wolf, or lick the back of her hand and purr like a cat. As I flipped through the book, I came upon an inscription from decades before:

To Allie— Sing your truth, even if your voice shakes.
Veronica ☺

I choked down a sob and pushed the book back on the shelf, then spotted my leather diary. I skimmed entries that read like vignettes that could have been titled "All the Reasons a Black Girl Must Leave Birmingham When She Comes of Age."

I had written about the time men began to look at me in a certain way at the corner store. One passage described this perverted store clerk who'd eye my chest when I leaned forward and rested my elbows on the glass counter. Another recounted when my hips became too curvy to fit in my older cousin's jeans.

Next, I pulled down my freshman yearbook. When I flipped through, a photo fell out, of a girl named Leah Pearlman. She had moved here from Germany when her father was hired at Birmingham University. We bonded over soccer and Michael Jackson. I don't think anyone in the world knew his lyrics as well as she did.

There was this one time on our way to lunch we
became engrossed in a conversation about whether
or not Michael would ever do another album with his
brothers. We sat with my cousin Tasha and the other
black kids in my grade. A few moments passed before I
noticed everyone looking at us, whispering.

I casually suggested we eat outside on the grass
hill that sloped down toward a parking lot. When we
stood, everyone went back to talking as if nothing
happened. Leah seemed confused. I started to explain
but chickened out. I didn't have the courage to tell her
the unwritten rule that split our cafeteria down the
middle like a stone wall. It wasn't until years later when
we met for lunch in Germany that we spoke about that
day. She told me that she intentionally defied the rule
and sat with me and my cousins. But, rather than make
me feel uncomfortable, she acted as if she had no idea
why everyone got so quiet.

I pushed the yearbook back on the shelf and went
into Grandma's study to search her closet. There I
discovered an accordion folder tucked with other files
with girls' names and dates. This had to be more of
Grandma's research. Over the next hour we went
through the contents of boxes and folders, making piles
on the dining room table, and examined all we had.

I heard a knock on the front door on my way into
the kitchen. Mrs. Davis had arrived with five other

women, who brought banana bread, crackers, and farm-fresh cheese. My sister made sweet tea and we gathered around the living room, as I'm sure they had when my grandmother was still alive. They went around the room and introduced themselves, then we went over what we found in the boxes, some of which even surprised them.

Based on her research, my grandmother believed the next kidnapping would happen in Jefferson County, but she hadn't outlined the specifics of this theory. Mrs. Davis assumed she had planned on sharing these details at their next meeting, but she passed away. Having never surveyed all of what my grandmother had discovered, Mrs. Davis and the other mothers were astonished by the boxes and folders that covered the dining room table. One box had maps, newspaper clippings, and interview notes organized in such a way to make it easy for anyone to pick up where she left off. I pulled out a folder with notes on loose-leaf paper, photos of the girls, and interviews with mothers.

I'd always thought she gave up hope trying to find out what happened to Mom. But after going through myriad boxes of her research, I knew she'd kept her faith that one day she would. I realized anytime someone confessed to murdering a woman in Alabama (or anywhere in the Deep South), my grandma searched for ties to my mother's disappearance.

These older folders were separated from the ones from the recent kidnappings she'd been investigating. As she thumbed through piles, Janice wiped tears, shaking her head with a "Lord have mercy" after reading the gory details about how and where investigators found body parts or corpses of women who'd been murdered. After a while, I couldn't stomach going through those files. I was terrified about having nightmares: these women sitting around my kitchen table with their legs crossed over bruises, nodding their hacked heads. It was clear that even though Grandma didn't talk about those torturous days, for *years* after my mom went missing, she endured the pain like shrapnel lodged in her chest. She never let go of it.

An hour passed and Mrs. Davis suggested we take a break from the research. She invited the mothers to tell us about the days before each of their daughters disappeared. One said her daughter was last seen dropping her younger brother off at school. Another said her daughter took a bus to visit her cousin at Southern Methodist University. A few days passed. When she called her nephew, he said her daughter never showed up.

As they spoke, some of the moms pressed their fingers together, or massaged their arms, as if they felt the loss of their daughters like a severed limb — something missing that was so painful, so irreplaceable, that to conjure the memory continued to cause physical discomfort. They described arguments with their daughters over values, who they hung out with, how they spent their time, and other things that now felt as inconsequential as choosing not to wear a raincoat when clouds threatened above. Some wished they could rewind back to that last time they saw their girls and apologize. Janice and I met eyes across the room; she was tearing up just as I was.

We devoted another hour to trying to piece together the evidence in order to come up with a theory about where the next abduction would take place. Although we hadn't come up with anything solid, Mrs. Davis decided we should meet with the sheriff anyway, and give him a summary of these notes with a map Grandma created that showed the towns where each of the girls disappeared.

On her way out, Mrs. Davis handed me a manila folder with a rubber band to keep it closed. "These are other research materials and up-to-date lists of missing girls your grandmother compiled for our next meeting with the sheriff."

When Mrs. Davis and the mothers left, Janice pulled out the notes, photos of missing girls, and summaries of the conversations my grandmother had with the mothers.

"I still can't believe Grandma never told you about any of this," I said.

"Me, too."

"Maybe she didn't want to worry you."

"I admit I've been preoccupied, you know, with Davon's trouble at school. But still—"

My sister paused, then held up a newspaper clipping:

Forty Years Later: No Peace for Families of the Victims of the Atlanta Child Murders

I glanced at quotes from the women who'd organized a fortieth-anniversary rally. My childhood memories of the terror came back. I had always been haunted by the fear of a racist predator in Alabama like the one in Atlanta, luring children into his web, cutting up their bodies, and burying them in some earthen dam.

"Do you remember?" Janice asked.

"Oh yeah," I said. "That's him." I tapped on a photo of Wayne Williams, the black club promoter convicted of the crime.

"Think Grandma found some connection?"

"It doesn't seem like it from what we have here. The girls Grandma investigated are from all over Alabama. Wayne Williams only killed children in Atlanta."

"Didn't some people accuse the Klan?" Janice took the photo from me and examined it.

"That was one theory circulating in the news at the time," I said. "Some thought the Klan hoped to start a race war. The FBI denied this theory. Not to mention half the Klan are FBI informants," I said.

"Maybe she feared it was happening again—but in Birmingham? With all these protests over removing the statue downtown, maybe they *are* responsible for what's happening now."

I handed Janice a list of the girls' names and where they had last been seen—or, where they allegedly went missing.

MISSING GIRLS

1. Olivia Houston DOB: 8/11 Missing: 1/4 Montgomery, Montgomery County
2. Riley Anderson DOB: 12/19 Missing: 1/11 Pleasant Hill, Dallas County
3. Dominique Washburn DOB: 10/26 Missing: 1/18. Mobile, Mobile County
4. Brenda Roberts DOB: 6/14 Missing: 1/25 Letohatchee, Lowndes County
5. Paige Cuttingham DOB: 9/23 Missing: 2/1 Demopolis, Marengo County
6. Tasha Harrington DOB: 3/23 Missing: 2/8 Canton Bend, Wilcox County

7. Nicole Bennington DOB: 5/1 Missing: 2/15
   Anniston, Calhoun County
8. _____? Missing: 2/22
9. Jeanine Osborne DOB: 4/3 Missing: 3/1
   Tuscumbia, Colbert County
10. Diana Fleeming DOB: 3/11 Missing: 3/8
    Union Springs, Bullock County

"Wait," Janice said. "Each of them was kidnapped on a Friday? Seven days apart..."

"What?" I moved my laptop onto the coffee table, took the paper, and studied the dates.

Oh my God.

I searched my phone for Cynthia's last text message. Thursday, February 21. This seemed impossible. I grabbed my bag and took out the first letter. The date was Friday, March 1. I looked back over the list of girls. No others were abducted on the twenty-second.

We called Mrs. Davis and asked if my grandmother had brought up any ideas about why there was no person listed on that date. Mrs. Davis didn't recall, but she told us something we hadn't known. Right before she died, our grandmother discovered all of the missing girls had family from our town. She suspected whoever abducted these girls might be from here.

"Here? You mean Elysian?"

"That's what your grandmother said."

"Did she explain more? I mean, is there some person she had in mind?"

"No individuals. Though over her many years traveling the state as a social worker she paid attention to the more outspoken Klansmen and white supremacists. She said she had her eye on a few, but never mentioned any names."

Mrs. Davis suggested we bring this to the sheriff in the morning.

After I hung up, Janice hugged me for a long time. Regardless of how strained our relationship had been, I felt connected to her in a way I hadn't since we were kids. I realized I needed this. I'd felt so empty and closed off for so long; I'd been avoiding the pain I felt coming back, being here. But not anymore.

BOOK III

ASCENSION

*...he ascended into heaven and is seated at the
right hand of the Lord.*

—NICENE CREED

[MY OLD MASTER'S] DEPARTURE FROM THIS WORLD DID
NOT DIMINISH MY DANGER. HE HAD THREATENED MY
GRANDMOTHER THAT HIS HEIRS SHOULD HOLD ME IN
SLAVERY AFTER HE WAS GONE; THAT I NEVER SHOULD BE
FREE SO LONG AS A CHILD OF HIS SURVIVED.

—Harriet Jacobs, *Incidents in the Life of a Slave Girl*

FIVE DAYS BEFORE MY ABDUCTION

After Janice discovered all the girls had been abducted on Fridays, we knew their disappearances had to be linked and time was running out. We spent the next few days spreading the word of the missing girls throughout the state. Janice came up with a multipronged approach. First, we asked Mrs. Davis and the mothers' group to contact all the Parent-Teacher Associations in Alabama and spread the word among parents in their districts. Given that many of those abducted were in high school, we had them contact the high schools first. Next, I asked my cousin Daryl to reach out to women he knew in black sororities at Birmingham University, where he worked. Black women were advised to travel in groups and avoid riding in cabs or any other hired vehicle for fear that this would be the easiest way to be abducted. Then, Janice reached out to the sheriff with the hope he would coordinate police throughout the state. I tried calling Detective Landers too but had to leave a message.

We felt confident that by Friday we had done everything in our power to prevent another kidnapping. What we hadn't considered—something impossible for us to know at the time—was that Matthew Strong had his eye on a specific girl. Regardless of how hard we worked, he had set his plan in motion months before, and his next victim would be gone before anyone had a chance to blink.

Janice and I met Mrs. Davis in the sheriff's office waiting room. A few minutes passed before the sheriff waved us in. Sweat circles soaked the armpits of his unbuttoned shirt. He reclined in his chair and fanned himself with his hat as I explained that he had missed several important pieces of evidence during his initial investigation.

"With all due respect, Professor, I'm not quite sure I appreciate your tone," the sheriff said.

"My tone?"

"That's right."

Mrs. Davis placed on the sheriff's desk my grandmother's map with the dates and locations where the girls disappeared.

"See here, Sheriff," she said. "These ten young ladies vanished over the past few months. Seven days apart. On Fridays."

The sheriff leaned onto his elbows and examined the list.

"And how are you certain they were kidnapped? You do realize my office gets over a dozen calls a year from parents claiming their child's been abducted? When in reality they're nearby, just messin' around. I told you this last time."

"But were all those women black?" I asked.

"Oh please." The sheriff sighed. "You trying to make this a race thing? There are more white children than black missing each year in Alabama."

"That may be the case, Sheriff. But our girls are all around the same age. Abducted one week apart from one another," I said. "That certainly warrants greater attention from this office. Doesn't that look like a pattern?"

"Professor, you got some political agenda, here?"

"No, not at all."

"Well I'll be damned if at the end of my career I'm gonna to let you bring racial politics into this office. I've been sheriff for over twenty-five years and, the Lord as my witness, I have never made a law enforcement decision based on color."

"Sheriff, no one's interested in tearing you down," Mrs. Davis said.

"Then why waltz in here accusing me of being some racist? I've contacted local law enforcement in every town on your grandma's map. Hell, I even went ahead and called the National Center for Missing and Exploited Children. Spoke with the Alabama state director just the other day. Until we have evidence to the contrary, these girls and young women are missing, not kidnapped."

"I'm sure there's more that you can do. If my grandmother's calculations are right, there should be another abduction on Friday. That's just in a few days."

The sheriff sucked his teeth. "You want me to call the National Guard to protect every black girl in the state on Friday?"

"That's not what I'm suggesting. But you can search harder for clues to catch whoever is responsible for kidnapping the others."

"Where we gonna start searching? You have any new leads?"

"What about the Oak Mountains?"

"Oh Christ!" the sheriff blurted, then rolled his chair over to the wall. He tapped a map with a pointer.

"See this here map? How do you suppose we're gonna search all of these mountains without any clue where to begin?

"What about the State Patrol?"

"Let me be clear. We've done our initial investigation. Local police interviewed family, searched the homes and premises, and established these as missing person cases. That's not nothing, you hear? We need some new leads. Now, you can go on and speak with any law enforcement agencies in the state. Hire a private investigator. Whatever. But at this point, there simply ain't any more this office can do."

"Can't you contact the sheriffs in the other counties? Ask if they'd help us search?"

The sheriff shook his head as he went to the door. "Dexter! Wyatt! Kenny! Get in here!"

Three men sauntered into the room. "Now, these ladies believe we have not done our due diligence about these missing girls."

"But, Sheriff..."

"Now, hold on a minute, Kenny. I know you've already looked into it. But I'd like you to go back over them folders and see if you can compare this map with the list of locations we've already searched."

"Yes, sir."

The sheriff turned to us. "Now, we're going to give this our total attention. You hear that? Our complete and total attention. For one day."

"One day?" I said, shocked. "That's it?"

"Indeed. For one *full* day the sheriff's department is going to hold off on all these other complaints and concerns of the citizens of Jefferson County and focus exclusively on these cases. Consider it a way of paying respect to your grandmother."

"And then what?"

"If we find any leads—any direction at all—I'll coordinate with the highway patrol's chief myself."

In the sheriff's parking lot, we contemplated our options. Mrs. Davis explained that the problem was as much with the system as with the mentality of law enforcement when teens went missing. I didn't fully understand what she meant.

"'Cause most of the girls are over sixteen, the police approach these cases as voluntary flights. They don't take those as seriously as if they were children."

"But none of these girls had any real reason to run away."

Mrs. Davis nodded. "Yes, that may be true. But without eyewitnesses or evidence of foul play, the police rely on family and friends."

"What about the media?"

"Spoke to the local stations, and they all said until the police officially list them as kidnappings, they can't run a feature about them. All they said they could do was post photos and contact numbers on their websites."

"What about the governor?"

Mrs. Davis put her hand on her hip. "You serious? Given how reluctant the sheriff has been, you think the governor's going to want to get involved?"

"But with the upcoming election against Thomas Turner you'd think the governor would be more concerned about his image with black people in Alabama."

"I guess you're right."

I turned to my sister. "Janice, didn't you say state senators have children who attend the Oak Mountain Academy?"

"Yes?"

"Can't we speak with them about it? At Thomas Turner's event?"

"Maybe. But I don't think many will be there. Most of them support the current governor."

"Seems like we're gonna have to mobilize on our own. Start with the churches and schools. Get some young people involved," I suggested.

"Let me check with our cousin Daryl over at the university. Ask him to organize college students to help spread awareness, maybe get a search party going," Janice offered.

"In the meantime," Mrs. Davis slipped her key in the car door, "I'll organize a meeting down at the AME church in Birmingham with community members. We ain't going to let one more girl disappear from under our noses."

FOUR DAYS BEFORE

The next morning I sat on the back porch and called Detective Landers in New York and told him about our meeting with the sheriff and that Janice and I had discovered a pattern in the disappearances of young black women and girls across Alabama on Fridays. The only Friday without an entry was the day Cynthia went missing. They still had no leads on who ransacked my apartment, but he said I needed to consider the possibility that I, too, might be a target.

I didn't have all the puzzle pieces, but I observed a faint outline of something I knew instinctively to fear, like fire or heights. As David Hume argued in "On the Reason of Animals," animals lacked humans' ability to reason, but observation and instinct provided them with enough wisdom to avoid actions bound to cause them harm. Humans' instinct to comprehend what they deem unusual phenomena actually puts them in greater danger than lower-order animals. Our curiosity. Desire for understanding is often our undoing.

When I came inside, Janice handed me a package that had been tucked into the screen door with my name written in black marker. *Not again.* I brought the box to my ear and listened for a ticking, then tore through the tape. There was a stuffed cougar and a letter.

I handed Janice the stuffed cougar and read the letter aloud.

Dear Professor Douglass,

I do hope you have found your trip back down to Alabama refreshing. While disappointed I have not yet heard from you regarding the event we have planned in Warrior, I recognize the timing is, perhaps, not ideal. Nevertheless, those who have joined my cause remain eager to discuss with you our movement. Despite misrepresentations in the media, our mission is proactive rather than reactive; it is based on rational reasoning rather than hatred.

You know quite well that successful revolutions throughout history have always been rooted in ideas derived from measured contemplation and reasoning. Unfortunately, until now, many of those who share my veneration of my ancestors' struggle have failed because they focused on instilling hatred rather than inspiring others by a higher purpose, a divine cause. A man driven by such a cause is more valuable than one motivated by hatred.

I admit, professor, you have written intelligently, if inaccurately, about the ideas that animated my ancestors' struggle in the face of more overwhelming odds than any other generation in our nation's history.

I look forward to the opportunity to speak with you about the philosophical foundation of our contemporary movement to reclaim this nation from those who abandoned the ideals our ancestors died to protect.

For the cause,
William Shields, Esq.

I looked up and Janice had covered her mouth.

"Lord have mercy, Allie. Whoever is sending these letters is really messing with you. And how does this man know you're staying *here*?"

"I have no idea."

I scanned the letter with my phone.

"What are you doing?"

"Sending a copy to Detective Landers."

I forwarded the scanned pages in a text to the detective. When Robert came in through the side door, I jumped.

"Sorry, Allie. I didn't mean to startle you," he said, pulling off his coat and dropping his keys on the kitchen counter.

"Allie has a stalker," Janice said, holding up the cougar and the letter.

"You're kidding." Robert went to the fridge for sweet tea before coming over to see for himself.

"Her apartment was broken into last week. Now this?"

I explained about my graduate student's disappearance, and the detectives who arrived at my door with a strange letter and a copy of my book found among her things. The part about my book didn't make sense, so I told him about the notes and lists inside the book and my suspicion that the guy who wrote the letter may have been the last person with my student.

"Do you think we should go visit Cynthia's mother and, you know, see if we can find some answers?"

"I don't know, Janice. I mean, shouldn't we focus on organizing?"

"We can mention Grandma's work. She should know other women are going through the same thing as she is."

"Well, Detective Landers cautioned against it. Especially since someone ransacked my apartment. I don't want to put her mother in danger."

"Oh, please. The police are always telling us to stay out of it, but in the end, they're just like you and me. Why do you think Grandma organized the mothers' group to begin with?"

After someone left the creepy stuffed cougar and letter at Janice's place, I knew I had to go stay at my grandma's. People with this level of fanaticism weren't beyond tossing a rock in your window or burning a cross on your lawn. Or worse. Neither Naquasia nor Davon should have to awake one night to something like that. I had no intention of dragging Janice's family into a feud between me and some racist who hated my book. And given the notes in my book and the letters corresponding with Cynthia's disappearance, whoever this was might just be the psychopath behind the kidnappings as well. He was evidently there now, in Alabama. Although Janice pleaded for me to stay, I convinced her this was best. Not to mention, I told her, living there would afford me more time to examine the missing girls' files.

Although I was born in Birmingham, we moved onto our land in Elysian after my grandfather retired from the church. "Started with our struggle over this land," my grandfather would say. "Our lives have always been defined by our relationship with the land. Planting, hoeing, and harvesting. Our blood, sweat, and tears fertilized this very soil, and our lessons, our philosophies, our stories, are preserved like fossils beneath this rain-soaked earth." For this reason, he always planned on moving back to this rural hamlet when he retired.

He had always been a natural storyteller, who prefaced his stories with "I once heard someone say," as if they derived their authenticity from how those who came before recalled a particular event. Granddad stitched a tapestry of tales based on the community's recollections rather than scholarly authority. Our past, he'd say, offers us a constellation of lessons we can read like stars. As far as he was concerned, our nation never paid for our founding fathers' sins, and this caused the specter of racism to continue haunting Alabama.

When I arrived, I settled in my old bedroom, shoved my clothes in the old wood dresser, and hung my dresses in the closet beside my grandfather's favorite Sunday suit. I was surprised my grandmother never gave it to one of my cousins. I pulled out the dark blue suit, still preserved in a thin plastic dry-cleaner bag. I held it out, ran my fingers down the covering, picturing my grandfather Sunday morning, pressed clean, fixing his tie, and mouthing his sermon in front of the bathroom mirror. I began to feel guilty for even considering selling the house and the land.

That evening, Janice picked me up to attend a fundraiser for Tommy Turner's campaign for governor. I couldn't believe she planned to support a Republican, even if Tommy was a childhood friend. On the drive over, Janice told me everyone knew months before that Thomas Turner would run as a Republican candidate.

Most were confident he would be Alabama's first black governor. The time had come. He ticked every box in a way that seemed contrived, if not scripted. That's what terrified Democratic opponents, as well as those who couldn't stomach a black governor. And the board of trustees at the school didn't hide their sense of responsibility for Turner's political rise from one of its first African American graduates to mayor, and now a candidate for governor.

I hated schmoozing with rich white people, especially Republicans. But I wanted to support Janice and see if I could meet anyone with connections that might help us. I took a glass of wine from a waiter circulating around the room, then went out onto the deck to get myself collected before I searched for Tommy Turner.

"Making friends?"

I turned and there he was, black tux, wineglass in hand.

"Yeah, right," I said. "Actually, I did hope some of your friends might be able to help."

"With what?"

"My sister and I have been investigating a spate of recently missing girls across Alabama."

"She had mentioned that. Picking up where your grandmother left off?"

"Yes, that's right. Did she mention anything to you?"

Tommy Turner glanced away, as if contemplating.
He shook his head slightly. "No, not that I remember.
But in all honesty, I haven't had a moment to spare in
months. And, from what Janice told me, there haven't
been any missing girls from Birmingham, so it was
never really under my purview."

"That's true, but—"

"Seems unlikely your grandmother would have asked
me about it, then." Turner shifted the conversation back
to me. "You know, Mrs. Maddie mailed me your book.
Who knew when we were kids you'd grow up to be a
genius."

"Well, I wouldn't go that far."

"Who would have ever imagined how far you and I
have come in one generation. We embody the progress
our people fought for."

"Are you practicing your speech?"

He smiled, leaning his forearms on the railing. "I
guess so. But I confess, most people would never be
willing to make the sacrifices I've made to get here."

"I know something about that. Tell me, are you
one of those socially moderate, fiscally conservative
Republicans?" I asked.

"Honestly? I'm a Christian first. Businessman
second. Republican third."

"So, being Republican is a business strategy?"

"Not entirely. I guess you'd call it 'pragmatism'?
Our chains have been off for over a century and it's

about time we do what we need to do in order to exploit opportunities from those who respect grit and a strong work ethic."

This sort of talk usually riled me, but I wanted to keep our conversation cordial, which meant I shifted the topic away from politics. Instead, I asked about his unusual ascension to mayor of a southern city. He told me about his stint in the Marines after high school, then his football scholarship to the University of Kansas, which led to a short-lived NFL career. Short-lived, he explained, because of a medical condition. Princeton Law School, then he returned to Kansas to marry his college sweetheart. He said he never thought too much about politics until his father-in-law—a Republican state representative in Kansas during the 1990s—pushed him. He was a huge Kansas Jayhawks fan and he'd admired Tommy since his days as a star football player. In fact, his wife liked to joke that if they hadn't married, her father might have adopted him.

"Excuse me, Mayor?"

I turned and I couldn't believe my eyes. It was Martha Jefferson's nephew, Wallace, who accused me of plagiarism. My face burned as he grinned at me, sardonically. Wallace put his arm around Thomas like they were the best of friends.

"Wallace, meet Professor Allie Douglass."

"We actually know each other quite well, Mayor. Don't we, Professor?"

"I wouldn't go that far," I said, seething.

"Me and the professor don't see eye to eye." Wallace smiled.

"That's good." Turner patted his shoulder. "I've always found it best to surround myself with critics. What's that saying, 'Keep your friends close and your enemies closer'?"

"I'm not familiar with that one," Wallace remarked, his arms folded.

"Sun Tzu. *The Art of War*," I said.

Turner nodded. "You never cease to impress me, Professor."

"Now, Mayor, if you're done with her, I'd like to have a word with the professor."

"By all means." Turner stepped back, probably sensing the tension now.

The mayor's wife took his arm, leaving me with Wallace. I searched for my sister and he followed me.

"If you have a moment, there's something I'd like to show you."

"I'm afraid I don't," I said, spotting Janice.

"I'm certain you'll find it quite interesting."

I paused, thinking to myself that maybe it would feel good to confront him about this bullshit claim. Maybe the wine gave me an unusual cockiness.

"Fine."

Wallace outstretched his hand toward the headmaster's office. I glanced over at my sister and

Robert chatting and laughing with the few other black couples. Looking back, I admit the stupidity of following Wallace into the headmaster's office. Given his disdain for my work and my selection for the Jefferson Chair, he was one of the last people I should have been in a room alone with.

Wallace shut the door, then walked over to a huge painting of a distinguished southerner hanging on the wall behind the headmaster's desk.

"You recognize him?"

I looked closer. I recognized that particular grimace—a face I'd come to know well, being from here. "Andrew Shields?"

"That's right. He was one of the founders of this fine institution. In fact, this building was one of his many original properties. There are only a few other restored plantation homes like this one. Most are in disrepair. But I have a relative who's made a hobby out of fixing these places up."

"Speaking of relatives, wasn't Andrew Shields's son, William, arrested for assassinations and kidnappings after the Civil War? Doesn't seem like such a noble family."

"We all have relatives who disappoint us, Professor. Besides, William Shields was brought to justice. No need to condemn the father for the sins of his son."

Maybe it was him, I thought. Not just the accusations against my book; he sent me those letters signed "William Shields." To intimidate me. But how would Cynthia have gotten the first letter? Had he brought it there and run into her? I knew Wallace was in New York that day, and perhaps he got my apartment address from the university. But then was I to think he also had something to do with Cynthia's disappearance?

"So, Andrew Shields's reputation has withstood the disgrace of his wayward son? Are his descendants involved with the school?" I asked.

Wallace smiled. "You're looking at one."

What a *bastard*. His disdain for me made perfect sense. The student protests against Andrew Shields's statue; his aunt selecting a black woman to hold a chair named after his family—not to mention my book's criticism of his forefathers' ideas. Things were changing, and he was watching his entire world fall apart. But why the hell would he kidnap Cynthia? Even if he despised me, how did Cynthia or any of the missing girls fit into this?

I needed to dig deeper. And seriously watch my back and look out for my family. I took a small step away from him. I should have left right then, but it occurred to me that if he was behind all of this, I might say something that would provoke him to tell me a clue, or puzzle piece, I could use to locate Cynthia and the other girls. I recalled Davon and the students who protested the statue.

"I'm sure you don't appreciate the students' protest against the Andrew Shields monument downtown?"

He guzzled his drink, set down the glass, and wiped his mouth.

"Our youth have lost their way. It's as if they spit in the faces of men who built the hallowed institutions that saved this state. All this hooting and hollering is a symptom of a much greater problem that calls for creativity and a new approach."

"Does Turner as governor fit into this 'new approach' somehow?"

"Indeed he does. With Tommy as our governor, we'll return things to how they used to be."

"Is that right?" I laughed. "I would think Tommy Turner would be more interested in the future than the past. Especially the past when people you glorify did all they could to keep black people from positions of power."

Wallace crossed his arms and nodded, slowly. "Despite what you may think, I'm no racist, Professor. I'm talking about returning things to the 1980s, not the '50s. Our greatness doesn't depend on racism. My generation learned that. We accepted desegregation as a part of our state's evolution."

"So, you think Turner will return Alabama to the 1980s? I'm not sure many black people agree the Reagan era was one of national progress."

"Perhaps they don't, but I know from experience you can plug up a hole, but the water will run in circles until it finds a crack and floods in. My point is that this so-called open-minded culture of political correctness we see today has set our nation on course for its moral demise."

"Protesting a monument is about civic engagement, not our nation's moral demise."

"Maybe not. However, we've descended from a superpower to a pauper nation. You must admit we're no longer the world leaders we once were. The Russians own the White House, the Chinese, Wall Street—we sold our nation to those we once defeated."

"Oh, so this is about our nation's wealth? You seem to be doing just fine."

He smiled. "Traditions are more important than money. And this is the reason it's crucial we speak frankly about our dilemma."

"Dilemma?"

"That's right."

"What, are you going to send me more threatening letters signed 'William Shields'?"

"I haven't the faintest idea what you're talking about."

"I figured you wouldn't admit it. Look, I'm not interested in your games. If you don't approve of your aunt's decision to award me the Jefferson Chair, take it up with her."

"That's another matter I'll come to in a moment. I'm sure your sister mentioned the financial burden of sending Davon to this school. Am I right?"

"What does that have to do with anything?"

"Turns out there's a pretty simple solution."

"Let me guess. It involves me turning down the Jefferson Chair?"

"No, actually, my associates and I have been expanding our property borders near where your grandma lived. Putting in nice homes. Your grandmother's residence extends into the woods. We'd like to buy the entire property."

"Her home?"

"That's right. Now, your sister wasn't all that excited by the idea. But only a fool would turn down our offer. I was hoping you'd be able to talk some sense into her."

"How do you know I don't want to keep the house, as well?"

"Professor, we both know you have no desire to live in Alabama. And with your new distinguished chair, you're on an upward trajectory. Not to mention, it seems our families share a destiny."

"Destiny?"

"I mean your career. You go on and do some more distinguished works with the money we've donated for your research. Don't you feel that this is the least you can do?"

"Selling you our grandmother's house?"

"The property, really. Our offer will improve your family's financial situation, as well as assist Davon in his future academic pursuits."

"Seems Davon's doing just fine, and so is my sister."

"My wife is an active board member and a big fan of Davon's. But after the stunt he and some of his friends pulled downtown? Spray-painting the statues of one of our most distinguished citizens? You may want to reconsider my offer. There are board members who would like all those who knew about it but didn't name the culprit expelled. Maybe selling the house is in Davon's best interest as well."

He was blackmailing me. I tried to keep my composure. I didn't want to appear intimidated.

"I guess that's up to my sister. But, excuse me, I should get back to the event," I said, turning.

"Before you go I thought I'd show you something I brought with me, in case you need some coaxing."

He put a folder down on the desk. Inside was some sort of computer-generated document with symbols and words organized like code.

"I had my research and development department analyze your book using software designed for counterterrorism. Notice the patterns where you used other scholars' analyses."

"So, this is the big evidence you have against me? Everyone does that. Academic scholarship depends on building upon previous scholars' ideas."

"But your word choice and the organization of the composition is identical to those you've cited."

"That's not plagiarism. Anyone who knows anything about research knows that."

"I guess it depends on how you define the term."

I had enough. I turned back to him. "Are you blackmailing me?"

"I'm not that crass. But I'm willing to do what's necessary to help you see our shared interests."

"Look, Wallace, it's been interesting talking with you."

I turned to leave and he called me back. "Remember, there are alternatives. This will kill three birds with one stone."

"You can't intimidate me. Maybe I'll let Mayor Turner know about this bullshit."

I stormed to the bathroom to get my bearings. The fucking nerve. I folded a paper towel and dabbed beneath my eyes where tears had started to leave streaks. I was intent on depriving Wallace of the satisfaction of knowing he upset me. Plagiarism? Patterns of words and sentence structure that resembled other philosophers' writings? I had seen more blatant acts of intellectual theft ignored— especially if the book won a prestigious prize.

When I left the bathroom, I searched for Janice to get out of there. But everyone had gathered in another room. I followed applause into the main dining room. I couldn't believe my eyes. Wallace was in front introducing Turner. I'd always considered myself ambitious, but now I realized how self-serving Thomas Turner really was to get caught up with a corrupt asshole like Wallace.

I found my sister seated in the first row close to the podium. She motioned for me to sit beside Thomas Turner's wife. No way I was about to pass through the entire room, so I took an empty seat closest to the entry.

Wallace took the microphone. "When I first approached Tommy about this opportunity, he nearly spit his bourbon all over my feet."

There was laughter.

"But soon what had begun as a casual conversation became one about our state, crumbling beneath the weight of political opportunism and corruption. It's clear we need a man with Christian integrity more than ever."

Applause.

"Now, before I get out of the way so he can speak for himself, let's just take a moment to recall our progress in the great state of Alabama. No one can deny it's been challenging. Yet, when me and Tommy entered the Oak Mountain Christian Academy we both accepted that the future of Alabama depended on unity rather than division. Almost thirty-five years later, we have an opportunity to unite this state in the same way we've united Birmingham. Not only through our shared past, but by our values. Christian values. American values. And Alabama's values. Now, without any further ado, your next governor of Alabama, Mayor Thomas Turner."

The room burst into applause.

"Thank you, Wallace. I'm not going to take up too much of your time. In fact, I'd like to echo the sentiments of my friend and classmate here. When this institution's leaders voted to admit me and two other black teens, they acknowledged change had come. It wasn't an easy decision, and there were some white families who pulled their sons. But this school is like the great state of Alabama and the South generally: its leaders focused on the road ahead rather than behind. While we hold our traditions sacred, we also are driven by Christ's love. While we may allow fear to shroud our duty, when we open our heart to the Lord, we allow ourselves the opportunity for his wisdom. Our clenched fists and closed eyes become open to the light. We are children of this very light, which shines in all of our hearts regardless of race.

"Now, I know there are plenty of people—black and white—who are still bitter from the past. Generations of my black forebears tilled this soil, in some cases worked in some of your families' homes. Yet, it's time we focus less on past wrongs and more on future opportunities available to all who accept personal responsibility and abide by the teachings of Jesus

Christ. We have a destiny that must be fulfilled. I'm humbled by your encouragement today. It's time we come together, heal this state, and return America to its rightful position as a beacon of hope all around the world.

"With your blessings, tomorrow I will announce my run for governor of Alabama."

People leapt to their feet, whistling and cheering.

Wallace gave Turner a bear hug and took the mic.

"Now, if you all will take your neighbor's hand and bow your head in prayer."

A young white woman, probably a student, took my hand and smiled.

"In the name of Jesus Christ, our Lord and Savior, we pray. Lord, bless Mayor Turner. Give him the strength to do what is right, be merciful, and walk humbly before God. Amen."

The woman beside me shook her head, beaming. "He's something else."

"He sure is," I said, trying to hide my gut feeling Wallace and Tommy's performance masked something sinister. Wallace was not a person to be trusted.

On the drive back, I sat in the back seat brooding. I was flabbergasted that Wallace had the gall to try to blackmail me into selling Grandma's house by accusing me of plagiarism. I still didn't know how well my sister knew him, and why she hadn't mentioned that Wallace approached her about buying Grandma's house already. I wanted to ask, but it wasn't a good time.

Janice was livid because the associate dean pulled her aside and said a student accused Davon of spray-painting "#blacklivesmatter" on the Andrew Shields statue. Given the intensity of the recent controversy around the statue, as well as the publicity surrounding Turner's bid for governor, the school was under more scrutiny than usual. In order to prevent anything worse, the headmaster discussed with the board the possibility of expelling "troublemakers" who put personal politics before the reputation of the school.

We parked and Janice slammed the car door and raced into the house. When Robert and I came in, there was Davon sitting on the couch, arms folded, hood up.

My sister paced from one end of the living room to the other.

"How could you do that?!" she shouted, ready to unleash the wrath of God. Davon replied with short one- or two-word answers that did little to help explain his reasoning.

"You know the sacrifices we make, boy?"

He shrugged his shoulders, his eyes fixed on the coffee table. This was a safer response, but it didn't matter.

"Look at you. You think you're a man?" She kicked Davon's foot, forcing him to look at her.

"Go on then and act like a man!"

Davon's cheeks ballooned, then he exhaled, slowly.

Robert gestured for my sister to sit next to me, then took over where she left off.

"Son, this is not just about you. You're aware of that, right?"

"I don't know why you're so mad. It's not like we knocked it down."

"Don't you dare minimize this, boy," my sister shouted. Robert gave her a look as if to remind her it was his turn. She took a deep breath, folded her arms.

"Davon, this sort of behavior is what they expect from us. How many black kids go to your school?"

"I don't know. A few."

"And each one of you has opportunities that aren't shared by the majority of black people in this state, right? Son, your actions jeopardize the entire Sloss Fellowship Program, which your mother and I fought to create. Not to mention, this behavior threatens your participation in track for the rest of the season."

Davon's eyebrows jerked up, then he sat forward, resting his elbows on his thighs.

"Dad, like, we were just joking. Why do you guys need to make this into some big thing?"

"Big thing? Spray-painting on a public monument? That's a joke?" my sister scoffed.

Davon glanced over at me and for a moment, I thought I noticed beneath his defensiveness a little smirk. My sister and Robert missed it, but I'm sure I saw it. He was playing them.

"Look. It wasn't even my idea. Jessie's the one who—"

"Jessie?" My sister cut him off. "That white girl I see you with after practice? Oh, you didn't think I noticed her always cuddling up on you?"

Robert stepped forward.

"The point is, Davon, you can't allow other people to influence your decisions. We don't have that luxury. Who knows, Jessie's father may own half of a damn steel company. Rich kids love pulling stunts like this."

"Why do you two care so much about a statue that's going to be removed anyway?"

"Have you understood a word your father and I've said? This isn't about a statue or a white girl who's going through her chocolate phase. This is about you and this family. This is about our sacrifices to scrape together enough money for your tuition."

He exhaled, clearly exhausted by his parents' lecturing.

"Can I be excused?" he asked.

Robert looked over at my sister, who flicked her fingers in the air.

"Go on, then," she said.

Davon glanced at me as if he'd expected me to say something or to intervene somehow. I raised my eyebrows sympathetically as he passed on his way upstairs.

"I'll call the dean back. Let her know we spoke with him," Robert said, going to the refrigerator and getting a beer. He pulled up a stool across from us.

"Will they suspend him?" I asked.

Robert took a swig. "He's on probation already. Now, with this incident, I don't know."

My sister went over to the cabinet and took down two glasses, then poured us wine.

"Twenty thousand dollars flushed down the toilet because this boy trying to impress some girl by acting like a radical?"

Janice sipped her wine, then went on to recount the strings she pulled to have Davon accepted, and with enough of a scholarship to make it affordable. She told me about Davon's learning disability, which hadn't been diagnosed until eighth grade. By that time, his performance in school had suffered. My sister was thrilled, though, when he'd been accepted into the Oak Mountain Christian Academy provisionally. This act of generosity reflected my family's reputation and the need for certain powerful elements around Birmingham to reconcile the racist practices of the school before the civil rights movement.

"Well, I mean, at least they're letting their views be known," I offered.

"Oh please. This ain't the sixties, Allie. And that boy cares about two things—sports and girls. He even admitted he joined those little wannabe activists in the Students of Color Association because he liked some girl. Probably, Jessie.

"Not to mention," she continued, "this wasn't any public protest or standing up for something. Spray-painting a Confederate statue is nothing but attention-seeking behavior of the worst kind."

"So, wait. Are they really taking it down?"

"It's complicated," Robert explained. "The city council voted to remove the statue about a month ago. Since then, the governor signed a law."

"Heritage Preservation Act, he calls it," my sister said.

"It essentially makes it illegal for local organizations and city municipalities to remove 'southern heritage,' claiming these monuments and memorials represent our past and deserve protecting. The city council in Birmingham—about half of whom are black—plan on removing it anyway."

"So, he spray-painted a statue that's going to be removed and they'll kick him out of school for that? Seriously?"

"Allie, the Republican state senator who wrote the bill has a daughter at the school."

"Sounds like the students found a pressure point. I admire them for pushing it," I said.

"You know good and well that there's no place for this sort of vandalism. Demonstrations are one thing. But what he did is illegal and is going to get that boy in serious trouble."

THREE DAYS BEFORE

The next morning my sister asked me to go with her to the Oak Mountain Academy and meet with students to convince them not to participate in the rally in Linn Park on Sunday. Apparently, the Students of Color Association had joined with black colleges and clubs to hold rallies in Linn Park to counter those who came from all over the South to demonstrate against removing the Andrew Shields statue. Given the missing girls and increased racial tensions, Janice hoped I'd be able to persuade the students—especially Davon—against antagonizing those who continued to rally around the statue. With the fiftieth-anniversary civil rights march scheduled in a few days, Janice feared the students might cause a riot. Maybe I could convince them to write an article

for the newspaper instead. Use their words? She
suggested.

Their teacher expected an academic like me to be
objective, detached, unflappable. She hoped I would
tell them I found their provocative behavior unwise,
perhaps dangerous. Even if I admired the students'
courage, I couldn't go against my sister's request.

When we arrived, Janice met with the headmaster
while a student escorted me to the James Sloss
Conference Room, where the Students of Color
Association, SOCA for short, met each week. I looked
up at the clock, noticing portraits of Andrew Shields
and Jefferson Davis side by side. Some students sat
in a semicircle on the carpet, others on desks, or atop
radiators running along the wall. There were eight
students: two white, six black. The faculty advisor, Ms.
Adams, was white, in her early twenties, and wore hip
clear glasses. She rushed over with her hand extended.

"Professor Douglass. Wonderful to meet you." Ms.
Adams motioned to a black woman who stood near the
whiteboard. "You've met Dr. Langston, our associate
head of school? She and you both attended the same
university."

Dr. Langston smiled shyly like a friend from high
school waiting to see if I recognized her.

"Nice to meet you, Dr. Langston."

We shook hands.

"Pleasure's mine, Professor Douglass."

Ms. Adams turned to the students who had been laughing, joking, and talking about things that dominated teen life—friendship drama, relationship drama, parent drama.

"Okay, y'all." She clapped her hands twice to get their attention. "Let's make Professor Douglass feel welcome."

I looked over to my nephew, one of four boys in the group. He sat beside a white girl who I figured must have been Jessie. Now I understood what my sister meant about Davon's transformation from gamer to activist. I remember Janice saying in high school the best way to recruit young black men to social causes was flirtation and the promise of a party. I'd thought that was a male thing, until I found the same dynamic as an undergraduate.

Ms. Adams gestured to a student, prompting him to introduce himself. The other students followed suit. When my nephew's turn came, the girls sitting beside him giggled as if he'd said something funny.

The laughter died down and Ms. Adams began:

"Although there are some of you who have decided to take matters into your own hands, respect for other people's opinions is a crucial part of advocating for change. This includes challenging immoral laws, not vandalism. Furthermore, even those like Martin Luther King Jr. adhered to a court order despite how unpopular it made him with some young activists."

She went on and on; one moment she looked like she pitied them, and the next like she despised them. After a dramatic pause, she reminded the group of the importance of atoning; apologizing is simply not enough. All of them needed to reflect on the possible consequences for the school and for the group. "Consider what those who embrace hate gain from stunts like this."

"An education?" one of the boys said, eyebrows raised as if he was serious.

A black girl with short braids slapped him on the arm. He pulled his arm back— "Ouch!"

"No, Michael. Fodder. Fodder for those who preach hate."

Ms. Adams paused, scanning the faces of the others.

"Despite your noble intentions, spray-painting a provocative slogan on public property only adds fuel to the fire."

A few of the students chuckled, then pushed one another.

"Sam? Do you have something constructive to share with the group?" Dr. Langston asked.

"Ah, no."

"Please, enlighten us? Or perhaps, Lillian, you'd like to share what's so funny?"

Lillian brought her hand to her mouth, muffling her laughter. "It's just, I thought that they were going to remove the statue."

"Excuse me?"

"What she means is," Davon sat up, pulling down his hood. "Isn't the city council going to have the statue removed?"

"And how is that relevant? You suppose this line of reasoning makes your actions any less disrespectful?"

Davon's friends' head nods roused his confidence. He shrugged. "I mean, is it really a big deal someone spray-painted on something about to be removed?"

Dr. Langston glared at Davon, then glanced over to Ms. Adams, who gripped a desk as if she was on one of those carnival rides that drops you straight down.

"If that someone is you, Davon, then yes, it's a big deal."

Ms. Adams exhaled dramatically. Davon scowled as if poised for a fight. I stepped to the front of the room and snatched a marker from Ms. Adams's desk. I wrote "freedom" on the board, then turned to Davon.

"You raise several important issues that I'd planned to address. You see," I took a few slow, careful steps toward the students sitting on the rug, "the ethical issue here is about expression and ownership. Should people in a free society be permitted to express unpopular views publicly? Even if such expressions break the law?"

"Yes?" someone piped.

"Perhaps. But we must consider the implications of public forms of expression, such as graffiti on public buildings, within a context. This isn't about private property, is it? These monuments represent the general public—the collective will of the community, right?"

I wrote "Athens" on the whiteboard, then "Socrates." I explained Plato's analysis of Socrates's act of civil disobedience by refusing to participate in the public worship of Greek gods.

"Are there certain contexts in which defacement of idols of the tribe is appropriate? Yes. It seems, though, the more important issue is the meaning of the painted remarks, #blacklivesmatter, rather than the actions—in this case, spray-painting on a public statue."

They looked at one another as if unsure where I was going with all this. Maybe they were figuring out if I supported them or not. Ms. Adams came forward.

"Okay, then. Thank you for your thoughtful words. You have certainly given us plenty to consider. Can everyone thank Professor Douglass?"

One student started to clap and the others joined in. I nodded as Dr. Langston held out her hand for me to shake. She pulled me close. "I'll walk you out."

We made our way to the headmaster's office to meet Janice.

"That was an interesting lecture, Professor," she said, nodding slightly as we walked.

"How so?" I really couldn't gauge if they'd understood a word of what I said.

"I mean your talk certainly put things in perspective."

"Well, I hadn't intended on giving a lesson about ancient philosophy, but it seemed appropriate."

"Professor, these kids are at an age when they act before they think. Your lecture gave them something to think about. If they're going to deface public property, they might as well have an intelligent reason for doing so rather than a dare or prank, which I think this was really about."

"Oh, come on. You don't think at least some of them knew full well what such an action would cause?"

"Maybe. But, I doubt they were aware of the broader implications. The recent controversy over the memorial downtown has put all of us on edge—especially the black students at this school. It wasn't too long ago few black families could afford this school, let alone get in. For us to lose our foothold here seems to me like a step backward. Our alums and board have been clear to administrators about their expectations for students responsible for the spray-painting incident. And anyone who participates in this controversy."

When we came to the office door, she turned to me. "Listen, Professor, all of us are thankful for your time. But the last thing we need is our students of color embroiled in this controversy and being expelled from such a prestigious school."

"I understand, but I'm not sure that censuring them will send the right message. Don't you think it'll just embolden them?"

She shook my hand and smiled. "It was a real pleasure to meet you. And when you return to campus in New York, please send my regards to Cynthia Wade. I'm sure the philosophy PhD program isn't so large that you two haven't met."

"Excuse me? You know Cynthia?"

"Of course. She taught history and civics here for two years before leaving for graduate school. I don't blame her. But it's not easy recruiting talented faculty of color like Cynthia."

I felt like a car had just backed over my foot. I must have looked startled, because she put her hand on my shoulder, tilting her head to the side, concerned.

"Professor? Is everything alright?"

I paused and took a deep breath to regain my composure. Why hadn't Cynthia mentioned she taught here?

On the drive home, Janice told me Cynthia had been one of four African American faculty members at the time, and one of the most beloved among students. There were rumors that she and another young female teacher—a math teacher, as my sister recalled—were caught being a bit too friendly once before school. Nevertheless, these were just rumors.

By the time Janice turned down her street it was pouring rain. Storm drains overflowed, potholes were pools, and each crack became a creek running down the street. A clap of thunder startled me as I opened the car door and glanced skyward.

Janice and I covered our heads with coats and rushed in the house. I went to the bathroom, and when I came out, Janice was in the kitchen texting frantically.

"Janice, what's going on?"

"Naquasia isn't home."

"What?"

"I'm texting Barbara, our neighbor. Maybe she went over to her house after school."

I went into the living room and glanced into the backyard, thinking about my walk with Naquasia searching for her cat. She surely wouldn't look for it when it was raining so bad.

I returned to the kitchen, and Janice was on the phone with Barbara.

"Yes, okay. No, not yet. Maybe she's with Robert. Thanks, I'll let you know." She hung up, her eyebrows pressed together. "Barbara said she drove her home from the bus stop so she wouldn't get soaked." Janice nervously scrolled down her phone.

"Do you think she'd walk to Grandma's? Or go looking for her cat?"

"Stop asking so many questions! I need to think!" Janice snapped, then went upstairs and called again for Naquasia. I heard her phone ring as she came down the steps.

"Mm-hmm...mm-hmm."

Janice pressed her phone between her ear and shoulder as she put on her coat and went for the door.

"Janice? Where are you going?"

"Barbara's daughter said Naquasia talked about finishing a project at Bernadine's. I called, but no one answered so I'm going over there. I can't reach Robert but I doubt she's with him at work. That wouldn't make any sense."

"Do you want me to come with you?"

"Nah, you stay dry. Ooooh, girl. When I get my hands on Naquasia...ain't she got enough sense to leave a message or a note? All that's been happening with these missing girls!"

Janice pushed open her umbrella and skipped around puddles on her way to the car.

I went to the living room, my heart racing. I imagined the other mothers, first realizing they couldn't account for their daughters' whereabouts. I wondered if they told themselves it was simply a miscommunication. Their daughters would text back, or call. Hours later, they may still have figured their daughters would turn up, guilty as sin, for sneaking off somewhere with a boyfriend or friend. I wondered when they first felt a sense of terror that they might never see their daughters again.

I couldn't just stand there and do nothing. I called Mrs. Davis, gazing through the window at rain pulsing

down from the pale gray sky, pummeling the leaves
in the backyard. No answer. My eyes came upon
Naquasia's bike slumped near the path into the woods.
An alarm went off in my mind.

I dialed Janice while I pulled open the sliding
glass door and rushed through the backyard toward
Naquasia's bike.

"What's going on, Allie?"

I struggled to speak clearly as I splashed through
puddles. "Her," huff, "bike," huff...

"Huh?"

"Near," huff, "the trail..."

Janice gasped. "I'm on my way!"

Rain drenched my shoulders as I raced into the
woods, cuffing my hand around my mouth to amplify
my voice.

"NAQUASIA!"

I hadn't run far before I saw Naquasia's backpack
floating in a puddle off the trail. I sloshed over and
grabbed it, shouting her name again and again. I
thought about the creepy shack at least fifteen minutes
farther along toward Grandma's house. I prayed
Naquasia didn't go that far.

Then I glimpsed a yellow boot caught beneath a
fallen tree.

There she was.

I trounced over to Naquasia, lying on her
stomach, arms out in front like she'd been reaching

for something. I glanced around terrified, imagining someone standing behind the tree ready to strike. When I reached her I fell to my knees.

"Naquasia, wake up!"

I shook her shoulder.

"Honey, please wake up!"

I pulled her onto my lap and noticed the left side of her head was drenched in blood. I wiped her cheeks gently with my thumbs.

Her eyes blinked open.

"Auntie Allie?"

She rubbed her eyes like she'd woken from a long sleep.

"Jesus, Naquasia. What happened to your head?"

"I don't know."

I wiped rainwater dripping near the wound. She winced so I drew back my hand.

"Sorry."

I helped her stand. But when she tried to walk, she reached for her ankle in pain.

"It's probably twisted. Let me get you back," I said, helping her limp back to the house.

When we came into the backyard Janice dashed toward us. Not long after Janice called, a police car and ambulance pulled into the driveway. The paramedics rushed inside and over to Naquasia, who lay on the couch with ice wrapped in a washcloth and pressed against her head. Janice spoke to the deputy, and I stood beside the paramedic as she checked Naquasia's pupils with a small flashlight.

I heard the front door slam, and Robert rushed into the living room.

"What's going on?" he asked breathlessly, pulling off his coat and dropping it on a chair.

"It's okay. Everything's fine," I said. "She fell and hit her head."

"I tripped, Daddy. On a tree branch." Robert came to Naquasia's side and took her hand.

"She lost consciousness," the paramedic said. "But she's okay. A mild concussion, but nothing too serious."

Robert kissed her forehead, gently. "My girl hit her head?"

Naquasia nodded with her lips turned down, frowning.

"We covered the cut with a bandage. The ice will reduce the swelling." The paramedic pulled off her rubber gloves and put her equipment in a bag.

Janice and Robert listened as the paramedic gave them instructions for Naquasia's ankle and the protocol for a concussion. The police officer came over and asked me what happened. I mentioned the shack near my grandmother's house, Naquasia's quest to find her cat, Athena. He nodded, jotted down a few notes, and went over to Janice and Robert.

"Seems that our little darling likes cats," the officer said.

"Cats?" Janice folded her arms.

"Yeah, Mommy. I saw Athena. Her paw musta got stuck on something, because she was limping real bad. I followed her, then tripped. That was the last thing that I remember until Aunt Allie woke me up."

"Don't tell me you're still searching for that cat." Robert glanced at Janice with a guilty look.

"Daddy said you'd be mad," Naquasia said.

"Mad? I'm furious! Where's your sense, searching for some cat ALONE in the WOODS with all that's been going on with these missing girls?"

"I don't want them cougars to get her."

"This is too much. You stay out of the woods chasing cats. And you," she pointed to her husband, "you need to choose a new bonding experience. Fishing, golf. Whatever. Long as it doesn't have anything to do with cats and woods."

The officer closed his notepad. "We've made a bunch of calls to families in this here area about avoiding feral cats. We've been having problems with cougars out here preying on 'em. We'd rather not have predators down this way. Avoid a tragedy."

"Yes, officer. We understand," my sister said.

Janice squeezed her lips tight and glared at Naquasia.

"We'll certainly stop doing anything that may draw them around here," Janice said.

"I saw a man." Naquasia repositioned the bag of ice above her eye.

"What? Honey, you saw someone? Who?"

"Couldn't tell. Looked a little bit like that man we'd seen with the police."

"You must be talking about Deputy Long. He's been setting traps to capture these cats. Once a week he goes out to check on them. See if we caught one."

"Even in the rain?" I asked.

"Well, miss, our taxpayers aren't all that interested in us working only when the weather suits us."

The officer put on his hat, annoyed. "Speaking of taxpayer dollars." He tucked his pen in his shirt pocket. "Best I'd be on my way. I'll fill out a report and email you a copy for your records. Y'all stay dry."

After the officer left, Naquasia went upstairs to take a shower. I gathered the towels we used to dry off and pushed them in the washing machine while Janice and Robert argued in the kitchen. When I returned Robert had gone, and Janice sat at the table with her face in her hands.

"You okay?" I asked, hesitantly.

Janice turned, tears in her eyes. "Why didn't you tell me about her wandering in the woods after that cat?"

"I mean..."

I took a deep breath and sat beside her, straining to think of something that'd make sense. I figured I'd stop with excuses and just tell the truth.

"Listen, Janice, I promised Naquasia I wouldn't tell you. She swore she wouldn't search in the woods again without an adult. At the time, I believed her."

"At the time? Was this before or after you learned about the pattern of missing girls? Didn't you think with all that's going on you ought to tell me my daughter's been *wandering in the woods* searching for some cat?"

"I know, it seems ridiculous."

"Stupid is what it is."

"I'm sorry. I understand how you feel. If I had a daughter and she was found like that, I'd be terrified too."

"If *you* had a daughter? How dare you act for a second like you understand how I feel. You don't know shit about how hard it is to keep your son from doing some dumb shit that'd end up costing him his future... or keeping your daughter safe from all that's out there trying to harm her. Maybe if you took a second from your busy schedule to call or visit once in a while you'd have a clue, but you don't. Period."

And there it was. The judgment. The condescension. I felt blood rush to my face, tears coming. No matter how hard I tried, she always despised me for making sacrifices for my career rather than running home every time she or Grandma called. And now the truth burst from her lips, soaking me in vitriol.

I gathered my coat from behind the chair and walked away, my tongue paralyzed, my mind awash

with grief and anger. I had to get out of there. As I held
the front door open, I turned back.

"You're never going to forgive me, are you?" I said,
holding the doorknob.

"Forgive you? Oh please. Don't be so self-righteous."

"I knew I should have stayed at Grandma's house
from the start. I'm not welcome here. Janice, you ever
try to understand my perspective?"

"What's there to understand? You've put your career
before your family. I don't even know how David puts
up with it."

"David? You're bringing him into this?" I snapped.
"You know how many goddamn hours he spends
working on his cases? I'm tired of this fucking double
standard!"

All my grief over Grandma's death converged
with my guilt for missing so many birthdays and
Christmases. Everything I'd missed over the years.
I could've had so much more time with them. With
Grandma.

"This ain't about a double standard, Allie. I'm
talking about you. *Your* choices. Your fixation with
getting awards and writing a damn book that disgraced
your family. When will it ever be enough? When will
we ever be enough?"

"I'm done being here. I have enough to deal with
trying to save my job and marriage in New York."

"Once again, here you go running away the first time someone calls you out for being selfish."

"Selfish?"

I stomped down their driveway, dialing a cab to pick me up.

"Allie? Stop. Come back..."

I ignored her.

"Alright. Be that way. Do as you always do. Run."

Back at Grandma's I packed, then searched for flights—any flight to get the hell out of Alabama. On my way to the airport, I called David, told him about my argument with Janice, and said I was coming home.

"Do what's best," he said, "but remember your progress rebuilding your relationship with Janice and her family. If you leave now, what message does that send to Naquasia and Davon?"

Like the great litigator he was, he placed before me facts I was unable to dispute, in spite of my anger. I had told Naquasia I'd stay for her birthday party Saturday. I'd committed myself to finding out the pattern of missing girls. The more he spoke, the more I felt myself wavering on my decision to leave.

Shit.

I knew deep down he was right. Was I really about to let my ego destroy what I had reestablished with my niece and nephew? With my sister? And what about Grandma's house? The mothers' group? Janice had lashed out and hurt me, deeply. But she was scared and I got that. So was I.

As I wrestled with the logic, I found myself falling into an old, comfortable pattern (yes, the very one Janice called me out for): avoidance.

By the time I arrived at the airport, there was only one flight left to New York. I waited as the man behind the airline counter asked about standby, and my phone vibrated. I glanced down. *Janice.* Not now, I thought, silencing my phone.

All of what I wished I'd said to her flooded my mind. I fought my urge to return her call. She was right, though. I should have stayed better connected to the family. But admitting I was *wrong* did nothing to help change her opinion of my struggle to succeed in a competitive profession. Despite my anger, I no longer wanted to distance myself from my family. I sighed and told the agent behind the counter to forget about it and went outside to find a cab.

On the drive back to my grandmother's, I thought about Naquasia's secret missions to find Athena, filling a sandwich bag with Athena's favorite food, and leaving a trail from various points in the woods back to her yard. I admired her hope despite the dim odds. I couldn't help but wonder if my lack of interaction with children had made me cynical.

When I got home and flicked on the lights, I noticed the drapes fluttering in front of the sliding glass door. I scanned the room and called out for my sister, thinking perhaps she came over to check on me. Maybe she went onto the patio. But how could she forget to close the sliding glass door? I crept into the kitchen to find something to protect me. I pulled a knife used to skin fish from the kitchen drawer, then tiptoed through the living room, wielding the knife with two hands like a sword.

"Hello? Anyone there?"

A cat dashed from behind the couch, through the drapes and out the door. I shrieked, jumped back. A few moments passed and when I regained my composure, I slid the glass door closed. I felt relieved until I noticed a manila envelope on the coffee table.

Another letter.

I unclasped the envelope, my heart thumping.

Dear Professor Douglass,

Do you believe everything happens for a reason? Most people die never having fulfilled their mission on this earth. I find this unfortunate.

You have a purpose greater than you realize. And when the time comes and we commence our revolution, mark my words, your purpose will be fulfilled.

For the cause,
William Shields, Esq.

I fumbled through my purse for my phone. Three voicemail messages from Janice. I dialed her, trying to calm myself. She answered after one ring.

"Allie? Oh my God, where are you?"

"Janice, there's another letter!"

"Just tell me where you are!"

"Grandma's."

"We're on our way!"

My sister and her family arrived with the state police and two FBI agents who introduced themselves as Agent Washington and Agent Tyler.

Everyone congregated in the living room. I told them about the open door and the cat and the other letters signed "William Shields."

"Why does that name sound familiar?" Agent Tyler asked.

"You know Andrew Shields? The 'father of Birmingham'? That's his son. After the Civil War, William Shields became infamous for an assassination campaign—he considered it 'redemption' for the South losing the war."

"How do these letters from someone calling himself William Shields connect with one of your students who was kidnapped?"

"I'm not sure, but I think they do. Before I came down here she disappeared. Detective Landers of the NYPD has been investigating the case."

"What was her name?"

"Cynthia Wade."

I explained about Cynthia's disappearance and the first letter and the book they found with Cynthia's possessions. The strange fact that she once taught at Davon's school.

"Can I have a look at the letters?"

I went into the other room and returned with the letters. Agent Tyler read each one intently, then passed them to Agent Washington.

"These letters. When did you receive them?" Agent Tyler asked.

"The first came a couple weeks ago. It was found with Cynthia's things. Then, there was a letter left at my home in Westchester. Just yesterday a letter was delivered to Janice's house. Now, this one."

Agent Washington finished reading and asked to borrow them. I nodded. I'd taken pictures of them all already.

Agent Tyler showed me a photo. "Have you ever seen this man before?" He had a beard that extended a few inches beyond his chin. His silver hair fell to his shoulders in the back, the front combed to the side. He had a determined gaze; his lips, taut like a military officer.

"He looks like the guy I saw after my book signing."

"Are you sure?"

I examined the photo closely.

"I think that's him."

"Do you remember his name?"

I tried, but nothing came to me.

"No, I'm sorry. I don't."

"Professor." Agent Tyler pointed to the photo. "We believe this man may be responsible for kidnapping a girl. Some people recalled seeing a man who looked like him when searching the woods near a rundown shack close to here. Your sister mentioned you and your niece were there recently?"

"Yes, that's right. But tell me something. Why mobilize the FBI over one girl? We've struggled to get the authorities across the state to coordinate a search for nine other young women who've been missing since the beginning of the year."

"She's not just any girl. She's Mayor Thomas Turner's daughter."

BOOK IV

REDEMPTION

For I know that my redeemer liveth,
and that he shall stand at the latter day upon the earth.

JOB 19:25

I FEEL SAFE IN THE MIDST OF MY ENEMIES; FOR THE TRUTH IS POWERFUL AND WILL PREVAIL.

—Sojourner Truth

TWO DAYS BEFORE

Agent Tyler of the FBI explained that Odessa had been visiting her grandmother Madeline Turner in Elysian when she disappeared. Her grandmother called her down for breakfast and when she didn't answer, Mrs. Turner went upstairs to her room. Her bed was made. There was no trace of her. Mrs. Turner called all her neighbors to ask if she was over there playing. No one had seen her.

The police officer who took the initial report did a basic search around the property, then radioed other officers to search parks where Odessa was known to play. Meanwhile, about two dozen members of the Bethel AME church showed up to help search the wooded area. One parishioner approached a man walking near the shack that I and Naquasia had found, and asked if he had seen a girl. He hadn't, but later someone spotted the same man jogging toward a red and white van parked about a hundred yards down the road. Before police had a chance to question him, he was gone.

Agent Tyler asked us to contact her if we saw or noticed anything unusual. In these situations, she explained just before she left, residents who notice something out of the ordinary often provide authorities with the most useful tips that crack the case.

Robert took Naquasia and Davon home, while Janice waited for me to update David about these new revelations. Seconds after my text, David called.

"Allie, what's happening?"

"Odessa Turner has been kidnapped."

"You're not serious."

"FBI agents just left."

"What did they say?"

"Witnesses saw a man near the shack where Naquasia goes—out in the woods behind Grandma's house."

"Jesus, Allie. Everyone must be terrified!"

"Of course we are. Scared shitless."

"Look, I think you need to come back to New York."

"What about the lecture you gave me when I was waiting to take a flight back to New York? Rebuilding my relationship with my sister and her family?"

David was silent for a moment. "You're right. Do you want me to fly back down?"

I sighed. Part of me wanted him to, but part of me knew I had to be here on my own. "I'll be okay, I can take care of myself. I just wanted you to know what's up."

"Allie, I'm serious. This is in the FBI's hands now. Focus on your own safety and let the authorities investigate the missing girls and young women."

"David, I'll be careful. But we can't just stop now."

He sighed. "Fine. Do y'all have a plan that doesn't include chasing this guy?"

"We're discussing one now."

"Let me know what's going on, okay? I love you, Allie Douglass."

"I love you too."

When I hung up with David, I came back into the living room to see Janice on the couch, looking solemn.

"Sorry for blowing up on you." Janice teared up. "I was scared and angry. But that's no excuse. It wasn't fair."

"Hey." I sat beside her, and put my hand on her shoulder. "I realize you were right to call me out about all of it."

"It's not about being right. You never had anything to prove to me. All them degrees and awards don't matter. You're always going to be my baby sister who I'm going to do whatever it takes to make sure she good."

Me and Janice embraced. Our fight had been inevitable. Both she and I had to get all of that off our chests before we could move forward.

"So, what's our plan?" Janice asked, motioning to the box of files on the dining room table.

I shrugged. "I'm not sure." I went over and spread out our list of missing girls and the map. I tried to think about Grandma's next move. What hadn't we examined sufficiently?

"Janice, you mentioned that Grandma had been researching at Birmingham University's library with our cousin Daryl?"

"That's what Daryl said."

"Maybe I should go take a look. He could have something that brings all of this together. In the meantime, we need to mobilize the mothers' group and begin searching. Right away."

The next day we organized an emergency meeting at my grandfather's AME church to mobilize black communities throughout the state in order to prevent further abductions.

When I came into the church parlor, Mrs. Davis was engaged in what appeared to be a serious discussion with a few other women, perhaps from the deacon board, which my grandmother had served on for forty-five years. I nodded on my way to the table with cookies, coffee, and tea. I dropped a mint tea bag in a Styrofoam cup, poured hot water, and noticed my sister chatting with a woman I recognized but couldn't place. I felt edgy, my mind unfocused, having barely slept the night before.

Reverend Cary pulled me close.

"You know your grandmother would have been proud about how you and Janice stepped up."

"Thanks. But, to be honest, I haven't even really had a chance to organize all of my notes."

"Oh, don't worry. Just speak from your heart."

By the time Reverend Cary called the meeting to order, the room was packed. Davon arrived late with students from the Oak Mountain Christian Academy and joined the other late arrivals in the back.

I sipped my tea, feeling disquieted. I didn't want to disappoint Janice or the mothers. I whispered to Janice that I was nervous. She shook her head.

"Oh please. You're the one who got all this experience speaking in public."

After Reverend Cary gave a few words of introduction, she called me up.

I thanked everyone for coming, then introduced Janice, Mrs. Davis, and other mothers the group comprised. I recounted our efforts thus far; listed the missing black women and girls and where they were from. I told those gathered about our conversation with the sheriff and FBI. Then, I outlined our plan to spread the word around the state in order to prevent another kidnapping.

Before we broke into subcommittees responsible for contacting different organizations throughout the state, I opened the floor to questions. A teen girl near the front raised her hand.

"Has it only been girls?"

"Yes, so far. We've been trying to figure out how these girls are connected."

"But why not kidnap black boys, too?"

Good question. We hadn't come up with a theory why only young women had been kidnapped. I glanced over to Janice, who shrugged.

A teenage guy behind her said young women were more vulnerable. The sexist subtext of his claim caused an uproar among those gathered. Women shook their heads, and one disagreed, loudly, claiming young women would be wary of a strange white man. "And besides," she sneered, "black men cocky as hell. Y'all are easy targets because y'all think you so tough."

People applauded; others mumbled to one another for or against points made. Reverend Cary had to calm people down before I could call on a middle-aged woman in a large black sweatshirt with "Got Jesus?" written on the front.

"I was wondering if anything's come up with the local police? I'm not trying to start rumors, but some folk said they saw a police vehicle near Odessa Turner's house before she disappeared."

"I haven't heard anything about that," I said, thinking about my meeting with the sheriff.

She pressed on. "The reason I'm asking is that if you recall that mess in Atlanta, back in the eighties? At the time, my cousin Hyacinth lived there. She was saying she thought the police were involved."

"Mm-hmm, I remember that," someone called from the other side of the room.

"Once they got that man they just stopped looking into anyone else. Far as I'm concerned, they didn't even have any good evidence to get 'im. Y'all see that documentary 'bout that?"

A few people nodded.

"That's exactly the problem," added a woman with her daughter sitting on the floor between her legs. "These investigators love to focus on the evil of one individual, not the larger evil that's in all those who don't do nothing to stop stuff like this from happening."

"Preach, sister," I heard from behind her.

She continued, "Folk always looking to blame someone for their evil designs, but it ain't no use. There's plenty of evil in the world as it is. All y'all need to do is pause when you go into Walmart and look at

the faces of them missing young people plastered on
the wall. Shoot. They wouldn't've ended up like that if
someone would've said something."

Reverend Cary came forward, nodding her
approval.

"All these are good questions. Maybe Professor
Douglass will bring them up with the police when she
meets with them. Right now, we all need to break into
our groups and begin our work according to the plan."

People clapped, and I brought my palms together as
if in prayer and nodded. She closed her eyes:

"Dear Lord, bless us and give us the eyes we need
to see your truth, a higher truth. Give us arms to hold
that truth, and the legs to deliver that truth to all of
your children. In the name of our Savior, the Lord
Jesus Christ, who sacrificed his life for us, Amen."

"Amen" echoed in the hall.

Janice divided everyone into various
subcommittees. Some joined together to reach out to all
the churches in Jefferson County to warn people about
the pattern of missing girls. Mrs. Davis organized
volunteers to attend Girl Scout meetings, and other
school events where parents congregated. They
planned on knocking on the doors of PTO members'
homes in the towns where women disappeared. Some
volunteers agreed to post flyers with photos of the
missing women at local restaurants and stores, and
to make announcements at upcoming sports events

and social gatherings about the pattern in order to prevent other women from being abducted. Robert and the church deacon planned to organize men to patrol neighborhoods in the evenings, as well as establish a hotline for any young woman who needed a ride.

As people gathered their belongings, embracing one another on the way to different spaces in the church to meet, a couple came over with their teen daughter. The father took my hand.

"Professor, please know members of the senior group are here to support you in any way possible."

"Yeah, us too," his daughter said. "We have some Delta Sigmas over at Birmingham who are following you on Twitter. Any information you can share, please go on and send it to us so we can keep everyone connected."

I smiled. "It's great to see you taking initiative. And refreshing to know people besides a few dozen academics are interested in what I have to say. I'll be sure to share all of the information we have on social media."

When the young woman walked off, Davon approached with his friend Jessie. They told me a rumor had spread on social media that the white supremacists planned to disrupt the fiftieth-anniversary march when participants passed the Andrew Shields statue in Linn Park. With tensions rising, the Students of Color Association was divided over participation in the march. A few worried, given the headmaster's threat after the spray-paint incident, that if they joined the march they would be kicked out of school. Davon glanced at Jessie; then came the ask:

"The other students at my school were inspired when they learned about your background as an activist. I was embarrassed that I really didn't know much about it. Anyway, they asked me to see if you'd join us."

Davon dropped his hands in his pockets, his face yearning. My card had been pulled, as the expression goes. I'd never had a conversation with Davon about my activist past. I remembered Cynthia's expression when I wouldn't pressure the dean to change his mind about pulling her PhD funding. I still felt guilty for being so unsupportive. Even though I didn't think they understood how potentially dangerous their provocative behavior really was, I could see this meant a lot to Davon. I didn't want to dismiss his request outright, just like his parents and teachers probably had.

"Well," I said, spotting my sister over with Reverend Cary, "I'll consider it."

"That's all we ask. Just consider it."

I extended my hand to Jessie. "It was wonderful to see you again. Stay out of trouble, okay?"

When they walked off, I thought to myself that the last thing I wanted to do was to go behind Janice's back and support Davon's involvement. Especially after I didn't tell her about my and Naquasia's search for her cat. Yet, I decided to wait to see how things played out rather than put myself between Davon and his parents.

After our meeting at the church, Janice and I went to Birmingham University to see what our cousin Daryl had discovered based on Grandma's research.

When we pulled up, I saw Daryl waiting with his hands in his pockets just inside the library door. While we walked, he explained that Grandma had devoted hours to going through map collections and archival records of former plantations in the South. This included genealogical information about our family and property deeds from the 1870s. It appeared that she theorized the disappearances correlated with a recent project to restore old plantation homes. This information seemed vital—I'd have to study it carefully. There had to be answers somewhere in all this.

We approached a serious-looking white woman behind the circulation desk, scanning books and piling them in a cart.

Daryl nodded. "Is Lucas around?"

She looked over and gave an "It's nice to meet you" smile, melting away her authoritarian librarian vibe. "Let me get him. Is he expecting you?"

"Yeah."

She disappeared behind a door. Through a large window, we watched her tap the shoulder of a black

man consumed with reading a journal. He glanced
over his shoulder and Daryl waved. He hurried over,
smiling.

"'Sup, Daryl." They slapped hands. "You must be
Professor Douglass." He held out his hand. "I'm Lucas."

"Nice to meet you, Lucas."

"Can we take a look at the stuff her grandma was
working on?" Daryl asked.

"Yes, of course." Lucas turned to me. "I'm sorry I
didn't have a chance to introduce myself at the funeral.
Your grandmother was a truly blessed woman."

"I appreciate all the work you did with her."

"Oh, it's been my pleasure. Come on and I'll show
you where we left off."

Lucas lifted the wood divider and we followed him
to a back room. He gave us a mini tour of the archives
and rare book room, discussing the renovations and his
new role as assistant curator of the special collections.
Lucas's current project was on Birmingham University
during the civil rights movement. An alum himself, he
admitted enjoying uncovering documents that showed
the cowardice of administrators who denied students
the right to invite King to campus, while providing
full-on access to Klansmen, the White Citizens'
Council, and any racist who asked.

I must confess, I had never imagined Birmingham
University would give free rein to a civil rights exhibit
that criticized the university in this way.

Lucas took us into the conference room, where there was a map projected on a large white screen. He gave us a lesson about plantation homes erected during the apex of slaveholders' wealth and power and the new renovations all across the state.

"A few months back we had an exhibit on plantation homes in Alabama," Lucas said, clicking through slides. "If we move this map over the map your grandmother made of the places where girls have gone missing locally, what do we have?"

Lucas clicked to another map that merged the two previous ones. "Do you notice the missing girls are from the same towns where they are renovating plantation homes?" He shined a red laser pointer at the result.

I was lost for words.

After a pause he went on. "And look at this other map."

He clicked the mouse, and a map of the southern states from 1850 projected on the screen. "See that?"

A red dotted line appeared—beginning in Richmond and snaking through Tennessee, Georgia, Alabama, and Mississippi.

"This map is the Longstreet Slave Trade Map. We're using it for an exhibit next fall on slave trading in the Deep South. This line traces where traders transported slaves in coffles from the upper South through Alabama, selling them on their way to the large slave market in Natchez."

I followed his pointer as it traced each part of the path.

"A correlation," he said, smiling.

I had to tell the FBI.

After our alarming, illuminating meeting with Lucas, Janice dropped me off at the Justice Department building where the FBI had set up a field office.

Agent Washington met me in the lobby and escorted me to a conference room where Agent Tyler sat beside a pile of files. She popped up from her seat when she saw me through the glass window. Two other agents hovered beside her. After the formal introductions and hand-shaking, Agent Tyler waved for me to sit, then shut her laptop.

"What brings you by, Professor?" Agent Tyler leaned her elbows on the table.

"I wondered if you all had spoken with any of the mothers of girls who have gone missing?"

"The sheriff's office is supposed to send me a report, but to be completely honest, our attention needs to focus on the mayor's daughter."

"Yes, but we've found there's a correlation between the locations of the missing girls, old plantation home renovations, and a slave trading map."

I showed them Lucas's map that overlaid my grandmother's map of the towns where girls had vanished.

"But, Professor, you mentioned that Cynthia Wade had been abducted in New York?"

"I realize that, but she's actually from around here, and with the connection to Shields's plantation in Elysian—"

Agent Tyler cut me off. "Professor, please. We are interested in the letters coming to you, and how they can help us find Odessa. But this theory you have doesn't give us much to go on. You say the girls have been reported missing in the same towns with recently renovated plantation homes?"

"Yes, that's right."

"And these plantation homes are throughout Alabama?"

"Exactly." I pointed to the locations on the map.

She leaned forward, studying the dots on the map where my grandmother identified towns where girls had been kidnapped, then the line Lucas drew connecting these dots to the plantation homes. After a moment, Agent Tyler pointed to the plantation home once owned by Andrew Shields.

"This one here. That's near your grandmother's house, right?"

"Yes."

Agent Tyler shook her head. "Professor, we had the police check this entire area. In fact, this was where our initial search took us."

"But what about *inside* the plantation home?"

"The sheriff told me his deputies went over there and searched the house. They didn't find any clues. Given the renovation, it was still under some construction, but his men searched every part of the house they could access."

I recalled the weird interaction I had with officers near the shack Naquasia showed me. I also remembered how the sheriff's deputies looked at me with scorn when I questioned how well they had investigated the other missing girls. Maybe I was emotionally drained, but my judgment and intuition remained strong. Something was off.

"How do you know you can trust the sheriff or any of his deputies? They may be working with whoever's responsible for this."

The agents looked at one another as if my question was ludicrous. Were police involvement and police corruption, in general, really that unrealistic?

Agent Tyler crossed her arms. "Gentlemen, can you please give me and the professor a moment alone?"

After they left she pulled her chair closer to me. She reached for a pack of mint gum from beside her laptop.

"Piece of gum?"

I reached forward. "Thanks."

"So I spoke with Detective Landers in New York earlier," she said, crumpling the gum wrapper. "He said your grandmother passed away recently?"

"Yes, she did. Last week."

"You two close?"

"We were. She raised me after my mom disappeared when I was kid."

Agent Tyler had a pained look on her face. "Professor, with your grandmother's death, this missing graduate student, and these harassing letters, you must be feeling tremendous pressure. I can see how it would help if everything were connected."

I hesitated, feeling suddenly like I was in a therapy session. I let out a deep breath.

"Agent Tyler, I see your point. Yet, this isn't about my anxiety over my grandmother or anything else personal. I just think—I know—there's more to these cases than it seems. Someone is planning something."

"I get that, Professor, but your theories about police collusion seem off base. Regardless of their inaction, we're conducting our own *independent* investigation."

"Agent Tyler, I have no desire to step on your toes. I'm just trying to help."

"I realize that, really I do. But we have our own process and procedures. We need to build trust with local law enforcement and utilize them in ways that will allow us to investigate strategically. Not to mention, I'm not searching plantation homes all over the state without any solid evidence. And they're private property—we'd need search warrants for each one in order to get in. So for that we'd need compelling witness statements," she touched a finger, "footprints," she touched another finger, "or a vehicle parked close, plate numbers, images," she touched a third finger. "Anything that provides us with convincing evidence for a search warrant. What I'm saying is, we need more than maps that line up. I'm sorry."

Her eyes were wide, serious. Despite my eagerness, she was the professional and didn't need my help devising theories. She sought clues, tips, concrete things to build a case on.

"Okay." I nodded, deflated. "Thank you for your time."

She smiled. "No problem, Professor. And, like I said before, please send me any *hard* evidence you discover. You never know what might break a case like this. I really do appreciate your concern."

She walked me to the door. I paused, recalling Davon's previous activism against the Andrew Shields monument in Linn Park.

"Have you spoken with any students who plan to demonstrate against the statue in Birmingham?"

"The statue?"

"The Andrew Shields memorial in Linn Park?"

She brought her finger to her chin. "Do you think it's connected to Odessa Turner's kidnapping?"

"I think it's a possibility. Mayor Turner graduated from the Oak Mountain Christian academy. Cynthia also taught there. That means two people affiliated with the school are among the missing."

I could tell she was momentarily caught off guard, but she quickly regained her poise.

"I'll look into it. In the meantime, please keep yourself safe. If another letter comes to you, or you feel like someone's following you, please call us. You have my card, right?"

"Yes, thanks."

Agent Tyler had a point. I'd had so much on my mind I hadn't been paying attention to who or what was around me. Looking back now, it's clear I should have.

Despite the FBI claim that the police had already searched Andrew Shields's plantation house, Janice and I wanted to check and see for ourselves. I reached out to Reverend Cary to ask for volunteers to meet in the church parking lot the next morning.

People carpooled to the plantation house and parked outside the cast-iron gate, which prevented us from riding down the long dirt driveway.

"So, you're telling us that you think one of these plantation homes is where they're holding them girls?" Reverend Cary asked.

"I understand your skepticism. But this just can't be a coincidence," I said.

People looked at one another.

"I guess it won't hurt if we go on over there and check it out," Reverend Cary said.

One by one, we lumbered over a short rock wall and walked to the front porch. As we approached, I noticed the windows boarded up and a box with scrap wood.

"That's it, huh?" one of the mothers said.

"I thought they was done renovating it?" another said.

"Looks like they've gotten pretty close. No paint, but you can tell the front has been replaced. The door looks relatively new, even if the windows have boards."

"You don't suppose it's locked, do you?"

"Best we find out."

"Ain't we trespassing?"

"When we climbed over the rock wall," Reverend Cary said.

"Yeah, but going inside the house is something entirely different."

"I'll go," I said, stepping up the stairs. Stupidly, I rapped the door knocker as if a butler would invite us inside. I glanced at the others, and Reverend Cary motioned for me to knock again. I hit it again, then suddenly something rushed out of a corner and down the steps and behind the house. I jumped back as the others gasped.

A cat.

"It's just a cat," I said, laughing at myself for being so scared.

Then, I heard car tires behind us. A police vehicle raced up the overgrown driveway, lights flashing, sirens blaring. It pulled up onto the grass and the doors flew open. It was the sheriff and a deputy.

"Well, well. And to think we'd mistaken y'all for a bunch of teenagers." The sheriff smiled.

"Good morning, Sheriff," Reverend Cary said.

"Reverend. Some reason y'all over here?"

"Yes." I came forward. "We heard this might be a place we ought to look for Odessa and the missing girls."

"This home's been boarded up and locked since they stopped renovating, 'bout three weeks ago. Seems the land trust ran into some trouble paying the construction company and they've halted the renovation until they receive part of the pay."

"But," I said, walking down the steps, "the inside hasn't been fully searched? Right?"

"Professor, it's a construction site, and it'd be dangerous to go up in a place where they've only half built a new floor and steps."

"All we want is to be sure they're not in here. Then we'll leave, I promise." I pressed him.

"You just won't let this go, will you?"

He grinned, hands on his hips, scanning the faces of the others.

"Listen here. I'm delighted citizens feel compelled to step up and aid law enforcement as we try to handle this situation, but y'all wasting your time. What I suggest you do is collect information from your people about Odessa. Leave the rustling around in the woods and turning over stones to us. Is that a deal?"

"Yes, of course, Sheriff," Reverend Cary said. "We understand. Thank you for your attention."

"That's what we're here for. Now, some of you'd like a ride?"

"No thank you, Sheriff. We'll find our way back," Reverend Cary said.

He tipped his hat and we walked back to our cars.

On our way, Reverend Cary came beside me. "You okay?"

"I'm just exhausted. There's so much we still have to do, there's something I know we're not seeing. And frankly, I don't trust that guy."

"Sheriff's a good man, Allie."

"But there's something I don't trust about him."

"Trust in the Lord. Not men. But you know, your grandmother always found Sheriff Morgan to be attentive, even when he disagreed with her."

"Why don't you think my grandmother told me about the work she did to help other mothers with missing children?"

"Isn't it obvious?"

"No."

"When the time comes, it will be."

"Did it have anything to do with my mother?"

"Maybe. But you know something? One time she told me working with those mothers gave her strength. That's a gift. Like all the Lord's gifts, we have to embrace them if they're going to have any positive effect on our lives."

"I understand what you mean in theory. It seems that black people around here are always the ones who are reaching out to the authorities when the authorities should be reaching out to them."

Reverend Cary stopped and took my hand. "Allie, you weren't born until years after the bombing at the Sixteenth Street Church. Back then, it seemed most black folk abandoned coming together with white people. It took courage. But you know what? Your grandmother held a meeting with a few white women she'd known for years after the funeral. For the first time I watched as Mrs. Maddie encouraged the black women who had gathered to tell the truth about times when the white women's husbands and fathers touched them inappropriately, and even in some cases outright abused them. They told these white women how they had neglected their own families to help them raise theirs. Some even chastised them for participating in a system of inequality that was the work of the devil. There were tears shed, certainly. But in the end, those white women vowed to follow our lead and do what needed to be done."

"But look at everything that's happened now! Where are the white women to help us?" I asked.

"I'm not suggesting we achieved all of what we set out to achieve. But through it, we developed a sense of collective empathy."

"Honestly, Reverend Cary, I couldn't care less about gaining sympathy from those who did this to my Cynthia and other young women."

"Empathy is not the same thing as sympathy, and you know that. We may have imagined things would have changed more. But we haven't given up yet."

"Don't you think those mothers care more about justice?"

"Justice is an illusion, Allie. If you don't find empathy, you will never achieve anything more than revenge."

"You expect me to say that to those mothers with missing daughters? Should I ask them to be 'empathetic' toward the people who destroyed their lives?"

"Even the most wretched acts have a higher purpose. A wise person accepts that there are some things she will never understand. The foolish ones rush around driven by a belief that they can fully comprehend another person's actions. Some things are in God's hands."

"Well, I don't think me and God are on speaking terms."

"I'm not talking about speaking to God. I'm talking about listening."

"Listening?"

"Hearing, really. Not with this." She pointed to her ear. "But with this." She pointed to her heart.

THE DAY BEFORE

Palm Sunday. Although Janice had canceled Naquasia's birthday party the day before, she still planned to attend the fiftieth-anniversary celebration of the civil rights movement. Odessa had been gone for two days, and news of her kidnapping had engulfed the state. If the mayor's own daughter could be stolen, who was safe? Black families kept their children indoors. Parents organized carpools for when they returned to school.

The media reported some believed Odessa's disappearance and the planned fiftieth-anniversary celebration march and rally could not be a coincidence. After Odessa disappeared, the city council president called for organizers to cancel the march, especially since even more white supremacist organizations

arrived to hold a demonstration over the removal of
the Andrew Shields statue. A march now, the president
argued, would erupt into violence and potentially
roll back fifty years of racial progress. But Reverend
Wayne Morris of the Birmingham Council of Churches
refused, quoting from Martin Luther King Jr.'s "Letter
from Birmingham Jail" during the press conference.
They'd march, regardless of whether or not agitators
and racists taunted them. It was their right. To my
surprise, Janice and Robert still planned on attending
the event despite the potential violence.

When Robert pulled in front of the church parking
lot where the march would start, I noticed the sheriff
talking with two officers on motorcycles. I had emailed
him an apology the evening after he caught us trying
to search the plantation home, hoping to persuade
him to look at the map Lucas created that showed
a correspondence between the renovated plantation
mansions and the missing girls.

I caught him glancing my way, then turning toward
his squad car.

"Sheriff?" I jogged over.

He folded his arms. "Now, Professor, as you can see,
I got a lot on my hands right now."

"I just wanted to make sure you received my
email?"

"Your email, the mayor's email, the governor's email,
and every single citizen of Jefferson County who has

some extra time on their hands to tell me how to do my job."

"Look, I understand, but the information we found about the girls—"

"Pardon me, Professor, maybe I'm not being direct enough for you. I don't have time to discuss this with you. But if you insist." He pulled a black notebook from his holster, flipped open the leather cover.

"Olivia Houston: arrested for soliciting a police officer a year ago.

"Riley Anderson as well.

"Sugar—or Dominique—Washburn: arrested for shoplifting and more recently possession of a controlled substance.

"I found a warrant out for the arrest of Brenda Roberts in Florida for several burglaries—"

"Is there a point to all this?" I interrupted.

He nodded. "Despite your dissatisfaction with my performance, I am indeed looking into these young women. What I'm finding isn't pretty."

"So, these women's disappearance is of less concern because of their arrest records?"

"Stop twisting what I'm saying to fit your political agenda. I'm trying to be up front with you. I'm the sheriff, true. But local police aren't likely to search too hard for drug addicts and prostitutes who, more often than not, have been abandoned by the same sort of mothers who asked Mrs. Maddie for assistance."

I was so done with this conversation. I shook my head in disgust. "I can't believe you have the nerve to accuse these black mothers of neglect." It was as if his laundry list of accusations gave him a sufficient reason to ignore these missing girls.

The sheriff got in his car and started the engine. "Listen here, Professor. I've withstood worse critics than you over the past two decades. Fact is, the folks of color around here know I'm the only one who can hold all this together. Done it before and I'll do it again."

"It seems that your office is more concerned about protecting white supremacists than these girls."

"You been in New York too long. No one's concerned about them knuckleheads camping out in Linn Park. I'm less worried about them than I am protecting these kids out here like your nephew, Davon, who won't be content until they've stomped on the baby toe of every skinhead and neo-Nazi in a sixty-mile radius. For what? That statue been there for decades. It's not bothering nobody."

"It seems the Birmingham city council disagrees with you."

"Maybe so, but the voters need to make that decision, not no politician or civil rights outfit. We can't have outsiders stirring up trouble. You should watch yourself, Professor. These crazies are not beyond doing something regretful to you. Once they have a target, if you see what I mean?"

"Well thanks for the warning," I said.

He pulled shut the door. I tapped on the window and he rolled it down, looking exasperated.

"Please, Professor. I really do need to get back to work."

"One other thing. The girls were kidnapped in the same towns where old antebellum plantation homes have been renovated."

"And?"

"Have you ever heard of a man named William Shields?"

"Name rings a bell. What about 'im?"

"He's Andrew Shields's son. He organized the original Sons of Light and wrote a confessional in the 1870s recounting horrible things he did to black people and those whites who opposed him."

"Okay, a history lesson. Ma'am, I know all about those things done to black folk in Jefferson County in our past. No one's proud of 'em."

"This isn't about the past, it's about now..."

"Are you saying that William Shields came out of his grave and abducted them? I'm not very good at hunting ghosts, Professor."

"Of course not, but perhaps he's inspired—"

The sheriff cut me off. "The Sons of Light are just one of a handful of evangelicals. No different than Jehovah's Witnesses."

"But Jehovah's Witnesses don't preach white supremacy."

"You listen here, Professor," he said, then glanced around. "I have always had the utmost respect for your grandmother. And I have always—*I mean always*—done all in my power to help her in whatever way I could. Even back when your mother went missing. But neither that, nor this here, is part of any racial conspiracy. Tragic as it is."

Why did I keep trying with this guy? It was useless. "Well, Sheriff, I hope it's not."

I watched as Sheriff Morgan drove down Eighth Avenue toward a line of officers near one of many police barricades. I went inside the church and saw Janice and her family seated in the front pews, waiting for the pre-march celebration of the movement to begin. I looked around, admiring the church. I recalled Janice telling me they had completed renovations a year ago. The entire front was refurbished stained glass, and a large cross took up the center of the window. Gone were the wooden benches and ancient, half-broken organ. Now there were theater-style seats, wall-to-wall carpet, and six-foot floor speakers connected to an electric organ. Although the renovations were new, the congregation was old. These same families had been coming here for decades.

On my way to join Janice, I was greeted by Mrs.
and Mr. Jackson, the Patricks, and the Meyers.
They'd all known me since I was a little girl. My
Sunday school teacher Mama Peterson must have been
at least ninety, but she looked the same as I always
remembered. And, sure enough, old man Wright
hovered over the organ, moving his hands like he was
massaging a woman's back; intently, softly.

When the song ended, Reverend Cary began the
service recounting the legacy of my grandparents
for both this parish and the civil rights movement
in Birmingham. Then, she smiled, shaking her head
slightly. "Isn't God great?"

"Amen," people called out.

"I mean, it ain't saying much to affirm his greatness,
am I right?"

"You sure is!" a man said, clapping his hands.

"Preach, sister."

"God is so great, he knows exactly when to remind
us when we ain't been so great, doesn't he?"

"Sure does."

"That's right."

"I recall the late Reverend Douglass once reminded
me about the futility of striving to control those matters
that remain in God's hands. I'd like to share my insights
about the legacy of these two great Christians based on
a reading from Jeremiah 3:21–25, which was a favorite

of the late Reverend. Why don't y'all go ahead and flip to that page right quick."

Pages turned; my sister handed me a Bible. I took it, eyebrows raised. Did she actually expect me to read along with the others? She nudged me, then put her Bible on my thigh and used her index finger to trace the words the minister read.

"A voice is heard on the bare heights, the weeping and the supplications of the sons of Israel; because they have perverted their way, they have forgotten the LORD their God."

Reverend Cary looked up at the congregation with a smile.

"Ain't it something when you try hard to forget what the Lord saying to you? You get so caught up trying to do something another way, you wish you didn't hear the Lord, in your ear, that moment, 'bout to do something you sure know is best not to do?"

"Go on, now," someone shouted from the congregation.

"My brothers and sisters, it's not the loss of faith, it's not the blockin' out the Lord's voice time and again. No, it's those ways we behave that we know good and well that we can never find salvation from, yet we go on just behaving that way. Go on and raise your hand if you been there."

As I glanced around at the aged faces of people who had known me since infancy, I finally felt the faith that guided my grandmother through heartbreak and disappointment. Maybe it was sitting among my family and friends, swaying from side to side, one hand in the air, eyes shut, who had so few material possessions, but made life's lemons taste like peaches, accepted contradictions, embraced tragedy, all while singing about the Lord's triumph and his blessings despite man-made misery. In here, away from the eyes of their bosses, they found peace regardless of the societal sins that hemmed them in. Here, in this moment, my cynicism flaked off like dead skin.

After the service the congregants filed out to take their positions with the other marchers. Janice suggested we cut through the parking lot to the Civil Rights Museum, where a series of people were scheduled to give speeches. Initially, Janice said no when Davon asked to join some of his peers who marched. But when two students I recognized from the Students of Color Association the other day approached Davon and introduced themselves to Janice, she relented and let Davon join.

Although the mayor feared tens of thousands of demonstrators would overwhelm Birmingham, businesses welcomed the crowd. Once-abandoned storefronts had been rented and populated with ephemera, T-shirts, gear commemorating the fiftieth-anniversary celebration or with "#blacklivesmatter" written all over.

When we arrived at the Civil Rights Museum, a crowd of a few hundred were waiting for the marchers to complete their loop and arrive at the museum for the formal part of the program to begin. Mayor Thomas Turner had been scheduled to address the gathering, but after Odessa's disappearance his advisors cautioned him against attending. Instead, he made a prerecorded speech published in newspapers that celebrated racial unity and argued against those who called for the removal of a statue of "our shared heritage," as he put it. His suggestion to construct a statue of Martin Luther King Jr. across the street from the Andrew Shields statue instead caused some of those who waited beside us to suck their teeth and curse him.

We watched the marchers follow a police escort on motorcycles. They were on their way past the Andrew Shields monument, which was covered in black plastic, a piece of silver duct tape wrapped around its neck. Police in riot gear, shields attached to the brims of helmets, batons, and padded black gloved hands guarded the perimeter, daring the white supremacists to cross their yellow tape as the marchers followed the prescribed route and passed the park. Men with shaved heads, leather jackets, and army fatigues flanked it, poised ready to charge.

Meanwhile, black and white teens alike marched down the street shouting "Black lives matter," some holding placards in the air that read "Down with

Dixie." Other marchers raised their open palms to the sky and shouted, "Hands up, don't shoot."

As they passed, I saw a man pump a white knuckled fist in the air, shouting "White lives matter" in response.

I noticed women in the crowd, too. Some looked dressed for church with pamphlets in their purses just in case they met women with the right pedigree in the bathroom. Others wore their hair pulled back in slicked ponytails and tight, sleeveless black T-shirts with names like "high priestess of chaos" and "disciples of the devil" stenciled in gothic white type across the front. It seemed as if their breasts would flop out at any moment.

With them were tattooed men with slogans, slurs, and attire that showed they had picked over the carcasses of racist movements all through history. Some held banners or posters plastered with a diversity of clichés. Some real classics like "dreaming of a white Christmas," "love it or leave," "go back to Africa," "go back to Mexico," "go back to China," reminding onlookers that white supremacy was a global affair.

Passersby paused to snap photos of what they supposed would be a tweet-worthy image of confrontation between the two groups. When the marchers began to clot in front of the statue, the police shouted for them to keep moving, stick to the preapproved route.

Now I saw Davon standing with Jessie and the other students on the outskirts of the marchers. He looked purposeful. Serious. Proud. Someone near him pushed over a fruit cart and apples, kiwi, and pears rolled down the sidewalk. Students picked up fruit and hurled it at the white supremacists being pushed back by police.

This hail of fruit enraged one guy with a long white beard, shades, and a bald head. He kicked over a recycling bin, releasing cans and bottles to a group of skinheads who returned the volley of fruit with bottles and cans. Then I heard a boom and a recycling bin exploded into flames. A few teens who stood beside Davon grabbed books from an overturned stand and tossed them into the flaming recycling bin.

Janice shouted for Robert to get Davon, then Janice and I took Naquasia inside the Civil Rights Museum with others seeking shelter from the melee. The metal detector's red light pulsed and beeped as people pushed past the security guards in search of a safe place to wait for police to regain control. We held hands and forced our way into the building behind the others and to the front window so we could search for Davon. We watched marchers scatter from the street as a fire truck zoomed in, lights flashing, alarm screaming. Firefighters rolled a hose from the truck and sent a shower of water over the bin. They stomped the paper and books, smothering the flames with their boots and axe handles.

Police in riot gear stormed the park, forcing white nationalists to back up farther from the street. They wrestled resisters to the ground, cuffing them and dragging them to the police bus waiting on the corner. Some shook themselves free, chasing marchers who continued toward the Civil Rights Museum. But luckily, thankfully, the police prevented any further violence that day.

THE DAY OF

By some miracle, in all the mess Robert found
Davon and brought him and his other friends
inside for the fiftieth-anniversary celebration,
while outside the police arrested those who refused to
disperse. By the time the program ended, the police had
regained control of Linn Park and things cooled down,
but I could tell it scared my sister to death, the could-
have-beens going through her mind. What could have
happened to her son at a demonstration gone violent
like that. Janice was beside herself.

The next day I woke early to reorganize the files
of the missing girls in categories for another meeting
we planned with Mrs. Davis and the mothers' group.
I hadn't worked long before my phone vibrated on the
coffee table. It was Daryl.

"Good morning, Allie."

"How are you, Daryl?"

"Fine. I called to let you know Lucas received other documents Grandma ordered from Alabama State. There are letters, folders, memoirs—all info on the Shields family."

"Really?"

"Yeah. And there's a pamphlet. Lucas said it had been misfiled. Only going through Shields's family papers yesterday did he discover it. *Confessional of William Shields, Colonial Confederate States of America. 1873.*"

My breath hitched. This had to be one copy of only a handful, if not the only copy. The *Confessional*, in all my years of research, had been impossible to find. "You found an original copy of Shields's *Confessional*?"

"You've heard of it?"

"Of course. It falls exactly in my line of research, but I've never seen or read a copy of it. And by the way, the person who's been sending me letters signed his name William Shields."

"Wow, that's creepy."

"I know. Can you scan it and email it to me? I'll come over to look at the original later today."

"Yes, it's being done as we speak."

"Thanks, Daryl. I'll give you a call if I have any questions."

Daryl emailed a PDF with biographical info on Andrew Shields and his family. Next was a list of ex-slaveholders, including Andrew Shields, who borrowed millions from New York bankers to rebuild the South after the Civil War. I assumed these were the people whom William Shields accused of selling out Alabama for the benefit of a few. Then the *Confessional* came through—I was eager to read it, but something like that would have to wait. I didn't have much time before my meeting with the mothers' group.

Next, he sent a PDF of my family's genealogical records. This showed that our family had once been the property of Andrew Shields. Beneath those records were land deeds in my family's name, and a map of plantation estates from 1870, which were the same ones being restored now. As Lucas had showed us already, my grandmother suspected this correlation, but hadn't known if the girls were being held all in one place. We had checked the estate near Grandma's house, but I didn't see any sign of them. Then, I remembered a conversation I had with Mrs. Beatrice Summers, an elderly white woman in charge of the Jefferson County Historical Museum, a few months earlier. At dinner that evening, Mrs. Summers—or Bea, as she insisted I call her—linked the controversy over the Confederate monuments throughout the state to this new interest in plantation home restoration, as well as the increase in visitors to her little museum. Not that she herself believed in the Confederate cause, but she said that each community had the right to determine on their own who ought to have a monument or statues. This was no business of the governor. Just her opinion.

Bea told me several young well-dressed men arrived at her door a year or so prior with an offer to move her museum into a plantation mansion they had hoped to renovate and restore.

As she explained, these young men promised to include in the renovation airtight stone rooms in the basement where the Jefferson County Historical Society could store boxes of the museum's more precious letters, deeds, and diaries from the nineteenth century. Her own building was nearly collapsing and, until then, it didn't seem like anyone much cared if all those documents and photos simply disintegrated.

She was impressed by their conviction. When the time came, she recruited women from her church senior group to support their bid to purchase those century-old Gothic manors that more resembled haunted houses than the estates of cotton kings.

Restoring these plantation homes would inject a new spirit of southern pride throughout the region. Starting right here in Alabama. But what impressed her most was the men's passion for the ambitious project, which she found intoxicating.

When they began construction, the women from her church senior group would go out to the job site with iced tea and moon pie praline, refreshing the young men carrying plywood on their shoulders, or wielding nail guns on the tar-hot roofs. They, of course, appreciated it. After spending time watching them work, there were more than a few in her group who wished these young men would find their way to their granddaughters' front porches.

Now I know these men who flattered Bea, apparently into turning over documents she'd guarded with her life, were Strong's recruits. Had Beatrice any clue of Matthew Strong's real motives or the magnitude of his mission, I doubt she'd be so admiring. In retrospect, all of my experiences analyzing southern ideology became much more than a theoretical exercise.

Maybe she could provide more insight into these correlations and perhaps offer an update on the renovations. Perhaps the girls were being kept in one of the most finished estates, given there'd be fewer people working the area. I scrolled down my email for her contact details and called her.

"Good morning, Mrs. Summers? This is Allie Douglass."

"Professor Douglass, how wonderful to hear from you. How's the big city?"

"Actually, my grandma passed away, so I've come back down."

"That's terrible news, Professor. My condolences to your family. I'll be sure to keep you and yours in my prayers."

"I appreciate that. Really."

"Nothing to it."

"So, I wondered if you could help me with something."

"What is it?"

"I'm sure you've read about Odessa Turner and the recent kidnappings?"

"Sure have. It's just awful."

"Well, I recalled our conversation about the renovation of a plantation home near you?"

"Yes, in fact it's done."

"Really?"

"Chambers to store our most precious documents in the basement are almost ready too. Should be able to move our operation over there within a month or so. At least, that's what they've told me."

"Do you know anything about similar renovations in other counties?"

"Actually, yes. A dear friend of mine runs the historical society in Jefferson. They supposedly finished 'bout seven renovations throughout the state."

"Seven?"

"That's right. I guess some wealthy family went and raised a bunch of money in order to restore them."

"Do you know anything about the funding?"

"Not much. Although I do believe I have a card somewhere. Hold on a moment."

She put the phone down and returned a few seconds later.

"Yes, I sure do. Nebraf Inc. They own all sorts of companies. Home Health Aide. They own SOL Inc. I met the man behind all of this. But I don't recall his name. He joined us on our trip to check out the renovations of the Andrew Shields plantation mansion. In fact, the man said he was related."

Wallace? I remembered him mentioning he was a descendent of Andrew Shields.

"Are you there, Professor?"

"Sorry. I was just thinking. Do you remember if the man's name was Wallace Jefferson?"

"No, that's not it. Wait, now that I think about it, he asked if I had some extra copies of your book for sale at my museum. From when you gave a talk here? He had me mail him two copies. I still have his address on a brochure. He's a minister. Let me see."

I heard her rustling through some papers.

"Yes, here it is. Matthew Strong, Sons of Light Ministries, 124 Main Street, Warrior, Alabama."

"Excuse me? You said his name is Matthew Strong?"

"That's right."

It hit me. The man who asked me to sign his book after the celebration for the Eli Jefferson Chair. I replayed in my head our encounter. Janice had just left me the urgent message about our grandmother when he introduced himself in the elevator.

"Did he have a gray beard?"

"He sure did. Handsome man. I wasn't surprised when someone told me he was behind these young men fixing up these plantation homes. They got just as much charm as him."

I thanked Beatrice for her time. The pieces were falling in place. I emailed Detective Landers and Agent Tyler that the man behind the renovations and who asked me to sign his book was named Matthew Strong. I assumed this was the same guy who sent me letters signed "William Shields." I searched online for the Sons of Light Ministries, recalling that William Shields had first organized a group with this name in the 1860s based on a European sect during the Middle Ages dedicated to preserving the "Kingdom of Light" from the "Kingdom of Darkness," or ignorance and social disorder. Later, some scholars argued that William Shields's Sons of Light inspired the Nazi Party's use of occult rituals.

Then I moved on to a Southern Poverty Law Center website entry for the recent group Matthew Strong organized using the same name. The Sons of Light Ministries recruited white youths with the usual justifications—black people were getting too numerous and Mexican immigrants were flooding into white neighborhoods.

Originally, I thought Wallace had been behind the letters and the plantation renovations. Given what I

read about the Sons of Light, the timing of Cynthia's
disappearance and the first letter, what Beatrice told
me, it now seemed clear Matthew Strong was behind
all of this.

I called Janice, but it went straight to voicemail.
I texted her to call me and then I went onto my
grandmother's back porch. I needed a cigarette, bad.
As I smoked, I checked Facebook. I had shared photos,
the map, and my theory about the plantation homes
on Facebook and Twitter. Now, my messenger swelled
with questions and comments about missing women.
I felt close to finishing what my grandmother started,
but there was something I still was missing. Where
were the girls? Could they be in that mostly finished
plantation home Beatrice had mentioned?

My phone vibrated and it was Detective Landers.
He told me he'd searched the National Crime
Information Center database and found a man named
Matthew Strong with multiple outstanding warrants
for minor crimes from Richmond, Virginia, to
Greenwood, Mississippi. His last known address was
Warrior, Alabama, and he had affiliations with several
white supremacist organizations, but currently was
listed as a minister of the Sons of Light.

Detective Landers said he was still waiting for the
crime lab to return with a report on whether my book
and Cynthia's items held any DNA evidence. There

was none in my ransacked apartment, to everyone's
surprise. Whoever had broken in used masterful
technique, leaving no trace. He told me he planned on
calling the Alabama highway patrol and FBI agent
Tyler about this connection as well. They still hadn't
found Cynthia, but finally recognized it might be a
connected case, given her ties to Warrior.

"Bottom line, Professor, if Matthew Strong is in fact
the man responsible for Cynthia's disappearance, and
he's the one who has been sending you those letters, you
need to be careful."

Right after I hung up, my sister called, terrified.
I summarized the evidence Daryl emailed me and
my conversation with Beatrice. All arrows pointed
to this Matthew Strong, who, according to Detective
Landers, was a member of a white supremacist group in
Alabama.

"Allie, you shouldn't be alone. Robert's on his way
home from work to get you. We want you here with
us."

"Wait, Agent Tyler's on the other line. I'll call you
back."

I clicked over. "Agent Tyler?"

"Yes, I just received a call from Detective Landers
about this white supremacist Matthew Strong. Where
are you?"

"At my grandmother's house."

"Okay, I'm sending a patrol car over there."

"Thanks. I've found some important correlations about where he might be holding the girls."

"Good. Explain more when you get here."

When I called my sister back, she had become frantic. I told her Agent Tyler was sending over a police car, and suggested I have the police pick her up as well. She balked.

"I'm not the one receiving crazy letters. Anyway, Robert is on his way home. I'll call Mrs. Davis and meet you at the FBI field office."

A police car pulled into the driveway as we hung up. I was so eager to gather my laptop, maps, and the manila envelope with the letters, I didn't think through how quickly they'd arrived.

I met them on the front porch. They were polite, serious as they led me to their car and closed the door behind me. Reminded me of my graduate students. I figured I was just any other routine assignment.

I buckled in next to another officer and we drove off. We had only been driving for five minutes when my phone vibrated and I glanced down at the screen. It was Agent Tyler.

Where are u?

I texted her back, *On my way.*

Why not with the state highway patrol?

I'm with them now.

???

Highway patrol said no one answered your front door.

I'm with deputies from the sheriff's department.

I felt a hand on my arm and I glanced up. The one sitting beside me appeared concerned.

"Everything okay, Professor Douglass?"

"Yeah. It's fine. Just a mix-up."

"How so?"

"I guess Agent Tyler sent the state troopers also. Wires must have crossed."

The man appeared to be reading my expression. Then a thought came to me. Why send three deputies? I caught the driver looking at me warily through the rearview mirror. I needed to stay calm. This was probably just a miscommunication.

I felt my phone vibrate again. I glanced down.

I didn't call the sheriff! Get out of the car!

My face must have changed once I realized these were Matthew Strong's men. The man beside me leaned forward, head tilted to the side, looking concerned again.

"You sure you're okay, Professor?"

"Yes, I'm fine. Hey, can we go back? I realize I forgot something."

"Can't do that," the driver said. "We have our orders."

The doors locked and the man thrust me against the door while the one in the front reached back and jabbed a syringe in my thigh.

"What are you doing?" I shrieked, kicking, punching with all my might. But as each second passed I lost feeling in my legs, then my arms. Everything became blurry and I lost consciousness.

BOOK V

✣

REVOLUTION

He will come again in glory to judge the living and the dead,
and his kingdom will have no end.

NICENE CREED

FOR AS THE BLOOD OF CHRIST HAD BEEN SHED ON
THIS EARTH, AND HAD ASCENDED TO HEAVEN FOR THE
SALVATION OF SINNERS, AND WAS NOW RETURNING TO
EARTH AGAIN IN THE FORM OF DEW—AND AS THE LEAVES
ON THE TREES BORE THE IMPRESSION OF THE FIGURES
I HAD SEEN IN THE HEAVENS, IT WAS PLAIN TO ME THAT
THE SAVIOUR WAS ABOUT TO LAY DOWN THE YOKE HE HAD
BORNE FOR THE SINS OF MEN, AND THE GREAT DAY OF
JUDGMENT WAS AT HAND.

Nat Turner, *The Confessions of Nat Turner*

WE OF THE SOUTH WILL NOT, CANNOT, SURRENDER OUR
INSTITUTIONS. TO MAINTAIN THE EXISTING RELATIONS
BETWEEN THE TWO RACES, INHABITING THAT SECTION
OF THE UNION, IS INDISPENSABLE TO THE PEACE AND
HAPPINESS OF BOTH. IT CANNOT BE SUBVERTED WITHOUT
DRENCHING THE COUNTRY IN BLOOD, AND EXTIRPATING ONE
OR THE OTHER OF THE RACES.

John C. Calhoun, US senator

DAY ONE

"You look scared, Professor. You ain't afraid of me, now are you?" Matthew Strong said. He lit a cigarette, then motioned for the men with guns to leave. He wore a white linen shirt buttoned all the way up his neck, and he rolled his sleeves up to his mid-forearm. On the table were the Bible and my book.

"Of course I am." I felt a shortness of breath, my body responding to the sudden image in my mind of him from before.

"Fear is irrational. People fear what they don't know. You know all about me. You don't have nothing to fear. Not to mention if you're frightened of me it'll make it more difficult for you to do what you need to do. Tell me something. You believe in the devil?"

"What?"

Sitting this close I noticed his cleft upper lip beneath his white mustache. His beard was thicker than I recalled from when I stumbled into him three weeks before. Now it consumed his pale face like cotton, blanketing his sharp cheekbones and narrow jaw.

"The devil? Do you believe in him?" He tapped his cigarette on the edge of a soda can.

"Yes, I do."

I acted strong—as strong as I could—but as you may imagine, I was terrified. By now I knew what he was capable of. He picked up my book, flipped it open, and appeared to read the inside jacket. "Tell you one thing, you sure can write. You may be the smartest damn Negro in the world. That's what you think, don't you?"

What did he expect me to say? I thought about the letters he'd left for me over the prior three weeks. I glanced around the room. No windows, only piercing fluorescent lights overhead. White banker boxes stacked on metal shelves pressed against the sidewall reminded me of the archives I visited to research for my books.

"Are you going to tell me why you kidnapped me? Don't you have everything you need?" I still had no idea how much of my grandmother's research he'd uncovered.

"Oh, Professor, you know good and well I don't have everything I need. Besides, I already told you

I'm a fan of your work. There is use for you here. And don't you want to find out about what happened to your grandma, as well as your momma? Don't that make this worthwhile?"

My *mother*? She disappeared decades ago. How could this be related? I figured this was another one of his head games.

"Under these circumstances, not really," I said, with a measured tone.

"Maybe you'll see things differently when you take down my story."

"Your story?" I sat up in my seat, unsure what he meant.

"That's right."

"Is that what this is about? You're going to confess why you're doing all of this?"

"Don't you think you're most qualified to analyze my mission? Maybe write it down? For posterity, of course."

"You expect me to write a modern-day *Helter Skelter*?"

"Manson was a moron. Crazy too. Hitler was a sissy. No, Doc. I'm from an entirely different line of men. Honorable men who don't get the credit they deserve. You know something, Professor, I have some men who'll die for me. Hell, they're waiting for it. But when it comes to capturing the nuances of this mission they're not so useful."

"What do you want me to write?"

"That's exactly it. I'll get to talking and you write some of those pretty words—'obfuscation' and 'indomitable.' Make it sound sophisticated. We're about to begin a new chapter in the story of this fallen land, and I want to make sure it sounds how it ought to sound."

"Why not make a recording and post it online?" I remembered organizations like his often made podcasts and posted lectures online to recruit new members.

"You're going to write to the unborn millions. Think about it. No one had no YouTube a thousand years ago, did they? Hell, not even fifty years ago. Pen and paper. Stored properly. The rise of the Sons of Light, our mission, my ideas alongside the ideas of our forefathers. Archived for eternity."

"I don't understand why you trust me."

"Haven't you been paying attention, Doc? You believe in truth. It's your, what'd they call it, professional obligation to tell the truth. Ain't that right?"

He was insane. I took a deep breath. I realized why he had me. If they caught him or killed him, people would believe the authenticity of his words if written by an academic—especially a black academic who he figured would spare no detail. He had already galvanized his base, and now he wanted his ideas published beyond his circle. He wasn't about to allow the FBI or any of his enemies to prevent his ideas from being published.

Matthew Strong ran his index finger down a page in my book, then turned it around.

"See this right here?" He tapped a footnote. "*Confessional of William Shields*?"

"What about it?"

"You know where I might be able to ascertain the whereabouts of that pamphlet?"

"No, I'm not sure," I lied.

"Seems strange, wouldn't you say? Quoting from a book you ain't never seen?"

"Ah, well..." I hesitated a moment, thinking about the box of pamphlets and other files Lucas and Daryl discovered in the university archive. "I never used the actual pamphlet. That Shields quote in my book came from a dissertation I read online."

He creased his eyebrows. "That there pamphlet means a great deal to me. And it's best you think harder about where you found it. For the sake of the girls, of course."

At the time, I didn't understand why it was so important to him. I knew the *Confessional* had inspired revolutionaries, but he appeared to need it desperately.

Matthew Strong leaned onto his elbows. "You see, me and my men have been through nearly every Podunk town historical society and archive in Alabama looking for an original copy. You can imagine how tedious that's been, as a researcher yourself."

"Why do you need it?" I asked hesitantly.

"We'll get to the why once you help me with the where, Professor."

"I told you. I quoted a dissertation. I never actually used the original pamphlet."

He chuckled. "Come on now, Professor. Truth. Remember?"

"I'm telling the truth! Maybe if you tell me what you need it for, I'll remember a passage from the dissertation that quoted it."

He sneered. His eyes probed my face, as if trying to figure out whether I was telling the truth. *Relax, Allie. He can't read your mind.*

"Well, I guess you need a little incentive."

He stood abruptly and walked to the bookshelf, turned some sort of crank. As he did this, the bookshelf revolved, and there was another room that reminded me of a wine cellar with its concrete floor and stones protruding from the walls. A black girl lay on her side. Her wrists and ankles chained. She lifted her head and scanned the room as if orienting herself. Matthew Strong's boots echoed as he entered the cavern. When he untied a gag around her mouth, she begged.

"Please, God. Don't hurt me."

It was Cynthia.

"Cynthia!" I shouted. Matthew Strong came back into the room, then turned the crank again, and the bookcase replaced the hidden passage. Cynthia extended her chained arms.

"No, wait! Please!"

My stomach convulsed, then I vomited on the floor. The door opened and a woman emerged to mop around my chair. Once she left, Matthew Strong set down a glass of water, then leaned against the table with his arms folded.

"What are you going to do with Cynthia?" I wiped my mouth with the back of my hand, trying to regain my composure.

"You cooperate, she'll be just fine. Before you take down my story, I'm going to have you take a look at this."

He handed me a manila envelope, and I pulled out a pamphlet wrapped in plastic used to preserve old documents.

"What is this?" I scanned the pamphlet.

"Paid a pretty penny for that. It's the only original I could find."

"Wait—this is the *Confessional of William Shields* in German?"

"So it seems." He motioned to the pamphlet. "Seeing how acquainted you are with the philosophy of William Shields's generation, you'll have no problem translating that into something I can read."

He motioned to the pamphlet and smiled. I hadn't figured out why he needed me to do such a laborious task. But even if I didn't know why, I knew I *shouldn't* translate it. I decided to bluff.

"You expect me to translate this?" I shook my head. "It's been years since I've translated German."

"Professor, I'm surprised. Thought this would be no problem for someone with your intellect."

"Why don't you kidnap someone who actually speaks German?" I asked, continuing the lie.

"I haven't found no one I trust who does. Plus, I got you right here, don't I? And God forbid it fall into the wrong hands."

I fixed my eyes on the faded pamphlet, deciphering the letters.

"And you trust me?"

"I trust you're smart enough to know better than to lie to me." He went to the bookshelf, and I feared he'd turn that crank and torture Cynthia until I agreed. Instead, he pulled a German dictionary, then came over and dropped it on the table.

"Use this to brush up your skills."

I shook my head, trying to stay strong and defy him. "It'll take me weeks. And my translation won't be very good anyway."

"I'll make you a deal."

"A deal?"

"Two options, really. Translate Shields's *Confessional* into English, and I swear on my momma's grave, I won't kill you. Or, keep refusing me, and each day you do so, I'm gonna kill one of them girls—then you, of course."

Thoughts of Cynthia chained on the floor crowded my mind. "What kind of choice is that?" My voice stammering. My eyes wide.

"The kind you love, Doc. Save yourself and the others, or hold to your principles and die a martyr. Simple enough, don't you think?"

He was totally out of his mind! I hated being taunted. "No, not exactly. The choice isn't about me or them. It's about whether I trust you or not."

"I don't follow you."

"How do I know you won't just kill all of us after I translate the *Confessional*?"

Matthew Strong stood, smiling. "You are truly something special, Professor." He winked. "I knew you were the right woman for the job."

Matthew Strong adjusted the gun he had kept in his waist and called one of his men in the basement room to guard me.

"There's one thing you ought to know about me, Professor. I'm a man of my word."

———

After Matthew Strong left, I wondered how long he'd be gone and how many pages he expected me to complete per day. Seeing Cynthia, chained as she was, I knew she wouldn't resist him. It terrified me to think everything was going according to his plan. As frightened as I was, I knew I needed to throw him off and delay him long enough for the FBI—or anyone—to find us.

I flipped through the *Confessional*, assessing the task. Those who have translated a document know it's nearly impossible to do a decent job without living in the country and being exposed to its culture. For Matthew Strong, this pamphlet might as well have been written in Aramaic. As a graduate student, I'd worked nonstop for three days translating a nine-page document from German to English. But that was over ten years ago, when I lived in Germany. I'd be lucky if I could translate one page with twice as much time now.

The *Confessional* was twenty-seven pages total and composed of three parts:

Part I. Confessions of William Shields, taken by
    Nathanial Yarg, PhD
Part II. Evidence Submitted to the Court
Part III. Field Notes on Our Revolution
Appendix
Letters
Trial Transcript

I focused first on translating the TO THE PUBLIC statement before the main text:

> As permitted by the court of Jerusalem, Alabama,
> I interviewed William Shields and committed his words
> faithfully to the account that follows.
>
> Nathanial Yarg, PhD
> April 14, 1873
>
> Sir, for me to offer an accurate narrative of the
> motives which compelled me to commit those actions I've
> been charged with, I must begin with my childhood…

Over the next six hours, I read about Shields's life, how his family moved from Virginia to Alabama, his childhood growing up as the son of a prominent slaveholder. I was familiar with most of this background, which made translating the document a bit easier. But I worked slowly so Matthew Strong wouldn't suspect I lied about knowing German.

By the afternoon, I had finished only two pages—mostly background information. One passage caught my attention because he mentioned Brewer Cemetery, where generations of my family had been buried, as well as the Shields family, who once owned the surrounding land. Shields wrote:

> Brewer Cemetery was my refuge as a child.
> Sometimes I used to walk those rows and read for names,

*dates, and Bible verses on the tombstones. I would stand
over my sister's grave and ask her questions about what
it was like before I was born. She passed when I was just
an infant. I listened to relatives of mine who died over the
years tell me ways they amused themselves as children.*

*Once my father caught me coming up from Brewer
Cemetery, and he demanded I stop spending so much time
there. He told me if I continued, I might catch my death.
As a boy, I never understood this saying, "Catch your
death." I always thought death was trying to catch me.
Were we not all avoiding eternal rest? In fact, I believe
men fear inconsequence more so than death. Others fear
indifference even more. All men have their white whales
to chase and dragons to slay. Each man is driven in life
by a sense of purpose and can only pray he fulfills his
purpose before his eternal rest.*

"Sense of purpose"? I recalled the same rhetoric in
the letters Matthew Strong mailed me. As I translated
the pamphlet, I had no sense how important Brewer
Cemetery would be to how this all ended.

Once I completed the section on Shields's
background, I considered skipping to the appendix,
or combing through the pamphlet to uncover what
Matthew Strong thought he'd find to help his mission.
But I worried he might realize my secret.

I leaned back in my chair and stole a few glances
of my guard, who rubbed his eyes, then yawned. He

appeared impossibly serene; completely unburdened
by the weight of what he was involved in. I thought
about the difference between these men—disciples of
Matthew Strong—and the rebel flag–waving types who
wore General Lee baseball caps at my book talks; men
more interested in performance than ideas. The guards
rotating in and out of the basement were serious,
professional, seemingly uninterested in flamboyant
displays of pride.

I wondered what vulnerabilities Matthew Strong
exploited when recruiting these young men to join his
movement. After all, most looked like they were just
out of their teens. Midtwenties tops. Didn't they realize
they had their entire lives before them? I imagined the
high school dropouts, drug addicts, and those with
mental health issues who were waiting for someone like
Matthew Strong to give them something to believe in,
something to inspire them. There were also the ex-
military men. Maybe this group struggled to reorient
themselves to the humdrum routines of ordinary life
after some foreign military campaign? Or maybe
witnessing so much death and misery in the military,
they became cynical, and vulnerable to Strong's
darkness?

After a half hour passed, I tried to draw him into a
conversation.

"You don't have Google Translate on your phone, do
you?"

He glanced over. "You just worry about what you're doing."

"With a translator I'd be done so much faster."

He ignored me.

"Is that a friend you're texting? A girlfriend, maybe?" I smiled.

He shook his head slightly. "The Prophet said you was a cunning one."

"The Prophet? You mean Matthew Strong?"

"That's right."

"He doesn't seem much like any prophet I've read about."

He stood straight, gripping the handle of his automatic weapon. "Well, it don't matter what you think. When the redemption comes, millions will understand."

"Understand what?

He smiled. "The truth."

Truth? What truth? That Matthew Strong had exploited his naiveté to convince him to wage some suicidal war to return the South to the days of slavery? Please. In the past, I'd gained pleasure shifting people's mindset about slaveholders' ideas and showing them how slaveholders used them to reinforce a sense of southern nationalism among the non-slaveholding majority. Most southerners never owned slaves and therefore did not benefit financially from the institution. Those politicians and intellectuals

who did—"Prophets of Fire," as I called them in
my book—mixed Old Testament fire and brimstone
rhetoric with Enlightenment theory in order to
persuade uneducated poor white folk like this guy that
their liberty was in jeopardy from northerners under
the spell of abolitionists, who were responsible for
Lincoln's election. These slaveholders persuaded them
the Confederate cause was all about protecting the
principles of the Declaration of Independence—liberty
or death, right?

"Truth," I said, trying to sound earnest. "I can see
you have tremendous faith in him. My grandma used
to say, faith is the substance of things hoped for, the
evidence of things not seen."

"She must know her verse. That's St. Paul."

"Do you have a favorite Bible verse?"

He smiled, then closed his eyes and began: "And this
man shall be at peace, when the Assyrian shall come
into our land... And they shall waste the land of the
Assyrians with the sword, and the land of Nimrod in
the entrances thereof: thus shall he deliver us from the
Assyrian, when he cometh into our land, and when he
treadeth within our borders.

"That's from Micah," he said, beaming with pride.

"Wow. I'm impressed. You memorized that entire
passage?"

"Sure did. Used to recite it all the time back when I
was captured by some Islamists."

"You were a prisoner of war? Where?"

"Oman. Seventeen days. My vehicle was bombed by one of them IEDs. An Arab woman came every day and read to me from the Quran. Those days were long. I prayed. And God's voice came to me. Told me I had a mission. A calling."

"Is that right?" I said, watching as the guard relaxed. My effort to establish a relationship seemed to be working. This was exactly the break I needed, or at least a good start. "What did God say?"

"You are the flame."

"You're the flame?"

"That's right. *You are the flame.* It was a sort of booming voice, with an echo. Like when God spoke to Abraham and told him the Ten Commandments?"

"What do you think it meant?"

"I wasn't sure until I was back home from my service and I heard the Prophet speak and I joined the Sons of Light on the spot. Gave my life to the Lord Jesus Christ. And my people."

"He must be a powerful speaker."

"Sure is. He told me I had the gift, too. I never had no interest in that kind of stuff, but it wasn't long before he had me out there preaching. College campuses were my favorite."

"Why's that?"

"Ain't many places more rife with folk who lost their way than on a college campus. More than sports events or carnivals. Recruiting in them parking lots was easy. College campuses are some of the saddest places I've been. Men dressed like women. Girls kissing girls. Tell you one thing, you walk through Alabama College and you about to see things you've never seen in your life."

"Is it difficult to recruit them?"

He smiled. "Yeah. But like the sun: Don't matter if you believe or not. Its light shines on everybody."

I caught a sense of thrill in his eyes. He cherished his chance to tussle with me, show me up. This was survival. I knew I needed to use this apparent desire to prove me wrong in order to make him question his beliefs.

"That's poetic."

His expression shifted to one of contemplation. He rubbed his chin, sized me up. "Look, ma'am, I know what you're trying to do."

"What's that?"

"You think you're going to befriend me and I'm going to help you. But ain't no one can help you but yourself.

"Tell me something," I said. "Wouldn't killing me go against what you believe?"

"Nope. I'd do it in a second. That's the only way. Cleanse those who forsake God. Start again. Blacks. Mexicans. Arabs. Murders, rapists, and terrorists. All the same."

"But doesn't violence go against your Christian beliefs?"

"Just like the Prophet always says. Folk like you are always using your intellect as a smoke screen for moral failings. Factual doubts are one thing, but the volitional kind are what concerns me."

"But this movement. Kidnapping girls? Can't you see how all of this violates the teachings of Christ?"

"I don't expect a person like you to understand."

"I can tell you're a compassionate person. And you believe deeply in all of this. But please, I want you to understand that there are other ways to accomplish what you seek." I glanced at his gun, then back in his eyes. "You don't need that."

He shook his head, as if I wore him out. "You go on and get to doing what you need to do, you hear?"

He put his headphones in his ears and scrolled down his cell phone.

NIGHT ONE

That night his men blindfolded me and brought me two flights up to a bedroom. I wondered where he found these men. I wondered how they came to know him, how he manipulated them to join a futile fight against overwhelming odds much greater than the odds faced by those he admired from generations before. Most of all, I thought about how I could convince one of them to help me escape.

Once they left, I pulled down the blindfold so it hung around my neck. The room was empty besides the small lamp on the floor near the head of a stained mattress pushed into the corner. The walls were a bright white; the wood floors appeared recently waxed. I walked to the window. Three two-by-fours nailed across the outside frame prevented all but a sliver of

light from passing through. I figured this was one of
the plantation manors Matthew Strong had convinced
Alabama's Historical Society to let his men restore with
the intention of reopening them as museums. The smell
of fresh paint meant they were nearly done with this
particular renovation.

As I sat on the edge of the mattress, I imagined
this room over two hundred years before, with a
painted portrait of some slaveholder's daughter above
the dresser, a king-size bed hogging the center of the
space, and a large closet with silk dresses. There she
was, slipping on a dress with the assistance of an
enslaved black woman. Maybe a suitor was coming
over for a dinner party. Maybe her cousins had come
from their own poisoned plots of land and her father
wanted to show her off, informing them she was
nearly ready to be given away to the right sort of
southern gentleman.

I thought about my arguments with my sister,
Janice, a few nights before my abduction. I regretted
my foul attitude then, as well as the time she visited me
in New York three years before as I endured cancer
treatment. I regretted focusing more on my career than
on building a relationship with Davon and Naquasia.
Tears came the more I thought about never having the
chance to apologize to my sister for being so selfish.

This wasn't my first time lying in a bed, wondering
about my mortality. I'd faced death before, yet then I

could see the faint outlines on the CAT scan as cancer grew like the oak tree roots snaking beneath my driveway with an inner logic I would never understand.

There were times after a shower I'd run my index finger across the scarred skin where they stitched me up like a football, pondering whether or not my husband still felt attracted to me. Some nights I could still feel the needle pushing doxorubicin into my veins like a Roman legion in fourth formation, shocking the enemy germinating within, sapping cells of sustenance, sucking out nutrients. I recall those awful nights sprinting to the bathroom, falling on my knees, holding the toilet like a drunk, puking, coughing, crying, crying, crying for death to take me.

For a while, I couldn't even look at my scar without my mind thrusting me back to the day I lay on my back and was rolled down the hall to the OR, where men with rubber fingers stood, waiting to slice out the insatiable beast devouring me from within. And after counting to four, I'm out of my body, rising into the air, hovering above, watching them do as they've done to so many other women, sucking our blood, slicing away cells that grow and grow.

I remember dreaming that I am running behind my sister in a field as my mother chases us back to Grandma's house.

Now I am flying above my roof, gazing at the stars, decoding their messages.

I move my finger across my scar that reminds me my enemy did not win.

Reminding me I fought a good fight.

Reminding me war isn't cheap.

Reminding me life is worth the price.

I often avoided recounting my experience fighting cancer like some veterans avoid discussing war. Whenever friends or colleagues brought it up, their questions felt like bullets, and their pity, grenades. After fighting daily to regain control over your body you lose patience with frivolity and small talk. But I didn't hate them. I hated my body betraying me with each handful of hair or infection that wouldn't heal. I hated my throat aching from tubes, hated the foul smell during radiation therapy.

I resented my grandmother's constant reminders that "it's in God's hands," or when she'd say, "All you can do is pray on it," after I told her about new treatment options. Now I felt ashamed for my arrogance; ashamed for telling her I doubted praying would make a difference.

I also regretted how I treated my husband, David. Growing cold, resentful. Despite his support, I never appeared satisfied. Looking back, I think my behavior toward him reflected a fear he'd leave me for a younger, more attractive woman. No matter how often he said he loved me, my fear prevented me from believing him.

My resentment extended to my colleagues as well. I deleted their sympathetic emails and avoided them on campus. I remember one time sitting at my desk wondering how long it would take before these men, who'd dismissed my books, searched my desk for unpublished ideas they could claim as their own.

After my doctor told me I had beaten cancer, he seemed bothered that I didn't appear relieved. But the only way I survived the ordeal was by accepting death. I remember saying sarcastically I may have won this battle, but not the war.

I lay on the mattress unable to sleep, my mind consumed by trying to decipher how Matthew Strong planned to use the *Confessional*.

I finally dozed off, only to wake when I felt a hand over my mouth. Matthew Strong's finger was pressed against his lips.

"Shhh."

I attempted to flip him off me, but he pinned me on my back.

"Just calm down now," he whispered, holding me until I wore myself out kicking. My teeth chattered as an unnatural chill came over me. Every possible dark scenario flitted through my mind.

"You know, an undisciplined man would take this opportunity to fulfill his carnal desires," he said as he knotted a rope around my wrists. "But I'm the sort who believes a man's word is his bond. 'Bout all we have between two people is words and deeds."

He jerked the rope twice to ensure it held and finally got off me.

"Tonight, we're going on a field trip."

"Where?"

"That'll ruin the surprise."

"Haven't I had enough surprises?"

"'Fraid not. It's a full moon and I got to show you something."

Matthew Strong yanked the rope for me to follow him down the back stairs, past two men smoking and playing cards in a wood-paneled study—the only door we passed that was open. Once outside we walked along a brick pathway around manicured bushes and toward a wooded area. The farther we wandered, the more terrified I became. I glanced back over my shoulder and realized I hadn't seen the plantation house from the outside. It must have been at least six thousand square feet, with four center columns and a porch that wrapped around the second floor. A wide white staircase descended onto a brick patio. It reminded me of the plantation near my grandmother's house. But this seemed improbable because, when they kidnapped me, they drove far too long before arriving here.

We came to a clearing where someone had recently cut away the brush and stacked the branches in bundles. Here the moon shone over several rocks that looked as if they once formed the base of a chimney. Only the first layer of brick jutted up from the soil.

"You see," he said, pointing to the bright moon overhead, "my daddy used to wake me just like I woke you so he could take me out here to observe the peace and serenity that comes on this kinda night."

He looked up at the moon, then surveyed the space with his arms extended.

"This here is where the former owners were forced to live right after the war." He turned in a circle. "All of them crammed in a log cabin together like frontiersmen."

"That must have been tough," I said, mapping in my mind the distance from the house for a potential escape. "One day you're living like kings, the next you're out here near the slave quarters."

"What made it worse was how them Union men let their Negroes gallivant in and out of that plantation home like they owned the place. It's like the thief who, having failed to lift your wallet from your coat pocket, pulls a pistol and orders you to hand it over. What could not be accomplished through trickery would be done the way of Napoleon—the saber and the pistol replaced the petition and the soliloquy."

I searched for a trail off the property each time he looked away. For all I knew, since it was just the two of us this might be my only chance.

"Is that why you brought me here? To teach me about hope in the face of adversity?"

"Hope?" He squinted, then shook his head. "Listen here, Doc, I'm trying to teach you something. When my great-great-grandfather's generation declared their independence, they were on the path toward moving to the next phase in the expansion of the Lord's civilization."

The Lord's civilization? He was insane. The Lord did not enslave people or force others from this land. I'm sure these were the lectures he gave when recruiting followers. The more he lectured me on his vision for a new world order based on his own historical interpretation, the more I felt my anger push aside my fear.

"The Lord built that house? Gave your family all this land? You know, the Chickasaws from around here had their own gods. What did their gods say when colonists stole their land? And the enslaved Africans who built that house—did they believe God did all the work?"

"Once again, you've got it all figured out. That's what you think, ain't it? You think just 'cause you wrote a book about these men that you understand the circumstances that shaped them? But what none of you professors understand is that all of this was prophesied before you were even born. Even the invasion by the North."

"You mean the Civil War?"

"Please, Doc. You're smarter than that. There was nothing civil about the invasion of the Cotton Kingdom led by a bunch of Massachusetts and Pennsylvania radicals."

"I've never claimed to be a historian, but it seems to me that you have the facts backward."

"How you figure?" Matthew Strong clasped his hands behind his back.

"Your great-great-grandfather shot first."

He nodded, slowly, as if contemplating my critique.

"You seem unable to comprehend the circumstances as they were, Professor. You know, my great-great-grandfather's generation viewed the election of Lincoln like a thunderclap over the distant horizon. Them Northern dogs got it in their head that slavery was the problem. But my ancestors knew full well that slavery was not the problem: it was the solution."

"Solution to what?"

"Spreading the Lord's gospel. A positive good, really. These noble men brought them Africans from a savage land and taught them the virtue of work for the greater good of humanity."

"You think you're trying to defend your family's legacy, but this isn't 1860. Things have changed."

"Changed?" He snapped the rope hard and I fell forward onto my stomach. He rushed over and pulled me up by my hair. His lips were now beside my ear.

"Listen here, goddamn it! You ever been bit by a copperhead? Happened to me once. My daddy used to always remind me never to go into our chicken coop without making sure I tap a stick against the floorboards. One time, I was in a rush to meet some friends to go fishing over near the rock quarry. So I leaned my pole and tackle box against the coop and went in with Momma's basket. Sure enough, I reached my hand in the nest box, and faster than a crack of thunder I felt the fangs of a copperhead.

"My hand swelled up, my skin started turning green, and I was hollering, shaking my arm, and running from the coop to the house. Then, my legs went all rubbery, and the next thing I knew I was in bed, six minutes from knocking on death's door."

He leaned close, and I felt his breath on my neck. "You see, Professor, in life one must always be aware that sometimes the thing that has the most potential to kill you may be hidden behind something as harmless as an egg."

He released my hair. I fell forward, breathing heavily. Aching. Then, he drew his pistol. I raised my hands.

"Wait, no! Please! I'll help you."

Matthew Strong softened his grip on the gun and motioned for me to get up. When I stood I realized I'd wet myself. Under different circumstances, I might have been embarrassed. But I was sure this wasn't the first time someone peed themselves when he held them at gunpoint.

He shoved the gun in the front of his jeans, then lit a cigarette. After he took a drag, he held it out for me to take. Realizing I couldn't reach, he gave the rope slack. He sat on a large boulder and lit another.

"Professor, you got as much wit and courage as a honey badger lapping water beside a crocodile. You know that?"

I took a drag from the cigarette, blew the smoke from the side of my mouth. What the hell was he talking about?

He gestured to the house where he held us. "That plantation home was constructed identical to my great-great-grandfather's in Elysian. Whenever I pass by his old estate I think about people's disregard for plantation homes that once stood as testaments of the white man's progress in the Mississippi Valley. I made up my mind to raise these castles from the dead as physical manifestations of our own resurrection."

As he spoke, I massaged my chafed wrists, thinking how a moment prior he nearly shot me. Now, he acted like some moonlight and magnolia tour guide. I smoked and this temporarily took my mind off the discomfort around my inner thighs.

"On occasion, I'd go on out there and take a look, imagining ways me and the boys would fix her up, restore her to her glory. The paint was peeling off water-stained walls. Black mold everywhere. Warped wood. We'd need to tear down the entire back side.

"Over the last couple years, one by one we'd go on to renovate the estates until the entire southern landscape was dotted with these castles. Restored back to full glory.

"I knew I needed a hefty investment to see this through. This is when my cousin and the Jefferson family's wealth came into play. My cousin has a short attention span. But he agreed because he figured he'd use this 'favor'—he loved givin' out favors—to get something in return he didn't have the guts to get himself.

"Having procured the finances, I started right here with this house. I cleaned the cobwebs, clearing out the rodents and wildlife who'd made this place a sanctuary. I soon heard rumors from the locals that gang members from Birmingham would on occasion drive out to this mansion and do their dirt. So, I instructed the white folk around these parts to contact me if they noticed anyone who didn't seem like they belonged here.

"It was midmorning when I got the call. As soon as I came to the basement window, I caught a glimpse of three Negroes inside. I've always found it best to carry my sidearm and whip in case I stumbled upon a set of circumstances that seemed best dealt with by force. In my experience, you corner a Negro, you about to get his fangs. I shouted for them to come out. I could see them hiding behind a wooden bookshelf tilted on its side. I said there was no point hiding anymore. Then I realized they had assumed I was an officer of the law. They didn't budge.

"So I reached down and picked up a rock and tossed it in the window, then rushed over to the basement door and crouched down, waiting. Sure enough, they made a run for it. I shot about a dozen rounds at their lower extremities. Been justified killing each one of them snakes. But I sought to make an example out of them. One they'd bring back to the other Negro degenerates who live around these parts. Each one dropped to the ground, writhing in pain.

"They begged for mercy. 'Officer... sorry, sir. Please.'

"Their desperate tone most certainly fit the circumstances. I told them all that moaning and groaning would not get them any sympathy. I pulled my whip from my backpack and told them that, in the good old days, the owner of this home would give them all a whipping. To honor his memory, I was going to give each some leather. They glanced at one another, surprised, confused. I cocked my pistol and yelled,

'Strip.' Sure enough, they pulled off their shirts, and I wasted no time whipping their naked backs with 'bout twenty-five lashes apiece, moving from one to the other.

"I made them swear they'd cease living a life in vice and sin. As they gathered their clothes and hurried down the dirt driveway I remembered my father telling me you can trust a Negro not to steal about as much as you can trust a fox to stand guard of a chicken coop."

I felt as if I might throw up again. I took a breath, then another; deep and deliberate. Matthew Strong flicked his cigarette away.

"You know something, Professor, if the circumstances had been different we might have been colleagues." He wiped his mouth with the back of his hand.

"I wish that was the case," I said. I fought my desire to tell him he was a sick, sick man.

"Why's that?"

"Well, for starters, I wouldn't be here," I held up my wrists, "sitting with my hands tied together. Second, I would have been able to convince you how unnecessary all this is. I have no intention of getting in the way of your movement."

"Professor, you don't have a prayer of doing that. And I don't want to kill you. You know that, right?"

"And I don't want to die."

"Well, then. We're on the same page. You do as I ask and the others might make it out of here alive."

I took a deep breath, feeling relieved his calm, pensive tone had returned. I thought about when he lashed out at me. Out there under the moon it was as if he grew fangs and his skin glowed a paler, vampiric white. He may have enticed people with elegance and charm, but beneath this façade he was a monster.

DAY TWO

Most of the next morning I translated the *Confessional* in the basement room alone. When Matthew Strong showed up, he came into the room carrying an orange and white cat. The cat jumped from his arms when Strong sat down and stretched out her front paws, then lazily reclined on her side.

Matthew Strong scanned the pages I'd translated, becoming annoyed. He dropped the pages on the table in front of me.

"Read what you wrote."

"What?" I said, surprised.

"I told you to read back what you wrote!" He tightened his lips in disgust.

"Ah, let me see," I shuffled to find my last page.
"I...I...I."

"Damn it! Give it here!" He struck the table and some of the pages slipped from my hands. He picked them up and squinted at me.

"Listen closely," he jabbed the page with his finger, "all these squiggly lines don't make not a bit of sense."

I hadn't realized he wanted me to write in print rather than cursive.

"Read it back, now!"

I chose a random page I had just translated:

"These ideas for my mission go back to when I served in the Independent Company of Alabama Mounted Volunteers during the Civil War.

"Since I had spent so many years traveling the slave trade routes from Richmond to Natchez I was well aware of how to move through the heart of darkness to transport slaves to trading centers along the popular routes. I knew the creeks and caves and where all the good Indian hunting grounds were, as well as the trails through the Appalachians. I could go five days off of blueberries and wild onion soup made with horned beetles and toad legs."

I looked up and Matthew Strong motioned for me to continue.

"My last trip before the war I gathered a group who awaited transport to be sold in the New Orleans market. This was a special group indeed. Each one of them had killed their master

in some horrible and creative way, and the families figured it'd
be best to liquidate them on the New Orleans market rather
than burn them at the stake like in the old days.

"Despite my agreement to sell them, I chose a different path.
Not for my own wealth—in fact I lost a near fortune from this
trip—but for the greater good of society. Indeed, I was inspired
by a higher calling.

"In those days, young women like them were valuable for
breeding. Yet, these ones were no different from dogs that had
snapped at their masters. There was only one thing to do with
them: take them out back and shoot them. But before I did what
needed to be done, I wanted to ascertain as much information as
I could about the root of their evil. So, I deceived them. I pulled
them close and whispered that I came from the east to free them.
I said I had killed the slave trader who went by the name of
Ridgewood and used his letters of introduction and his identity
to purchase them. I told them I really planned on taking them
to Boston. But we'd have to move swiftly in order to elude
authorities.

"Them Negro wenches swallowed my lies like a teaspoon of
honey. They asked all sorts of questions. A couple even asked
if I would draft letters to their children and husbands that
promised when they got up north they'd raise enough money to
buy their freedom.

"Off we went through the backwoods following the Natchez
Trace—"

"Wait!"

Matthew Strong went over to a box near the bookcase and found a rolled-up map and laid it flat on the table. He ran his finger along a dotted line, then stopped.

"Did you just say 'Natchez Trace'?"

I glanced down at what I wrote, then nodded. "Yes, that's right."

He pulled a marker from his pocket and made several circles on the map. He probed the map, rubbing his chin, quizzically.

"Go on and read some more."

"I let their chains hang loose, saying this would allow them to slip out of the cuffs if we needed to flee. I taught them how to follow the moss and travel toward the moon. I helped them identify empty barns and bridges to sleep under during the day. At night, I called each of them over one by one to draft false freedom papers—just in case they'd been discovered.

"I built their trust so they'd feel comfortable enough to speak candidly about how they did their dirt. One bragged about setting fire to her master's house and another told about how she poisoned hers. Some said they had done it because their master had violated their womanhood.

"I listened, legs crossed like them Chickasaws, jotting notes in my journal as these devil women described the horror they inflicted on their dumb, improper masters who had no clue how cunning the Negro really is. I planned on using these stories for a book I hoped to write about slave trading and slave discipline.

"I traveled about two days, studying their minds and taking their stories. Then, it came time for me to execute my plan. I followed a trail through the back of the Appalachians—a mountain pass about thirty minutes off the Natchez Trace.

"Hold it."

He leaned over the map, then, again, followed a line with the marker and circled another area. I tried to see where he circled, recalling that the Appalachians extended thousands of miles northeast of Alabama. Searching for something over such a large distance would be as difficult as crawling around in the snow to find a lost diamond ring. He told me to continue, his eyes still fixed on the map.

"I made camp just down from a cave I scouted on my way up there to retrieve them from slave markets. After we ate, I read aloud passages from that dreaded abolitionist newspaper The Liberator, *written by a man who hated slavery and was trying to free them. When I came to the end, they clapped and broke into one of those simple songs based on a few Bible verses they recalled. I never in my life have heard a more pleasant sound than the singing of a Negro who believed she was on her way to freedom. Like the first time a bird is freed from a cage, they tweeted their hearts out. Soon I tucked the newspaper under my arm and joined in the clapping, singing the chorus loudly and joyously, thinking to myself that these Negroes were never going to see the light of another day.*

"Like rabid dogs they'd meet the fate they deserved. Death didn't seem appropriate on its own. They needed to suffer like the

white men they'd butchered, poisoned, or burned. They needed to feel the desperation those white men felt as they met their fate, fighting for their lives like a gator flipping in circles to free himself from a hook and line.

"When the full moon glowed, I walked them up to the cave I had prepared for them to sleep in. I showed them the straw beds I laid out, saying it was the least I could do after all that they had suffered under the bootheel of those men. Then, I returned to the campfire and laid my head on a log near the fire, figuring that I would wait until the last one fell asleep before consummating my plan.

"It must have been a couple hours later when I snuck back up to the cave. I attached chains to my horse's saddle and dragged several large logs in front of the opening. I could hear some rustling inside, but I had set up their sleeping accommodations deep enough so they couldn't get a clear view of the entrance. I ensured they would be less likely to be found that way. Then I stacked logs, shrubs, leaves, so the bundle would catch fire quickly. I dumped a small carton of kerosene I had packed all over those branches and brush, causing the fire to catch quickly just as expected. As the flames popped in the cool breeze, the smoke climbed toward the tops of the pine trees as the moon provided a perfect spotlight for my execution.

"Then I heard them coughing and crying for help. The choking and the cries gave way to the crackling of the sticks. Soon they'd be before God to attest to what they had done. I wondered whether or not they recalled the cries of the white men they had set fire to, or the sound of them choking as poison *coursed through their bodies. Did those Negroes cover their mouths, horrified by what they'd done? Did they feel one ounce of guilt watching those men stagger about, holding their throats, reaching and grabbing for anything that'd relieve the burning?*

"Then the strangest thing occurred. They began singing. I was unable to make out their words, but it sounded like a song the Negroes used to sing on our plantation. I waited until I could no longer hear them, then tossed my brown leather bag over my shoulder and made my way back to my horse.

"Must have been about a year or two ago when I found myself near that very same cave. Sure enough, those scorched logs still stood solid as the stone doors of a tomb. I attached two ropes around them and pulled open the front so I could have a look. When I crept inside I started thinking about how much money I sacrificed when I burned them evil wenches about a decade before.

"I never regretted what I did, or the money I lost. Those women had more than a tiny bite of the devil's curse coursing through their veins. To send them on to the New Orleans market infected as they were, and have them spread their demon impulses to some other man's slaves, seemed unethical.

"From then on out, I made regular stops there to remind myself of the cost of preserving our way of life. That cave became a sanctuary for me and others who believed in my vision and were willing to leave a little sacrifice—gold coin, rings or other jewelry, even stacks of bills. All of these were tributes to our cause. In fact, the Sons of Light was born in those caves."

"Alright. You can stop reading."

Matthew Strong capped his marker and leaned on the edge of the table, running the back of his fingers against the side of the cat's face.

The cat snapped up, ears twisting this way and that. Then, it leapt off the table past me and snared a mouse.

Matthew Strong grinned at my horrified look as the mouse dangled from the cat's jaws. "See that, Doc? It's their instinct. Nature has its way. Modern technology ain't got a damn thing on natural instinct. Send a man to the moon, but can't keep a forest full of field mice from getting inside your home."

He picked up the cat and went to the door, then turned back.

"So, like I said. You gonna write in a manner I can read. We clear?"

"Yes. Sorry."

"No use apologizing. I'm going to leave you here to rewrite all that and finish translating. When I return I expect you to be nearly done."

All morning I wrote out the *Confessional*, printing, as instructed, anticipating with dread Matthew Strong's return. I translated Shields's horrific descriptions of burning people alive, dynamiting municipal buildings, and drowning men in the Cahaba River. Shields invented an entire vocabulary to instruct his troop— the Sons of Light—on how to carry out any given execution. He called assassinations of Republican politicians and local leaders "storms." If he wanted a man drowned, he referred to it as a "flood." When he wanted a group of men shot, he called for a "hailstorm." A "lightning storm" was when he wanted a man burned to death. Kidnapping was a "windstorm." If that person died, he termed it a "hurricane." But there was something else.

Right before he had been captured in April 1873, Shields ordered the Sons of Light to execute the "secret six"—six men who had funded his mission but double-crossed him. He ordered his troop to cut off the right hand of each of these men for shaking his hand, then stabbing him in the back.

Although I feared Matthew Strong planned to commit these same acts on his path toward seizing control of the state, I found one section titled "Actions" particularly bizarre.

The section began with instructions:

To be chanted at midnight one day prior to redemption:
When witches dance with gods
On midnight mountain pass
stones bleed black gold
light breaks the dark
twelve swords
slice flesh
break devil girl's
curse
Waton brings forth

the light
Ostra brings
Thor to life.

Although I knew little about the occult or the dark arts, I was aware the Ku Klux Klan, the Nazi Party, and other white supremacists were inspired by pagan blood rituals. It dawned on me that Mathew Strong was so desperate for the *Confessional* to be translated into English likely for this very reason. Had he planned some cult ritual before he commenced his "redemption"? It made sense. While I thought, perhaps, he sought the cave with the money and jewels left as tribute to the Sons of Light's mission, I worried this section meant much more to Matthew Strong. If this passage that described cutting the flesh of "devil girl's curse" was central to a successful mission, then I figured this was the reason he kidnapped the girls. I had to locate the girls, and find a way out of the house.

I glanced over at the guard playing on his phone and pondered how I might best manipulate him again. Previously, I'd used the bathroom upstairs, but not the one down here. Maybe it had a window. Or even a crawl space into the vent? I had to try something.

"Excuse me?" I said, waving my hand to get his attention.

He raised his eyes.

"Bathroom?" I asked.

He shook his head, then returned to his phone, texting.

"No, I'm serious. Please."

"Yeah, right." He didn't even look up.

"I really need to use the bathroom."

"You'll have time later."

"Please. It's a woman thing."

He relented, put his phone away, and walked me down the hall. He motioned toward the bathroom on our floor, demanding I "make it quick."

I stepped inside and locked the door. *A window.* I rushed over, flicked the latch, and lifted. *Shit.* It was stuck. I shook the window frame, desperately.

I heard the knob rattle. The guard banged on the door. "Open up!"

"I'm not coming out until you let me call my sister and tell her I'm alive," I said, offering a reason that might buy me more time. I noticed that the outside window latch prevented me from lifting it all the way. I reached under and tripped the latch.

He tapped his knuckles, gently. "How long you planning on staying in there?"

"As long as I need."

I forced my shoulder under the window, hoping I'd have enough leverage to force it up. It moved a bit, but something else, perhaps the recent paint job, prevented the window from sliding.

"You go on and open this door and I'll personally ask the Prophet if I can contact someone on your behalf."

I pushed with all my might, but I couldn't move it. Then—

Bang!

Bang!

Bang!

Bullets tore the doorjamb beside the lock. I dropped to the floor and cowered in the corner, holding my arms above my head, terrified that one of the door-busting bullets would kill me. The guard burst in, grabbed my arm, and yanked me up.

"That wasn't such a good idea!"

I fought desperately, kicking, screaming. He brought his gun down on my head, knocking me sideways. My mind became woozy, eyes blurred. I must have lost consciousness for a moment. Next thing I knew, I was being dragged down the hallway, then pushed into a storage closet. I heard him mumbling "stupid bitch" over and over as he fiddled with the doorknob and it clicked. My body ached; the back of my head throbbed. I leaned against the wall and cried.

Trapped in the closet with no light, my mind grew incapable of holding a thought before racing off toward a new one. I cursed myself for failing to escape through the window. My actions now seem as irresponsible as tossing stones at a wasp's nest.

My stomach burbled, then cramped. I turned to my side, pulled my knees to my chest, hoping this would soothe my pain. I chewed my nails to the skin, then scratched my wrist, and my scalp. I felt like a hog pinned between boards with no space to move, no sense of time or when I'd meet my fate.

I tried like hell to stay awake. I shifted from one side to the other. I did sit-ups. I pinched myself, dug my nails into my thighs.

At one point I found myself reflecting on my relationship with David, using memories from the past few years to keep me awake. I thought about the time David and I decided to have children. During our baby-making phase, we made love each morning and before we went to sleep. As time went on, we even made love when he came home from work. But a year passed, and we worried there was something medically preventing me from becoming pregnant. Doctor after doctor offered options, but nothing we tried worked. Soon we fell back into our routine, which meant having sex whenever we (usually he) felt the urge.

Then I got sick.

It was strange shifting from imagining the possibility of growing something beautiful inside, to learning the only thing growing inside might kill me.

David once asked if I'd consider using a surrogate.
I couldn't imagine taking a child from a mother, even if
that child was a part of us. He even suggested visiting
adoption agencies. I caught him online looking at prices
for plane tickets to China after listening to a podcast
about overcrowded orphanages in Beijing. I laughed,
imagining the joy of raising a Chinese-American girl and
the stupid surprise on people's faces when she asked me
to stand and be acknowledged during her valedictorian
speech—me, that skinny, freckled, light-skinned black
woman with one breast and gray dreads. Of course,
you'd think they'd consider her smarts nurture rather
than nature, but no matter whether I held a PhD in
philosophy, I'm sure most people wouldn't fathom a black
mother responsible for such genius.

Last year, I'd resolved that after I finished my book
and became a full professor, I'd be ready to try again.
It was Friday the 13th and I'd returned from a book
talk in D.C. I waited on the couch downstairs, texting
David, wondering where he was, eager to see his face
after I announced I was ready. But I fell asleep reading.
When I woke and went to our bed, he still hadn't come
home. This was when I first suspected an affair. I had
no evidence besides his strange absence that night, and
the suspicious way he denied it when I asked.

Eventually, there in the closet, I lost my fight to stay awake, but was roused when I heard Matthew Strong shouting at the guard. I scooted back at the sound of heavy boots approaching the door.

"Well, you sure have surprised me."

My body tensed.

"It seems you and I are at an impasse. Maybe I have you all wrong. I thought we were on the same page. Sort of like one of them symbiotic relationships. I help you become more famous than any intellectual of your generation—sort of like what Hitler did for Nietzsche—and in return, you translate the *Confessional of William Shields*, then use that there brilliant mind of yours to capture my story using phrases that resemble Shields's generation. One of them win-win scenarios."

I stayed silent. I'd had enough of his games. I knew that, to him, I was no different from the other girls. We were tools in his imagined revolution. He wanted more than reclaiming the South; he wanted to make history.

"I'm not helping you anymore," I stammered, fearing losing my mind more than being tortured until I agreed to finish the translation.

I heard the flick of a lighter and smelled smoke waft under the door.

"I don't want to hurt you or none of them girls. You know that, right? While you may see me as a monster, I'm not. None of what I've done has been out of malice. Hell, I'm more like Thomas Jefferson than Stonewall Jackson."

I remained silent.

What did he expect me to say? That I thought his mission was noble? I refused to play along and stayed silent.

"Don't you want fame? Don't you want the world to know your name? Shoot, more people will read your words than any philosopher in human history. Now isn't that worth all the gold in King Tut's tomb?"

I clenched my jaw, expecting the door to open.

"You disappoint me, professor. I thought you were special. Not like the others. But if you intend on acting like 'em, I'm going to treat you like 'em. You'll regret your decision to deny me. Not for your own pain, which you'll have plenty of, but for our great nation. The civilized world.

"Before long, you'll be in a ditch. Undifferentiated. Anonymous. Body parts scattered alongside Route Twenty. No one could piece you together."

I continued my silence. Any moment he'd pull open the door.

"I see you need some more time to think it through. Fair enough. But remember this: you're not my primary concern. Like I said when you first arrived. We make a great team, you and me. Don't we?"

When he left, I took what felt like the longest breath of my life. I tried to hold myself together, knowing this faux patience was an olive branch. Next would come the sword. Or, in our case, the knife.

DAY THREE

I had no idea at the time how long Matthew Strong held me in that closet. I fell asleep despite my fear. When I awoke disoriented, I noticed a light passed through the cracked closet door, which I realized, to my surprise, was ajar. I leaned onto my knees and peered cautiously into the room. Three stacked crates with a plate of fruit and bread on top and a bottle of water were just outside the door. I glanced around, searching for his men, or the woman who usually brought me food. I figured this was another one of Matthew Strong's games, perhaps, a trap. But my hunger extinguished my fear and I crept toward the plate. I took it—carefully, quietly, steadily—and then crawled back into the closet.

I gobbled the bread, then cracked the seal on the bottle and drank desperately. He manipulated me by fostering a sense of hope, and trying to convince me that if I cooperated, did what he asked, if I helped him, he would let me live. I never believed him for one second. But, after I tried to escape, Matthew Strong figured this. He would surely try another strategy.

I heard someone outside, then keys. The door opened and two men stood there; one held a blindfold, the other handcuffs. I scooted away from them, screaming, kicking. When they got hold of my feet, they dragged me into the hallway and flipped me over. One held me down with his knee, the other pulled my arms behind my back, clicked cuffs on my wrists.

They carried me into the basement room where I translated the *Confessional*, then through the passage behind the bookcase, and into the cavern where I saw Cynthia. I searched the shadows for her, bloodied, or even dead, but she wasn't in sight. They plopped me in a chair, then chained my wrists to its arms and my ankles to its legs. Each time I inhaled my nostrils filled with musk and mildew. I heard the crank slide the bookcase back in place, extinguishing the light.

For what must have been hours I waited strapped in that chair. I had never felt so vulnerable, so terrified in my life.

I heard a clunk, clank, then the clatter of chains. Although it was impossible to see what made the sound, I heard a flick and a string of Christmas lights crisscrossed above sparked on, brightening the room.

Matthew Strong looked as if he just came from church. He wore a collarless white shirt buttoned up to his neck with loose linen sleeves, his gray hair pulled back into a ponytail, and his beard trimmed.

"This space once served as a place to discipline slaves, or wash them before sale."

He walked to some iron cuffs and chains drilled into the stone wall. I counted ten pairs. He inspected them, tugging the chains, turning over the cuffs.

"During the war, the plantation owner must have dug a tunnel from here that connects with mine shafts all throughout Jefferson County. He must have figured if the Yanks seized the house or burned it down, this provided him and his family an escape route through that iron door."

I closed my eyes and tears dripped onto my lap.

He kneeled down and ran his finger along steel tracks, then went over to a large iron door that I assumed led to a passage into the mines.

"For the past hundred-plus years these tracks have run beneath the Oak Mountains, ferrying out the coal and iron ore used to make Birmingham the most profitable city in the South.

"They called it 'progress'—'a New South.' What a disgrace. The elites' idea of progress depended on convincing poor white men to dig black gold outta these caves. Not their children or cousins. Nah. The fathers of Birmingham used poor white men to carve these caves, then left them sickened and starved with as little care as a bunch of Negroes."

Matthew Strong rubbed his finger gently across my lips, then leaned in as if to kiss me. I turned away, then he whispered in my ear.

"You see, Professor, this revolution is bigger than me or others carping on and on, from talk shows to podcasts, about all the evils of the world. The average American relishes the opportunity to be a part of something larger. Take the boys I recruited into the Sons of Light. It gives men a sense of pride to show their family and friends they've devoted themselves to a mission sent from God. A mission that'll benefit everyone, especially those who laughed at their failed business ventures, mocked their requests for loans, and shook their heads when they asked if they'd buy 'em a beer. These men? They have honor and purpose now. Like Shields, my movement seeks to redeem all those who have watched in shame the colonization of our land with Arabs, Mexicans, and them Asians."

He pulled his knife and cleaned the blade on his shirtsleeve.

"...I found thousands of 'em. Sitting on barstools in American Legions and Elks lodges, sipping beer and watching the news. Waiting for something to inspire them. From Richmond, Knoxville, Atlanta, to Natchez, Mississippi.

He unbuttoned his shirt, tied it around his waist. Despite his grays, his chest and arms were thick and muscular.

"And they had no clue how to direct that anger toward something useful. Instead, they beat their wives and neglected their kids, robbed each other, illustrating the tragic consequences of our lack of leadership. Seems we became so distracted by the bombast of a few demagogic figures that we forgot our obligation to those who lost hope anything could be done. But soon this will all change."

Matthew Strong brought his knife to my face, and I turned away.

"Now, you listen carefully. Our circumstances have been altered on account of the weakness of some of those who I thought could keep their mouths shut long enough for us to complete our preparation. But that's no concern of yours. This does mean you're going to have to work faster. You understand me?"

He looked over at the devices attached to the wall once used to torture slaves. My eyes jumped from one pair of iron cuffs to another.

I nodded.

"Okay. How long before you're through?"

I hesitated. I knew he expected something reasonable, but I feared being held to that time frame.

"I can finish in two days."

He appeared surprised. "Two days?" He grinned. "Is that right?"

His tone made me feel relaxed. For a moment, I thought I impressed him. Then, he slapped me.

"You goddamn bitch! To think you've only done ten pages since you got here and now you're saying you can do seventeen in two days?"

He ran his blade from my eyebrow to my lips, slowly. I blinked tears, fighting my urge to scream, holding completely still as he pressed the blade against my lower lip. I swallowed.

"Listen closely, Professor." He squeezed my cheeks. "I'm going to give you two days to finish. And if you don't, those sumptuous lips are gonna be mine."

NIGHT THREE

Falling asleep after my harrowing experience in that cavern was impossible. Having read the bizarre cultlike ritual in Shield's *Confessional*, I assumed Matthew Strong would use our murder to unite his men. Even though I found such rituals absurd, I thought about Le Bon's theory that, in groups, people are more likely to die for a cause. Throughout the ages, rituals have bonded human beings together when confronted with internal and external threats. I knew Matthew Strong had convinced his Sons of Light this ritual would help him win an impossible war. And he made clear the consequences if I refused any further.

I recalled a lecture I attended the previous fall on revolutionary movements. The scholar claimed

terrorists and patriots were twin historical actors
who recruited peers by identifying a specific group
responsible for social misery. Kings. Infidels. Capitalists.
Communists. When patriots and terrorists bomb
buildings or carry out assassinations, they justify
this violence as the only way to save their families,
communities, or nations from oppressive forces. Their
struggle becomes virtuous rather than vicious, noble
rather than treasonous.

I heard the roar of an engine, then van doors slam.
I went to the window and squinted through the slats
between the two-by-fours nailed outside. Two men
with machine guns opened the rear doors. A white
man wearing a tuxedo and an argyle scarf climbed out
with his hands tied behind his back. He was followed
by a woman, also bound, who wore an evening dress
with a black fur pulled over her shoulders. Her jeweled
necklace glistened under the moonlight.

The men pushed the two forward with the barrels
of their guns toward a figure who appeared from the
house. Even in the darkness I recognized Matthew
Strong's strut. They forced the couple to their knees.
The guy tried to squirm away, but the men kicked him
until he ceased resisting. The woman begged, but the
men ignored her, casually wrapping a scarf around her
mouth, muffling her screams. They did this in a slow,
relaxed way, as if all the pleading in the world would
do nothing to prevent what came next.

Matthew Strong knelt beside the man, unfolded a piece of paper, and waved it in his face. I wondered what the note said. Were they people who fed money to his cause with the hope of benefiting from his mission? What fool would trust a man like Matthew Strong? It appeared as if their generosity had come back to bite them. I wondered why.

Matthew Strong opened a small book that looked like a Bible, then one of his men shined his phone so Strong could read a passage. After, he snapped the book shut and stepped back as one of the guards pulled a knife. Then, as casually as shaving beneath his chin, the guard opened the man's throat. The woman tried to scurry away, but two guards pinned her legs. Matthew Strong came over and took her arm. She wriggled from his grasp as he bent close and whispered in her ear. I swallowed, and instinctively covered my mouth. Matthew Strong smiled when his guard lifted the woman's chin gently, then ran his blade from ear to ear.

I staggered backward, stumbled over the edge of the mattress. I crawled to the door and shook the knob. "Please! Help me!" I banged on the door. "Someone? Anyone!"

I realize, now, this response made no sense. I mean, who did I expect would free me?

———

Nothing prepared me for what I had witnessed. Neither David's horror movies, nor documentaries on serial murder, nor the violence in the news. Not even the first time Grandma called me outside our chicken coop to hold a chicken's legs while she wrung its neck.

I have tried before to convey the sheer terror coursing through my veins the night I witnessed Matthew Strong's men slice that couple's throats. It's impossible to fully describe. Not because of all the blood.

No. It was the woman's eyes; her hopeless, fear-stricken eyes. That was a sight I'll never forget.

The way they widened the moment she knew her life would end; the moment his blade gleamed, and terror extinguished the final flicker of life.

I translated five more pages that night.

Although I did not know for certain why Matthew Strong murdered them, my suspicions were later confirmed. Roscoe Tanney and his wife, Lena, owned a chain of fast-food restaurants across the South funded by an inheritance made from the time when Woodward coal mines coughed black gold, making millionaires out of men who shared a vision of a "New South." Like the father of Birmingham, Andrew Shields, the Tanney family invested in coal, railroads, and mines, replacing cotton, steamboats, and enslaved people's toil. Matthew Strong searched for the descendants of the men who'd double-crossed his relative William Shields.

It was as if Matthew Strong was exacting some intergenerational revenge. He searched them out and forced them to donate to the Sons of Light. The couple never used their real names when donating to the Sons of Light Ministries, nor did they appear on any list of supporters. Yet Matthew Strong squeezed them of cash, and when Roscoe Tanney refused to donate any more, Matthew Strong's men kidnapped him and his wife when they were leaving a rally for Thomas Turner in Tuscumbia, Alabama. No one ever saw them again. When the FBI found their bodies, the investigators were puzzled by the absence of Mr. Tanney's hands.

DAY FOUR

My fourth day I found Matthew Strong hunched over Shields's *Confessional* and my handwritten pages, his reading glasses perched on the edge of his nose.

I stood for a few moments as he read, mouthing the words as if practicing a speech. The man guarding me waited beside me until Matthew Strong waved for him to leave.

"Take a chair, Professor."

I noticed a notebook beside him with six names. I tried to read the names, but he flipped shut the notebook. He pulled cigarettes from his front pocket. He flicked his lighter and leaned into the flame. As I sat there, I thought about the murdered couple from the night before, and found myself contemplating whether it would be worse to die by strangulation, gunshot, or having my throat slit. Maybe he'd hang me from the large oak tree, or drag me into the cavern and gut me. Such morbid thoughts crowded my consciousness, suffocated my hope, drowned my optimism. I was out of options. Only a miracle could save me.

My haunted thoughts must have contorted my face, because he looked at me curiously.

"Do you have something to ask me? Perhaps about last night?"

I averted my eyes, staring blankly at the floor. He prodded and poked, testing me. "Go on then, ask."

I hesitated, knowing he wanted me to acknowledge I had watched him execute that couple. He wouldn't be satisfied by my silence. I thought maybe if I agreed with him he wouldn't torture me in the cavern behind the bookcase.

"Spit it out."

"I just wondered when you plan on putting me with the other girls."

He chuckled. "I'm not quite done with you yet. You still need to take my confession. Add a new chapter in the 'Book of Matthew,' so to speak."

"Well, I'm practically done with the translation."

"That's good news. Tomorrow when I return from delivering a speech, we'll get started on the next chapter in this struggle."

He stood and went for the door.

"Before you leave, tell me this," I said, sitting up straight. "How did you figure out my grandma was tracking you and your movement?"

A sly smile came across his face. "Oh, me and her go way back. Before you were even born. Your grandmother was a clever one. Bold too. Guess the apple don't fall far from the tree. You know, once I watched her follow my van from Woodward to Montgomery. I even caught her out at Brewer Cemetery when I was paying respects at my great-grandfather's tomb. Right then I knew she was onto me."

Tears formed in my eyes. Had *he killed her*? He gazed at me as if reading my mind, took a drag from the cigarette.

"I know what you're thinking," he said. "But no, I didn't kill her. Personally. Not saying I wouldn't have if the circumstances had been different."

As I translated the final pages, I recognized several passages from Shields's *Confessional* with methods he used to conduct a successful grassroots rebellion. I translated these descriptions, thinking how wrong the FBI's approach had been. They thought Matthew Strong was a serial killer who kidnapped young black women to satiate sexual or violent impulses. But his violence sought to inspire a race war, and he began by uniting white supremacists in the South to rally around the removal of the Shields monument in Birmingham. The authorities had no idea Alabama was on the verge of a racial storm worse than the one in Atlanta decades before.

Hours later, I held my breath when the basement door opened, terrified Matthew Strong had returned. But to my surprise—shock, really—it wasn't Matthew Strong. It was Wallace.

That son of a *bitch*. I knew he was involved in these renovations, but I didn't know he had been involved in the kidnappings and murders. Anger swept over me. I wanted to leap from my seat and jam my pencil in his eye.

Wallace dismissed the guard, saying Matthew Strong asked him to talk to me about something sensitive. I didn't know what he meant, but it seemed like a blow-off line to get me alone.

He poured me a glass of water. "Some water, Professor?"

I leaned back, crossed my arms. "I don't want anything from you."

"So be it." He placed my glass on the table in front of me. "A lot has happened since you left."

"'*Left*'? What do you mean, 'left'? You had me kidnapped."

"Regardless." He poured himself water. "It seems circumstances have changed."

"Are you here to gloat? I figured you were a narcissist and a bigot, but I must admit I'm surprised you would collude with a man like Matthew Strong. All that talk of family pride. What bullshit! Matthew Strong should embarrass you."

"I know what you must be thinking. But I have no animosity against you personally, Professor. I never did."

"All this bullshit about supporting Turner for governor? I thought you said he's your best hope to restore Alabama to the good ol' days. What a lie."

"There's a chance he still is."

"How about you help me get out of here and I'll make certain Janice and I sign over the deed to the house?"

"Too late for that."

"Did she sign over the deed? Or did you just go ahead and steal the land?"

"The land acquisition is secondary now."

"I can't believe you think anything good will come from aligning with Matthew Strong."

Wallace grinned, leaned in close, and whispered, "This isn't what you think. Pay close attention," he said, scanning the room as if ensuring no one was listening. "Tonight. I'll tell you more, but for now you need to start concentrating on remembering what he's told you. One question. Nod yes or no. Is Odessa here?"

Why on earth was he asking *me*?

There was a knock on the door, then it opened. The guard glanced at me and then Wallace.

"'Scuse me, sir, but we've been instructed to take her back to her room."

"Yes, of course." Wallace went over to the bookshelf and pulled a random book off and flipped through. The man ordered me to come with him.

NIGHT FOUR

That night I heard footsteps outside my room, then the door opened.

"Professor? It's me, Wallace."

He tiptoed into my room, then set a backpack on the floor beside me.

"What the hell's going on?" I asked.

"I need you to listen to me. We don't have long."

"Before what?"

To my surprise, he looked nervous. "Before Matthew Strong returns." He teared up. "This was never supposed to happen like this." He wiped his eyes with his sleeve.

"What do you mean? It seems like you've been involved all along."

"Kidnapping Tommy Turner's sweet Odessa? This is just plain insanity."

"You're telling me you had nothing to do with any of this? I thought you were funding things?"

"You may think I'm ambitious, and I may have values that don't sit right with you, but I'm no killer. I abhor Matthew's methods."

"What about the Sons of Light?"

"What about 'em? Nothing short of a cult."

"But how could you have supported them?"

"I gave him a loan to build parishes, as well as renovate these plantation houses. Terrible investment. I would have torn them all down, but he got me by romanticizing our family's past."

"What does this have to do with Thomas Turner and Odessa?"

"Turner was our path toward reclaiming power for the South. Who better to bring about our agenda than a black man? Cut taxes. Stop sending jobs to Mexico. Not everyone agreed. You can imagine what Matthew thought about it. Yet I was able to persuade him and other doubters."

"Why did you need my grandmother's house?"

"I couldn't give a rat's ass about the house. It was the land! Matthew told me your great-grandfather bought the land. Owned it outright. I mean acres and acres. Beyond where your grandma's house sits. Well, turns out much of the Andrew Shields estate had been on that land, including Brewer Cemetery, where the Shields and Jefferson families buried their dead. Seems Matthew just couldn't stand the idea of our ancestors' bodies buried in land owned by your family."

"So you had me kidnapped and destroyed my career to force us to sell the land? I'm sure some amount of money would have persuaded us."

"I tried to talk your grandmother into selling it. I told her she could keep the house and her immediate property. She wouldn't budge. But what was worse was when I learned she passed away and left the land to you and Janice. I figured I'd be able to talk some sense into you two. But that didn't work."

"Why didn't you just tell me all of this?"

"I didn't think I would have to. Anyway, we have ourselves in a huge mess, because, since Matthew learned about you and the Eli Jefferson Chair, he's insisted you're the one to tell his story, given your research. Now, it's time to end this. Tell me something, Professor. Did he say where he's holding Odessa?"

"I haven't seen her. He hasn't let me near any of them."

"I'm fairly certain they're down in the basement," Wallace said. "It's locked and his men refuse to let me in there."

"Alive?" I asked, hesitantly.

"For now, yes. But he's planning on killing all of them the night after the next. Says it's a part of some ritual. An official beginning to his mission." Wallace took a deep breath. "Professor, you have to get out of here. Get to the FBI and tell them what he's said to you and where we are."

"You expect me to waltz out the front door?"

"There's only a few guards right now. The rest went with Strong."

"Why don't *you*?"

"If I leave, he'll know I've turned against him. Many more people besides the girls will be killed. Plus, I might still be able to delay him until the authorities come."

"This is crazy. If they catch me, they'll kill me!"

"At this point, we have no other option. So I'll leave this door unlocked, and the back door. When you hear a disturbance outside, go for it."

"What kind of disturbance?"

"I'll think of something. Go out the back porch. Into the woods."

He flashed his light in a backpack he brought with him. "I found this in one of the rooms. In here there's water, a compass, map, and gun. Have you ever shot a gun before?"

"Not a pistol."

"It's not hard. Use two hands. Aim for the chest."

There were footsteps outside the door. Wallace ducked behind the bed. We waited. The feet outside the door moved on.

"Just do as I said," he whispered. "Get out of here and get the FBI. Tell them what he told you."

"I don't even know where we are. Do you?"

"They blindfolded me on the drive out here. I may have inadvertently funded this godforsaken enterprise, but never went out to see their progress. I'm not even sure which plantation we're being held at," Wallace said.

"What about you? Won't they suspect something when I'm gone, since you talked to me earlier?"

"Let's just hope you get the authorities here by morning. His plan will commence on Sunday."

"What's today?"

"Good Friday."

After Wallace left, I paced the room, processing what he told me. Matthew Strong wanted my grandmother's land because of the *cemetery*? Could it be true? I thought more about my conversations with Matthew Strong.

I heard car doors outside, and then arguing.

"...the Prophet said..."

"I don't care what your prophet told you. I'm leaving," Wallace demanded.

"You cannot leave, sir."

The front door slammed and I heard another voice outside. "Go back inside, sir."

"What? Are you going to shoot me?"

I heard guns loading. I went to my window and saw Wallace's hands were up as the three men pointed rifles at him. I grabbed the backpack and tried the door to my room. It was unlocked, just as Wallace said. I heard more arguing outside as I tiptoed down the hallway.

"Sir, we have orders."

"Damn your orders. He told me to follow him to Montgomery. Why don't one of you drive me, then? Why are you all doin' every damn thing the man says? He's not a prophet; he's just a man, boys. Just like you and me."

As Wallace pleaded his case, I crouched down and continued downstairs, and through the house toward a closed door. I leaned my ear against the wood and heard weeping. I turned the knob, but it was locked.

"Cynthia?"

I tapped on the door. No reply.

"Cynthia?" I whispered again. "It's Allie. Unlock the door."

Again, no response, only weeping.

Wallace shouted, "Let me go!" and I heard car tires crunching, then an engine shut off. Matthew Strong had returned. Time was up. I had no choice but to continue down the back staircase, crouching low in case someone came back in the house. I glanced around, then rushed out the patio door and fled across the grass as the moon shone like a spotlight atop a watchtower.

When I made it to the tree line, I ducked down behind a tree and looked back to the house. I felt terrible for leaving without Cynthia and the other girls. But what choice did I have? I had to get help.

The lights came on and I could see men positioning themselves around the house. One came onto the veranda, pulled his machine gun over his shoulder, and leaned over the railing.

I surveyed the vast wilderness ahead, terrified about going into the woods with no trail to follow. I almost turned back, thinking perhaps I could reason with one of them. But these were Matthew Strong's most trusted disciples. I had no chance. I continued into the woods, knowing once Matthew Strong discovered I'd escaped he'd begin his hunt.

The farther I trekked through the woods in search of help, the more I reconsidered rushing away as Wallace had suggested. This was absurd—the entire scenario. Where was I going? What if all of this was a setup? Wallace claimed to be unaware of Matthew Strong's plot to kidnap Odessa and the other girls, but how did I know he was telling the truth? Maybe he lost his nerve and decided to make it appear like he never knew. Not to mention, I had no idea how far Matthew Strong's men infiltrated law enforcement agencies. This

was one strategy Shields described in the *Confessional*.
In fact, Shields kidnapped high-ranking officials to
throw off authorities and instill fear among those in
positions of power who opposed his campaign.

I wandered down a steep slope, skidding sideways
a bit to catch my balance. Through the darkness, there
was a symphony of hoots in the trees, pitter-patters
and sticks cracking on the ground, crickets chirping.
I periodically caught a glimpse of eyes reflecting back
toward me and the blinking of fireflies. I figured I had
five hours or so before dawn; before Matthew Strong's
men brought me breakfast.

But after what felt like forever, I had to accept
that I was lost. I imagined David's reprimand for not
using the compass and map as he taught me. I unrolled
the map, held the flashlight between my teeth, and
surveyed the markings. I studied the topography,
focusing on rigged lines indicating an incline. If I
walked back the way I came and went northwest, there
appeared to be a flat area leading to a road. But this
was where the map ended, and I had no sense of what
was there. It was a gamble, but I had to try.

I heard a stick snap behind me. I froze, assuming
any moment I'd hear the clack of a gun and feel the cold
pain of a bullet piercing my skin.

I looked back for flashlights. When I didn't see
any, I thought about wolves, but remembered my
grandfather laughing when I told him I was afraid to

go in our woods sometimes because of wolves. "They don't hunt humans," he'd assured me. As a matter of fact, he never mentioned anything scary out in the woods; I grew up thinking they were safe until my mother disappeared.

I squinted, attempting to make out a shape in the darkness that resembled a large animal, but I didn't see any. Maybe it was a raccoon, I thought, continuing on. But then I heard something that sounded like a child's scream. I froze. Again, twice more. Now it sounded more like a screech. Lack of sleep, I thought. Maybe the stress. I was losing my mind. *Get it together, Allie.* I took two deep breaths before I picked up my pace. I hadn't gone ten yards before I heard the sound again, almost like a child wailing. I ducked behind a tree, sizing up its lowest branch. I figured I'd try to pull myself up and climb to a spot where I could see better. Just before I climbed, I cautiously peeked around the tree.

It was a cougar.

Never in my wildest dreams could I imagine that a cougar made such a horrifying sound. No lion's roar, nor tiger's growl could match a cougar's scream. *Stay calm.* I knew any quick motion would make the animal lunge. It began circling me with its eyes fixed on mine. I reached in my backpack for the gun, rotating with the animal, ready to shoot if necessary. It paused, then took a few tentative steps toward me, testing the water. It seemed puzzled. Did it wonder why I hadn't shown my teeth, barked, or growled? The animal had no idea I held something in my hand with the power to kill. But I'd never killed anything in my life. Even though I was terrified, I had no desire to kill the cougar. I slid off my backpack and held it over my forearm like a shield. If it lunged for me, it'd slice my bag. It leaned on its hind legs, poised to strike. Then, a sudden flash lit the sky, followed by a crack of thunder. The cougar flinched as if struck by lightning, then darted away into the darkness.

I felt a drop on my nose. I held out my palm. Shit. Rain. Seconds later, it poured. I ran for cover beneath a huge oak tree, but it did next to nothing to protect me. My clothes, the backpack, and my hair were drenched. When the rain finally eased up, it didn't take long before the mosquitoes buzzed and bit. I slapped my arms and neck as I stomped over wet logs and passed trees, dripping and dreary as the sun slowly began its ascent.

I thought about William Shields's descriptions of miners blasting these mountains, stripping rock face like skin from skulls, leaving caves like vacant eyes and open mouths. I wondered how many enslaved black people escaped into these woods, fleeing north over the Appalachian Trail. I pictured them ducking into caves, hiding in the shadows, listening for the howls of dogs or the galloping of horses. I imagined Shields in hot pursuit, detecting them, then cuffing their ankles and wrists for the long march to the New Orleans market.

I couldn't stop thinking about the twelve women he burned to death in one of these caves.

Hours passed, and then I noticed a low rock wall in the distance. I picked up my pace, spotting a stretch of grass rolling downward toward a white house, chimney puffing smoke into the dark. There was a fenced area with cows, horses, and a chicken coop. Though exhausted, I ran as fast as I could toward what I hoped would be my salvation.

I came to the back door and heard dogs barking. A male voice shouted for them to calm down and be quiet. A light came on in the front room, then outside lights; one pointed down at me, and the others illuminated the backyard. I heard a gun cock.

"Don't move!" a voice shouted from the porch.

"Please," I said, my hands shaking. "I've been held captive, just up..."

"I said don't move!" He stepped out and pointed his rifle at me, eye trained behind the scope.

"Wait! You don't understand."

"Keep your hands where I can see them!"

I held up my palms so he could see my hands were empty. He was halfway down the steps when I heard a voice from behind him.

"Marshall, what is it?"

I could see a woman approach, gray hair to her shoulders, pulling closed a maroon bathrobe.

"Go back in the house, Mildred," he said, annoyed. Protective. Mad.

"Please help me! I've been taken captive and escaped through the woods." I barely had any energy left to beg.

"She's terrified, Marshall."

"Would you be quiet and go back inside," the man said as he reached the bottom step a few feet from me. She pushed past him.

The man lowered his weapon and looked around, as if anticipating an ambush. With each step, alarm spread across the woman's face. Her eyes widened like she saw a ghost.

"Good Lord, child. What's happened to you?"

Just then, as if hit with a bolt of lightning, I felt my legs go weak and my eyes blurred.

I awoke on a couch with a blanket pulled to my chin and dogs licking me. I pulled myself up, and they backed away, tails wagging, panting with delight. On the coffee table was a glass of water. A fire glowed in the cast-iron stove, near where the wood floor met the white linoleum kitchen floor. In the room was a love seat, a potted plant near the door, and shelves with various baby bird glass ornaments. A painting of a deer grazing was on the largest wall.

My hosts whispered in the kitchen. The man's red beard burst from his face like a bush. The woman still had plenty of brown hair among the grays, like a winter dusting over soil. When she noticed me sit up, she came into the room and tucked her hair behind her ears.

"Marshall, put on the kettle," she called, then pulled a seat close.

"My name's Mildred, and that's my husband, Marshall."

"Please," I said. "I'm Allie Douglass. I need you to call the FBI. Ask for Agent Tyler."

"Calm down. You're safe here," Mildred said. She placed her hand gently on my arm as the man set down a tray with two teacups, honey, milk, and a sugar bowl.

"But you don't understand, we have to act fast. This man. Matthew Strong. He has hostages."

"Who, now? Hostages?"

"Yes. I was kidnapped. The mayor's daughter, Odessa, as well. You may have heard..."

The two made eye contact, then she looked back at me as if I just told her I saw aliens.

I took a deep breath to calm my nerves. Each time I tried to explain, one of them would interrupt me, astonished. Both of them stared at me, waiting for further explanation, but I was so woozy I struggled to hold steady the teacup, let alone give a clearer explanation.

I sighed. "There are twelve others."

"Mayor of Birmingham's daughter?"

"That's right."

They glanced at one another, then back at me. What in God's name were they waiting for? I knew I sounded crazy, but I was running out of time.

"Listen, I know this seems strange. But I was abducted by a man named Matthew Strong."

"This man, Strong, is it?" Marshall asked.

"Yes." I sipped my tea.

"He kidnapped you, but you got away?"

I became frustrated. The more questions he asked, the more time was wasted.

"Please, I'm begging you. You have to trust me. This entire thing is complicated, I realize that."

"Complicated?" He smiled. "Where's he holding them?"

"I don't know exactly. In an old plantation house that's being restored. I came through the woods down a slope. I have a map in my bag."

"Let me radio the police." Marshall rose to go into the kitchen. "It's early, but at least someone will be on call." The dogs followed him, their tails flailing back and forth, tongues drooping from excited grins.

I asked if I could use the phone, but Mildred explained they never had much luck getting any connection out here. No cell phone towers, no internet. I felt as if I'd stumbled into the nineteenth century.

"Why don't you go on and have a shower?" Mildred said. "I have some clothes my daughter-in-law left. By the time you're all cleaned up, Marshall will be ready to take you down to the police station. It's not more than a twenty-minute drive."

I nodded, aware this was an order rather than a request. What option did I have anyway? Twenty-minute drive was worth the shower. And, when I saw the police, I'd have Marshall and Mildred's good faith.

It would all happen quickly, I thought. Given the current search for the mayor's daughter, I was certain the FBI and police would have been mobilized throughout the state. Helicopters for sure. It wouldn't take long before they descended on the right house.

As Mildred led me to the bathroom, she told me we were south of Birmingham, near Woodward. Not too far. "We'll have you back home soon enough."

She placed a change of clothes and towel on the counter. "Once you freshen up, you'll feel much better."

I hadn't showered in a week, and the warm water felt soothing on my face. Marshall and Mildred probably thought I was out of my mind. Some frantic black woman shows up at their door in the middle of the night? Demanding they call the FBI? But here they lived less than ten miles from a white supremacist base camp and they had no idea.

When I finished showering, I heard the dogs barking again. I dried off quickly and slipped on the clothes and too-small shoes Mildred gave me. I opened the door but paused when I heard laughter and men's voices. My heart lurched.

Shit. Shit. *Shit.* Matthew Strong had come for me. How stupid am I! I should've made Marshall drive me down right away. Panic spread all over me as I closed the bathroom door and went to the window above the toilet. I pushed it open, realizing full well it'd be difficult to squeeze through.

"Ms. Douglass?" I heard a tap on the door. "Everything okay in there?"

I was panting now, thinking I should have never trusted them. Why, after all I had been through, after all I knew about the way Matthew Strong organized everyday white people, would I trust them? So close to where he held us? He probably planned this.

"Yes, I'm, I'm fine...just using the bathroom. I'll be out in a second."

"Okay, I finished cooking up some eggs and grits. You want more tea?"

"Ah...yes, thanks," I said, standing on the toilet, straddling the windowsill, then rotating so I was on my stomach. My legs dangled out the window as I lowered myself down with my torso pressed against the side of the house. If I lost my grip, at least I'd fall on my feet.

Now I was hanging by my arms, my fingers gripping the windowsill. I took a deep breath and let go, landing safely several feet down.

"Ms. Douglass?" I heard behind me. I turned and Mildred stood just inside the back door. She came outside, and looked up to the window, then at me, surprised. "My God, are you okay?"

Marshall appeared. "What's all the fuss?"

I recoiled like a hurt animal, glancing over each shoulder, plotting which way to flee.

Then two police officers came around the side of the house. One held my backpack and the other shined his light toward the woods, then at me, scanning me up and down. I thought about the men dressed as police who kidnapped me.

"Lieutenant?" the officer called, then pulled from my bag the pistol Wallace gave me.

Fuck.

The lieutenant motioned his head toward the gun. "You want to explain this?"

"I was abducted. I need the FBI. They will explain everything!"

"Yes, that's what you've told our friends Marshall and Mildred. Why don't you come with us and we can go down to the station and sort this all out?"

Mildred looked at me sadly, Marshall with disgust.

"I knew she wasn't telling the full story," Marshall said.

The officer unsnapped a black pouch, pulling handcuffs. The lieutenant rested his hand on his gun holster.

"Now, we aren't going to hurt you. It just seems that all of this is quite unusual." He stepped forward and I stepped back. He took cautious steps toward me. Now the deputy pulled his gun from his side, gripping it tightly.

"Why does he have his gun out?"

"Just calm down, Ms. Douglass."

"Calm down?!" I shouted. "Tell him to put his gun away! The criminal they want is up a mountain somewhere and we have to stop him!"

"Put it away, Clyde," the lieutenant said. He kept his eyes fixed on me as he waved his hand for the officer to lower his gun.

The officer did as he was told, but then began to circle me. I knew in a moment they would try to grab me. Only one option. I sprinted for the woods.

"Wait! Ms. Douglass! Don't run!" the lieutenant shouted, chasing behind me.

I made it to the rock wall and reached one leg over, but felt his hands on my shoulders. The other one pulled my waist and brought me to the ground. They held me down, brought my hands behind my back. I felt the cold stiff cuffs. Click.

"I'm going to lift you up now, no point in resisting."

On my feet, they marched me to the squad car parked in the driveway. The officer sat me in the backseat, then removed my cuffs. Marshall and the lieutenant chatted for a few minutes in the driveway before we drove off.

"Now, why would you go and run like that? Huh?" the officer hurried to ask.

"You don't understand," I pleaded. "We must get to the FBI or he's going to kill all the girls!"

"Where did you get that gun? You realize possession of a firearm without a permit is a class-four felony?"

The officer ran his eyes up and down my body, as if gauging whether my posture revealed the truth behind my words. Perhaps if he had seen me even more disheveled, no shoes, smelling like urine and sweat, my story might seem plausible. But showered and dressed in Mildred's daughter's clothes, I realized it seemed far-fetched. Not to mention the gun.

"If I was a criminal, why wouldn't I break into Mildred and Marshall's house and hold them hostage? Why would I leave my bag with a gun in the front room when I took a shower?"

I pleaded, praying the officers would realize it was more insane for me to make all this up.

"Well, I know one thing for sure, when we get back to the station, we'll look into all of this. If it turns out you made this up, we're going to make sure you do

every second of time for having that gun. It's one thing
to do something you shouldn'ta done, and another
to make up a lie in order to convince good folk like
Marshall and Mildred to take you in."

As they drove, I began to doze off in the lull of the
back seat. It had been a long, exhausting night and
my body and mind were completely drained. I jerked
myself awake each time but I couldn't resist and soon, I
was out.

I don't know how long I slept, but I woke up to
sirens. I noticed a white van stalled in the middle of the
road with the front passenger door open. There was a
man bent down searching under the car. The two officers
looked at one another suspiciously. I ducked down in the
back seat, my heart pounding as our car slowed.

"Please," I said. "That may be them! We have to
keep driving."

The deputy glanced at me crouched down, then
shook his head as if I was being absurd.

"When you say 'them,' you mean that you recognize
that man?" the lieutenant asked.

I peeked over the seat, then ducked back down.
"No, but there were similar vans where Matthew
Strong held me and the other girls."

"It's just a flat tire, sir," the officer said. "Maybe they
drove over a branch. I'll go."

"No, I will." The lieutenant opened the door as I
pleaded, "Don't! They'll kill you!"

The lieutenant glanced over his shoulder. "Now, Miss, this ain't my first rodeo. You just relax, let me handle this."

"Want me to come?" the officer asked.

"No, you stay with her."

The lieutenant approached the man wearing a white painter suit who had bent down on one knee, his head tilted so he could see under the van. When the lieutenant came beside him, he stood and seemed to explain something. Then, both men bent down and searched under the van.

A cat leaped from the open passenger door, and the man stood and chased it around to the other side. The lieutenant followed casually behind him.

When the lieutenant went out of view, the officer in the car sat up, leaned out of the window, and shined the police spotlight on the van. Seconds later, the lieutenant walked toward us cautiously with his arms out to his side, and the man in the painter suit followed right behind. As the two came closer, you could see the lieutenant's face was pale, his eyes wide.

"Lieutenant?" the officer called out in a high-pitched voice.

The man pushed a gun against the back of the lieutenant's neck.

The officer thrust open the door and went down on one knee, his gun drawn.

"Drop your weapon!"

"Clyde, put the gun away." The lieutenant's voice was shaky.

The van's back doors popped open and three more men in painter suits emerged wielding AR-15s. They walked casually toward the one with his gun against the lieutenant's head.

"Put the damn gun down, Clyde!" the lieutenant shouted.

I knew it. I felt my hands shaking, my heart thumping. I watched the officer point his gun from one to the other, rehearsing the order in which he'd shoot them. He glanced at the police radio, as if calculating whether to call for backup.

"Now, everyone needs to stay calm," the officer said in a steady, confident voice.

"Oh, we're calm," said the one with the gun to the lieutenant's head. "Lower your gun and maybe we'll let you two go on back to keeping this here part of Jefferson County safe."

The officer and the man squabbled back and forth. Then, I heard: *bap! bap! bap! bap!*

Bullets thumped the car, and with each thump I winced, anticipating the bullets hitting me.

When the shots stopped, I held my breath and opened my eyes. The officer was dead. I heard Matthew Strong's laugh, then spotted him as he emerged from the woods strolling beside a man in a blue camouflage outfit with a military-style helmet.

Strong wore jeans and the white linen shirt he always wore with the sleeves hanging midforearm. As he approached with his half-moon knife, the lieutenant pleaded, "Please, oh God. Don't do this!" In one swoop, Matthew Strong's blade sliced the lieutenant's throat.

I assumed they had come to search for me, yet the setup—the stalled van and the ambush—seemed too big of a coincidence. How would they know the police would be driving back down that road? Then, I remembered Marshall had called the police on a CB radio. Anyone with a CB could hear him. Rather than head off the police, Matthew Strong waited in an ideal location for an ambush. He didn't chase me because his men went to Marshall and Mildred's to finish the job. Tears came as I imagined Matthew Strong slicing their throats like the lieutenant and the couple out on the side lawn that night.

Several men stepped from the shadows hauling a long pole with a cougar tied upside down toward the van. Was it the one I saw when in the woods?

Matthew Strong approached my side of the car, pulling a cigarette from behind his ear. Just like the cougar, I was hunted, captured.

"Nice night for a hunt," he said. He motioned to the

ne of his men opened my door and pulled me from
e back seat.

"That's some specimen," he said, ensnaring his arm in mine and escorting me to the van. "They're real serious predators. I've always been a fan of cats. Hell, even a kitten will attack a grizzly if provoked. You know them Chickasaws would send their teenage boys out to track cougars with just a bow and a knife. Coming of age and whatnot. Them boys learn this young: You either the hunter or the hunted. Predator or prey. That's why it's important we come out to hunt regularly."

I could tell he enjoyed getting the best of me. It wasn't about physical power with him. It was about the power to control my mind; the power to break my will so I'd do as he pleased.

"Look here, Professor. Nearly forty years to this day God unleashed an awful hurricane that devastated downtown Birmingham. In fact, the Birmingham Zoo suffered such a hit that the warden spent the next month recovering all the animals that escaped. Most of them predators had been born in captivity, so they didn't go far. Even a tiger will scavenge before hunting if someone fed him all his life. Turned out, two cougars—a male and pregnant female—escaped into these mountains. Some hunters came upon the male a month later and shot him dead. But they didn't catch the female until bout '73. You know what that means?"

"I'm not sure."

"Them ones she birthed? They were born out here in the wild. By then, most of the cougars had gone extinct. Truth is, letting them live unmolested out here in their natural habitat brought liberals and conservatives together; NRA and radical environmentalists; the lions lying down with the lambs, so to speak."

I read somewhere that the moment before you die the body gasps one final time. From this comes the expression "last gasp"—a shudder, a final attempt to draw oxygen, a last attempt at life.

When Matthew Strong's men snatched me, I had no chance for a last gasp. I had no chance to call for breath. I was just another one of his flock with as little power as the chickens I held as a child in the backyard, the moment before my grandmother wrung their necks.

They sat me down in the van, my hands still cuffed, where I waited for God knows how long. I thought about my fight with Janice. How angry I had become when she accused me of putting my career before my family, and claiming I understood how she felt when Naquasia was found in the woods, unconscious. How close I was to flying back to New York in order to fight the allegations against my book in order to save my career. I felt guilty for the way my ambition blotted out my obligation to my grandmother's legacy and a community on the verge of a racial storm.

When the door finally opened, Matthew Strong climbed inside and the van drove off. I had expected his usual banter, but for once he sat silently. It occurred to me that I had never been in his presence when he seemed this pensive, aloof. This terrified me more than his taunts. I wondered about his next move. Would he finally follow through with his threat? Leave my body on the side of Highway 20? Or would he put me with the others?

We drove for about fifteen more minutes until the van pulled off the road. The doors opened and one of Matthew Strong's men poked his head in.

"Sir, we've arrived."

"Thanks, son. Professor, come with me."

We climbed from the van and walked across a stretch of grass nearly half the size of a football field toward the tree line. A Department of Corrections van was parked nearby.

"Did you know it's been a hundred fifty years since the Emancipation Proclamation?" he said as we approached a path into the woods.

"And fifty years since this Alabama was invaded by a bunch of hippie freaks, black nationalists, and gutless politicians willing to cower to the liberal establishment and destroy our way of life?"

I didn't respond, just followed the progression of men onto a path and into the forest. I heard chopping and digging as we approached a clearing, where four of Matthew Strong's men gripped machine guns. Standing to their left were two men who wore Department of Corrections shirts. And there was a deputy I recognized from the sheriff's department holding a cat-o'-nine-tails whip. The men stepped aside, and now I saw five naked black men with bags over their heads, arms handcuffed behind their backs. Blood and pus bulged from torn flesh where each had been whipped. A noose dangled above each of them.

Matthew Strong motioned for his men to remove their hoods. Tears and sweat glistened on their faces. One held his eyes shut, tightly.

As they begged for mercy, Strong pulled a Bible from his pocket, then put on his glasses.

"This here is from Proverbs 28, verse 9: *If anyone turns a deaf ear to the law, even his prayers are detestable.*" He tucked his glasses in his shirt pocket. "Each of you has defiled yourself and disgraced your maker. The time for waiting has come to an end. It's time for you to confess your sins to God, and pray for his mercy from eternal torment."

Matthew Strong instructed the guards to put the bags back over their heads, then a noose around their necks. I squeezed my eyes shut. I couldn't watch.

Once all the prisoners had been fitted, Matthew Strong gave the word and I heard a branch creak as his guards hanged each man from the huge oak tree.

I gasped in horror at this cruel spectacle. I flinched when I felt Matthew Strong's hand on my shoulder.

"Fact is, Professor, we all have our day of judgment. You can accept it, or fight it. You can even try and run from it. But it's as inevitable as the sun and moon. Come now, you still have work to do. Seems we're almost out of time. Wouldn't want you to have to watch them girls go through the same thing."

Months later, someone forwarded a link on YouTube of the news coverage from the day after the inmates were brought here for Matthew Strong's men to lynch. Originally, the authorities called their deaths suicides. Yet this many suicides on the same day made such a theory absurd. Lawyers from the NAACP and Equal Justice Initiative called for a federal investigation and prompted the governor's response.

The governor claimed prison officials were cooperating with the Department of Justice already, and he would post the complete investigation online. A journalist asked the governor to comment on rumors that this was another in a series of racial incidents that had sprung up around the state. Specifically, the kidnapping of young black women. But the governor deflected the question, pointing out that "the investigation was still ongoing." When asked why there was no video footage of the alleged suicides, he claimed technological issues with lights and surveillance equipment made it impossible to know exactly what happened. But the warden claimed guards found them hanging in their cells. Another reporter asked if there was any truth to a rumor that prisoners organized a hunger strike in response to the deaths, and the governor denied any knowledge about that.

Back in the van, Matthew Strong glanced over at me, smiling. "You disapprove of this, Professor? Those men were condemned to death. Should've done that long ago. Why waste tax dollars feeding them devils? Anyway, what we did was kinder than what they did to the girls they raped and people they murdered."

I wanted to argue with him. He was the one causing disorder based on a misrepresentation of Christian theology. Their crimes paled in comparison to what he planned. Despite having no desire to give him any pleasure debating me, I couldn't help myself from telling him I missed his point.

"That surprises me. Okay, think of it like this. Disorder breeds fear. Fear causes chaos. Chaos, Professor, paves the way for a new order. It don't matter your race, religion, or creed. Reestablishing the natural order of things unites folk who don't see eye to eye. Whether that means letting them cougars live according to how God commanded it, or executing men who defied the Lord's most basic tenets."

"Are you saying killing those men is according to God's plan?" I asked.

"That's exactly what I'm saying. There ain't a God-fearing man on this planet who don't agree that them men deserved to be killed for the deeds they done. Man-made institutions are just a façade. They can't protect people from predators. Only one thing that can."

"The Sons of Light?"

"Precisely, Professor. Precisely."

"Are you saying you've done all of this to protect people? Sounds like the justification Shields used."

"Shields brought more stability to the South than all them politicians and the occupying forces ever could. If it wasn't for them backstabbers willing to compromise with the enemy, we would have avoided the calamity the Supreme Court unleashed a hundred years later."

"Are you talking about the Brown decision? Desegregation? So, this is about returning to the days of Jim Crow? Recruit prison guards to lynch black men and enforce your form of justice?"

"Guards? They're easy. This goes well beyond them. Besides, inmates run the prisons. But you're right, we recruited within them. Searched for those with the discipline and dedication to a higher calling. Military experience was a plus. Formed alliances with other groups. Most came on board. Klan, White Knights. Other offshoots. But the Aryan Nation. They weren't so cooperative. We had to weed the garden, so to speak."

"Weed the garden?" I shook my head, outraged at how he trivialized murder. My face expressed my disgust, and he appeared annoyed. Matthew Strong reached into a bag and pulled out a syringe.

"Seems like all this has got you upset. Maybe a little medicine to calm you down. What do you think?"

"No, please, wait! Not this again!" I squirmed in my seat.

My eyes jumped from his eyes to the syringe. He inserted the needle in the bottle, then pulled back the plunger so the drugs filled the syringe.

Matthew Strong grabbed my arm and I pulled away.

"Please...you don't need to do this. I'll tell you anything! I'll tell you what the FBI knows and what they don't."

"Be still or we're going to have to do this the hard way." He reached for me again, but I tossed and turned.

"So be it." He lunged on top of me, pinning me down with his elbow on my neck. I choked, then felt the needle jab into my thigh. Moments later, my vision blurred.

When I finally came to again, I heard coughing and the rattling of chains around the room. Sensation was returning to my body, first to my lips, then my feet and hands. I felt heavy steel around my ankles as things slowly came into focus. I blinked, trying to shake the blurriness. I noticed the pale soles of brown feet poking out from the shadows into the center of the cavern. As they noticed me waking, Cynthia came over with a metal cup of water. I was too tired and scared to show my joy at seeing her alive, but I felt it. She massaged my neck, guiding the cup to my mouth. Although my wrists were chained, I could still lift my hands. Standing in leg irons was more challenging. When I tried, I stumbled. The others helped me stand, and someone said it was the drugs. They would wear off soon.

I tried to recognize the girls from the posters we'd printed, but the light was too dim. Anyway, they had become emaciated and their faces barely resembled the girls in those posters. When I got my voice back I asked them to say their names. One by one, they identified themselves.

Eleven total. Eleven female descendants of the one hundred enslaved black people the Shields family once owned. But that meant one was still unaccounted for.

Odessa.

"Where's Odessa?" I asked, my eyes racing from one face to another.

"They took her," Cynthia said. "This morning."

"Why? Where?"

"They've moved us a few times. Maybe they brought her to the attic? That was the last place his men had me."

Despite being worried about Odessa, I was relieved they were all alive. I also figured he'd keep Odessa alive to blackmail Turner. I wanted to comfort them, tell them we'd be okay. But I knew my words would ring hollow, given I had been captured, too. So instead I told them about their mothers' efforts to find them, hoping this would raise their spirits. I assured them that my sister and their mothers would continue looking, that they were close: just narrowing down which house we're in. But we couldn't be sure someone would find us before Matthew Strong held his sacrificial ritual. We had to figure out some way out of that cavern.

Cynthia suggested we rebel when the women came to feed us. It appeared she'd been formulating this escape plan for a while. As I listened, I remembered how intoxicating her charisma and creative energy had always been. Cynthia went over to the large iron door.

"I don't know where it goes, but it's our way out."

DAY FIVE

Our plan was to outsmart and overpower the man who came to escort the women who fed us. Then pray he had keys that would unlock the thick padlock on the iron door into the mine shaft. I wasn't exactly sure where the mine shaft led, but this plan offered a glimmer of hope.

The time came, and the guard shouted for us to sit in the center of the room as the two women pushed a cart and distributed bowls of rice and bottled water. Just as we planned, Cynthia made herself vomit, drawing attention from the guard, who motioned for one of the women to help her. When the guard's attention was on her, Dominique and Brenda sprang for his gun. He knocked them down, tried to reach his gun, but Olivia jumped on his back, pulling him

backward and knocking him out. I cranked the lever
to shut the bookcase and prevent the other guards from
hearing his call for help before his head hit the stone
floor.

One of the women who brought us food implored
us. *No, please. Don't do this. Our children.* She pulled a
photo from beneath her robe of two young boys. *You
don't understand. He'll kill them.*

I learned later that Matthew Strong used his
connections within correctional facilities around
Birmingham to release these women on "probation" to
earn money and for reduced sentences working for the
Sons of Light Ministries. But when they were released,
Strong held them hostage, threatening to kill their
children if they resisted. She wasn't lying.

As the man lay unconscious, I took the large ring
of keys looped onto his belt and rushed over to the
padlock on the iron door. One by one I tried them, with
no luck. Then I found a long silver key with two teeth.
It clicked, and the lock came off easily.

When I held up the lock, the girls' faces beamed
with excitement. I pulled the heavy door partially open,
and a small creature crawled into our room. Florence
cried out, voice high-pitched, as she hopped from foot
to foot. "Mice!"

I felt a mouse run over the top of my foot and I hop-
danced too. Though this was our only option, the girls
backed up.

"We have no choice!" I whisper-shouted, motioning for them to follow me into the tunnel. But I paused when I heard a screech and hiss. A mangy cat emerged that looked like one of the strays in the woods. First one, then two, then a half dozen bound through the opening, hissing, clawing, chasing around after the mice.

I backed away, shocked, and disoriented by the melee. When I regained my composure and I rushed toward the door, I noticed a cougar with a brass collar and chain trailing behind creeping into the room.

I shouted, "Get back! It's a cougar!"

Just then, the cougar lunged for a cat, caught one between its jaws.

Now all the girls were huddled near the entrance, and the bookcase revolved. Two men rushed in, gripping a high-powered hose. They flooded the room, forcing the cats and cougar back through the passage, then turned the hose on us, knocking Cynthia and Brenda off their feet. We crouched down and covered our faces as the water blast stung our skin. Drenched and disoriented, we were dragged into the middle of the room and our wrists cuffed behind our backs. Or rather, everyone but me.

After our attempted rebellion, his men blindfolded me and brought me to a room upstairs, where I waited for hours, reflecting on the fifteen years I spent studying men like Matthew Strong. I understood where he generated his ideas, and how he twisted these ideas in order to erect systems of thought that justified oppression and violence.

I know it really didn't matter if he justified his actions by imagining himself as a martyr to the cause of freedom for white people whom he claimed had been overrun by minorities. It didn't matter if he was a sociopath, a master manipulator with an authority-driven system that allowed him to kill without any remorse. It didn't even matter if I had stopped him.

His ideas were the real enemy.

There have always been men like Matthew Strong and people searching for someone like him to explain the root cause of their misery.

Moreover, I still wonder about the women who might have known his plan and said nothing. Was their silence a greater threat than the ideas used to persuade their husbands, brothers, or sons to embrace Matthew Strong's mission?

This is how it ends.

When Matthew Strong's men returned, they wore orange robes with white stars running down each sleeve. They escorted me into the cavern where he'd previously held me and the girls, lifted my arms above my head, and clicked my wrists into manacles chained to the wall. Candles flickered from the top of pikes, which encircled the same oak table where I'd spent so many hours translating the *Confessional*. Blue, red, and white candles were arranged in the center of the table in the shape of a Confederate flag. There were eleven chairs—five on each side and one at the head. In front of each chair was an empty silver ice bowl.

Minutes later, they marched in the girls, blindfolded and gagged, and divided them so half sat on one side and the other sat on the other side. Then, the men cuffed their wrists and ankles to their chairs. I could barely tolerate their muffled moans and desperate sobs. I had no idea why I wasn't blindfolded or seated with the other girls. Did he actually plan on keeping me alive to tell his story? Or maybe he wanted to force me to witness this scene for his own sick amusement.

A video camera rested on a tripod, capturing what was happening in our room. Above the video camera was a TV with a split screen. I peered at the eight squares on the television, displaying eight other rooms decorated like our room. Same type of table, silver bowls, candles positioned in the shape of the Confederate battle flag's stars and bars. This identical ritual was happening in other plantation homes all throughout the South.

Matthew Strong entered wearing an orange gown cinched with a white rope around his waist like a priest. Draped in front of his gown was a blue stole with white Confederate stars embroidered down the center.

He tapped his index finger on a microphone perched on a lectern.

"Please, brothers. We must begin."

The men positioned themselves behind the girls seated in front of silver bowls. On split screens, I saw men enter these other rooms with the same priestly garb. Other black women who I had no idea had also been kidnapped entered these other rooms, blindfolded and gagged. One man stood behind each of them, holding up their chins, exposing their necks. Each man held a half-moon blade in his right hand. Matthew Strong flipped open a book on the lectern, looked around the room, then fixed his gaze into the camera.

"Brothers, I welcome all of you to our passage from this world order to the next—a passage from darkness, to light. Indeed, brothers, we are here to fulfill our role as a dedicated few who've pledged our lives for the redemption of our people, this nation, and the civilized Christian world.

"The American Negro, through thousands of years of inbreeding in Africa, often in very small circles, has preserved his racial characteristics much more than the European. As a consequence, they are an alien race that is unwilling and, indeed, unable to shed their deficient racial characteristics. Despite the benefits of living in the greatest nation known to man, and even, in some instances, being able to have political rights as we ourselves do, this barbarous character remains.

"All of this has resulted in the Negro becoming a cancer on the nation. Our fathers demonstrated the benevolence of their Christian faith by allowing the Negro to remain inside this civilization rather than be deported to reintegrate into the godless, savage society from whence they previously resided. Our final objective is *not* the total annihilation of the Negro. But, when the time comes and we must carry out their extermination, we are prepared to act on behalf of our civilization.

"Yet, brothers, we cannot blame the Negro alone for the crisis we face today, even if he is the root cause of this nation's demise. Look at the dominance of illegals, homosexuals, baby-killers. Look at our politicians' indifference to the suffering of men who fought for this country. Look at banks preying on poor people. The Sons of Light will lead our nation toward a rebirth. Our national rebirth. This will only happen through leaders who refuse to be influenced by liberal dogmas or by catchphrases and slogans. Our revolution must be led by those with an unwavering sense of loyalty that supersedes personal interest. Our redemption will only happen when we return power to everyday people who

do not need dictates from Washington, D.C., about
how we structure our society to maintain social order.

"Now we must sacrifice the lamb. Words have been
spoken, prayers made. The time has come for us to
initiate our movement—a movement greater than any in
human history. Gentlemen, please raise your blade and
repeat after me..."

I'm numb, my mind so full of desperate energy, I'm
seeing the world in high-def—faces of David, Janice,
my mother, my grandmother.

Then: a loud *bang! bang! bang!* snaps me from my
haze. Everyone looks around. The men step back
from the chairs, faces alarmed. The banging grows
louder, closer to our cavern. Men put their daggers
on the table and pull guns from their waistbands and
shoulder holsters. We see chaos in the other rooms on
the TV screen, then more banging from somewhere in
this house. Matthew Strong motions for his men to see
what's happening. There are gunshots, then the sound
of automatic weapons, the pelting of bullets.

Matthew Strong closes the bookcase, then rushes
to the iron door, pushes in his key to open it, glances
back at me, smiling, then snatches the bag with the
Confessional translation, the map, and all the other
damning evidence of his nightmare cause, and pulls the
door shut behind him.

The gunshots outside the cavern grow louder,
louder.

"Help us! Help!" I shout.

The blasts stop.

There's the sound of a saw and chopping. An axe head bursts through the bookcase and FBI agents rush into the cavern, wielding steel cutters.

BOOK VI

REVELATIONS

And God shall wipe away all tears from their eyes;
and there shall be no more death,
neither sorrow, nor crying,
neither shall there be any more pain:
for the former things are passed away.

—REVELATIONS 21:4

THE AUTHOR OF A CRIME IS WHAT HE IS—HE KNOWS IT,
CAN MAKE NO MORE DEMANDS, NOR IS ANYTHING MORE
DEMANDED OF HIM. BUT HE WHO COLLABORATES IS
DOOMED, BOUND FOREVER IN THAT UNIMAGINABLE AND YET
VERY COMMON CONDITION WHICH WE WEAKLY SUGGEST AS
HELL.

—James Baldwin, from *The Evidence of Things Not Seen*

DAY OF MY REDEMPTION

Although the FBI technically rescued us, they weren't the ones who discovered the plantation manor where we were held.

Shortly after they freed me, Janice told me that she and the mothers' group had gone to Birmingham University to help Lucas and Darryl examine Shields's *Confessional* and his family's papers for clues. A break came when they found a letter written to William Shields's mother, Lily Jefferson Shields, from Joseph Monroe, president of Elysian Land Company. In the letter, Monroe mentioned that he promised to give William Shields an abandoned plantation home in Woodward right before the federal authorities arrested him. Given the strange connection between the missing girls and the Shields family, Lucas thought there was

a chance Matthew Strong held us in this plantation
rather than the other Shields plantation we had already
gone over to but didn't look inside.

Janice tweeted the discovery, and joined other
mothers and fathers, sisters and brothers, church
congregations and sorority sisters who drove twenty
miles along Route 280 searching for the correct
plantation home. Agent Washington wasn't convinced
by this theory. Again, she asked Janice for any
corroborating evidence. This came when Sheriff
Morgan learned that two police officers never returned
to the station after they had been called out to Mildred
and Marshall's house in Woodward, only a few miles
from where we were held. Within the hour, the FBI and
the sheriff descended on this plantation where Matthew
Strong had us.

Word spread not only across Alabama but through
the entire Bible Belt. More connected disappearances
across the states came to light. Finally, as similar
cases arose from Mississippi to South Carolina, they
listened. News spread and in just a matter of days,
masses of heartfelt communities came out to help with
the search. If it weren't for the hundreds of Muslim
women, Jewish women, black and white women, and
sorority sisters throughout the state, stepping over logs,
climbing through branches, avoiding pricker bushes
and black flies, who searched woods outside Mobile,
Anniston, Montgomery, Union Springs, Pleasant Hill,

Letohatchee, Tuscumbia, and Demopolis, the FBI
would never have found the others. I could almost
hear the cacophony of cricket calls, toad bellows, and
owl hoots that provided a soundtrack for their descent
through the darkness bearing the weight of the past
and the burden of the present.

Some of these women beat the authorities there,
at other estates across the South, then busted down
doors and found rooms described as having makeshift
altars on long tables decorated with candles. Rescuers
uploaded video footage of them breaking open latched
trapdoors and pulling to freedom terrified women
who'd been held like slaves in the bowels of these
unholy homes with blood-stained floorboards where
virtual kings had once dined, danced, and laughed
a hundred years before. Some were discovered still
chained to chairs. But alive. They—we—were all found
alive. Or, almost all of us.

The tweets of these rescues were like snowflakes
falling on a spring afternoon: a beautiful surprise,
catching a single, shared hashtag:

#alive

#alive

#alive

The Sons of Light members across the South all
fled into hiding after they watched the gun battle at
our location through the livestream video. But over the
next few months, the FBI burst into bars, businesses,

and people's homes, arresting men from all walks of life who had affiliated with the Sons of Light.

For six weeks, Matthew Strong eluded authorities in the mine shafts of Jefferson County. When they finally found him in a cave less than a mile from the plantation house where he'd held us, Matthew Strong was sitting on a stone just inside, smoking. He made no attempt to flee, or resist. He merely asked if he could finish his cigarette.

The FBI never found Odessa Turner. They searched the caves with dogs, then moved on to use autonomous drones, helicopters, a media blitz, but all to no avail. Although people throughout the state and nation rallied around the bereaved mayor and his wife, there was much more besides Odessa's whereabouts that remained unresolved.

6 MONTHS AFTER MY REDEMPTION

Everything I've told you is my best recollection of what transpired. Of course, whether or not it's the truth, the whole truth, and nothing but the truth so help me God is another thing. But I did my best, given the circumstances of trauma.

Matthew Strong was indicted on fifteen counts of kidnapping, as well as the murders of numerous women who'd disappeared all over the South, throughout the years leading up to his great revolution in towns where the Sons of Light had parishes. The national media labeled him a terrorist, but his defenders called him a modern-day Samuel Adams.

As the investigation progressed, the authorities could not find one person who would testify to Matthew Strong's participation in the kidnappings besides me. None of the young women held with me could identify him in a photo or pick him out of a lineup. They never actually met Matthew Strong. It turned out that he had his men do most of his dirty work. To make matters worse, a bomb detonated shortly after we were rescued, and the house where he'd held us burned to the ground. Thus, no fibers, no useful DNA samples, no ballistics—there was no forensic evidence to prove Matthew Strong's involvement. Before the FBI stormed in, the video and camera that'd been set up had been destroyed. If there were any recordings from the other Sons of Light outposts, they were never found.

The two men who survived the gun battle refused to talk at first. And, most importantly, no one was charged with murder, given that all the women had been saved, except for Odessa, who remained missing. At least that we knew of for sure. The older couple I witnessed Matthew Strong's men kill in the woods had yet to be found. I was the only witness to what happened those nights who would talk, but they needed more than my account to identify and charge everyone involved.

So, what did they have?

The letters he sent to me.

The Sons of Light's financial records.

Podcasts.

Notebooks seized with administrative files.

But no membership logs. No list of donors.

In fact, all of the Sons of Light Ministries records were neat and in order. This did nothing more than confirm that Matthew Strong was the leader of the Sons of Light, an organization that preached white racial superiority, vowed to save America from blacks and immigrants, and lobbied for conservative causes.

The largest blow to the state's case against Matthew Strong came when the two of Matthew Strong's men who survived finally confessed to the kidnappings. Each gave a detailed account about when and how they kidnapped each of the women. They produced cell phone footage confirming their statements, and these statements were corroborated by the girls' testimonies.

I refused to testify on the stand at his trial. I assume this will make some of you angry at me. You may even call me a coward.

But let me explain.

Matthew Strong's defense attorney petitioned the judge to block my testimony. But I decided I wouldn't testify, for a variety of reasons.

Let's start with the death threats. Upon his arrest, I became a target for those whom Matthew Strong inspired. A torrent of nasty emails was sent to my colleagues and university administrators. Anyone who collaborated with me on any project, or invited me on a panel or to give a lecture, received harassing emails and phone calls.

What made matters even less encouraging was the prosecutor's rationale for putting me on the stand. While I had tremendous respect for her, she believed that if I went before the public, crying as I recounted my experience being held in the home, this would persuade the jury of Matthew Strong's guilt. Who, after all, could question the authenticity of a black woman like me, who had endured such a horrific experience, speaking truth to power, condemning Matthew Strong's racist beliefs?

Not to mention, I wasn't interested in entertaining millions through my own recounting of Matthew Strong's wicked deeds.

David agreed. Despite the state attorney's begging, David said a conviction solely based on my testimony would only add to Matthew Strong's appeal. He thought it best I leave the prosecutors to make the case with what they had. I'd do what I could from the sidelines.

Meanwhile, Thomas Turner called on the nation to pray for his family as they continued to search for Odessa. All the national and international publicity raised his profile, and in these heartfelt speeches, the nation came to admire this man who sought to be the first black governor of Alabama. There were many who believed he would be a formidable contender for president one day.

Matthew Strong's trial dragged on until the week before the governor's election, and his attorney struck a deal with the prosecutors to reduce his charge to endangering the welfare of a child rather than multiple counts of kidnapping. This carried a maximum sentence of five years. In addition, he would serve this time in a minimum-security facility.

Perhaps there would have been greater outrage had there not been a revelation the morning after the election.

DAY OF THE ELECTION

Thomas Turner invited us back down to Alabama for the election party. On the way to his house David stopped at a gas station, and as I waited in the car, a thin black man with a bushy beard appeared by my window. I rolled it down.

"Miss? I think you may have left your bag?"

He held up a black laptop bag.

I shook my head. "No, you must have the wrong person."

David came to the man's side. "Can I help you?"

"That lady over there?" The man motioned to a woman climbing in a car with HOME HEALTH AIDE written across the hood. "Said she found your wife's bag. In the bathroom?"

David looked cautiously in the bag, then pulled an envelope with a letter addressed to me and a return address, "Federal Correctional Facility, Montgomery, AL." David took the bag from the man and climbed in the car. He rested his hand on my thigh.

"Hey, you don't have to open that."

"You're right. I'll send it to Agent Tyler after the party. I know this isn't over yet."

This wasn't the first letter Matthew Strong wrote me from prison. When I received the first one, I thought it might reveal Odessa's location. No luck. I opened his next letter, hoping perhaps he would tell me something about my mother's disappearance. But, again, his letter offered more ramblings about the past without a word about Odessa, my mom, or anything else I cared about.

A few hours into the party, I felt an overwhelming urge to read the letter. I stepped away from the crowd and dug in my bag, thinking I'd feel terrible if it offered a glint of information about Odessa's whereabouts. I glanced over at Mrs. Turner, who looked proud even if her joy had been blunted by tragedy. After six months, I couldn't imagine her inner turmoil over Odessa. I unfolded the letter and cast my eyes over Matthew Strong's distinct penmanship.

Dear Professor Douglass:

The time has come for me to tell you what you asked me. No games this time. The truth and only the truth. So help me God.

Tell me, Professor, can you think of a better way to gain the support of your enemies? Those Democrats willing to do anything to keep Turner from the governor's mansion? The entire state—even the nation—mourning with a black Republican nominee for governor who is the victim of a racist?

You still wonder why Wallace helped you escape? Given his ambition? Would you do anything to fulfill your ambitions, Professor? Even sell your kin like them Africans used to do? For the greater good. Can anything be bought and sold for the greater good? Come to think about it, Odessa just might have been saved from living with a father willing to go to any length for his own personal ambition.

You want the truth? Odessa's safer now than she has ever been. As long as I live, she will live. As long as I'm freed, she will be freed.

But confine me to a cell. Sit me in that chair. And all those who condemn me must accept their actions might be responsible for the death of a nine-year-old black girl who will have never had the chance to plant a seed in the garden out back of the governor's mansion.

Let the future governor lie in bed like King Dionysius. Let him remember I'm not only the sword, Professor. I'm the shield.

Remember what Micah said:

"Shall I give my firstborn for my transgressions, the fruit of my body for the sin of my soul?"

You may have arrested my men and closed the Sons of Light Ministries. But what was that your Negro extremist friend Winfred Cookman said? You can kill the revolutionary but you can't kill the revolution.

For the cause,
Matthew Strong

Matthew Strong's accusations were absurd. Despite Thomas Turner's ambition, I couldn't believe he colluded with Matthew Strong to have his own daughter, Odessa, kidnapped to win the governor's race—perhaps set him up for a presidential run. Yet, they were just the sort that might feed conspiracy theorists and populate online forums established by those drawn to Matthew Strong. Thomas Turner made a Faustian bargain with Wallace to become governor, and Wallace never imagined Matthew Strong had been using him the entire time. Matthew Strong figured they would never execute him as long as they believed he knew where Odessa was held. And this letter to me was an additional safeguard.

News came in that Turner had enough votes to win. There'd be no runoff. I tucked the letter back in the envelope and looked over as Tommy Turner kissed his wife and hugged his mother. I couldn't bring myself to share with anyone what Matthew Strong shared in the letter.

I pulled David's sleeve and told him I needed to leave immediately.

In bed that night, I worried if I told the world what I knew about Turner people wouldn't believe me. I needed time to think about the best way to respond. I decided to wait until we returned to New York before asking David for his advice.

In the morning, I went to Brewer Cemetery to pay my respects to my grandmother and grandfather before I left for New York. Naquasia came, too. She and her mother visited weekly to trim around the tombstone and leave candles on iron pikes around the graves.

As Naquasia relit the candles perched on my grandmother's gravestone, I glanced up at the Shields section of the cemetery, reflecting on my time with Matthew Strong in the plantation house. I heard car tires crunch the dirt road on the other side of the fence, closer to the tomb of Andrew Shields. A white woman in her mid-twenties took a picnic basket and blanket up the hill toward the tomb. It seemed odd. Who has a picnic in a graveyard? Naquasia tapped my arm when she noticed the woman dropped her sweater. When we went to retrieve it for her, the woman disappeared from view. I picked up the sweater and walked up the hill to return it to her. But she was gone. We walked all the way around the tomb, but still couldn't find her.

I heard a *click-clack* sound from behind the tomb door, which began to move. Startled, Naquasia grabbed my arm, and we ducked behind the side wall, waiting to see who or what would emerge from within the tomb. I peeked around the wall and noticed the woman who dropped her sweater emerge from inside the tomb. I couldn't believe my eyes. Why on earth was she in there? What was she doing? She pulled an iron latch bolted to the front of the door, and it began to close slowly like automated doors designed for people in wheelchairs. Gone were the bags and blanket she carried up the hill. I took a deep breath, relieved by her sight, and stepped from behind the wall.

"Excuse me?"

I walked toward the woman, whose eyes shifted from me to Naquasia. Startled.

"I think you dropped this?" I held out the sweater. She paused for a moment, glancing down at the sweater, then at us. After a moment, she hurried back down to the car and drove off.

I took Naquasia's hand and stepped to the front of the tomb with *Shields* engraved above the thick stone door. Etched below the name was an image of two hands cradling the sun with the phrase *I am the sword and shield* beneath. I realized the door had no moss, no vines. It looked as if it had been recently installed.

Then it hit me: *Odessa!*

I tossed my phone to Naquasia.

"Call your mom!"

I felt adrenaline pumping as I pulled the iron door handle frantically. I heard Naquasia tell Janice we found Odessa. I moved my fingertips along the crease, searching for some lever or button the woman might have pushed to open the door. My mind had been so focused on trying to find a latch or lever, I had no idea how much time passed before I heard the sirens, the fire truck's horn, and the highway patrol's car door slam.

A WEEK LATER

On our flight back to New York, we barely spoke. But the careful way he caressed my shoulders, ran his finger over my hand, and kissed me anytime he left my side said more than words. Nothing mattered more in this moment than his touch. Than being close. And safe.

When we got to the house, David fished through the pile of mail and showed me a letter from Thomas Turner. I turned away and went into the dining room for wine. David followed.

"Are you going to read it?"

I shook my head. "I'm too exhausted right now."

I had no desire to have anything to do with Matthew Strong. For now, I just wanted to vanish like my mother.

I pulled a bottle from the wine rack, rustled through the drawer for an opener, then dug into the cork.

"Do you want me to?" David asked.

I sighed. "Yes, fine."

David ran his nail over the top of the envelope, then read the letter aloud.

1108 Center Street
Birmingham, Alabama 35204

Dr. Allegra Douglass
498 Elm Street
North Tarrytown, NY 10595

Dear Allie,

I cannot express my appreciation enough for saving Odessa and preventing Matthew Strong from carrying out his mission. Although I had no idea Matthew Strong had woven his way into my political circle, my ignorance is no excuse. I allowed him to prey on my ambition and manipulate me through my friend. I have only myself to blame. I am truly sorry.

Now I have the inauspicious task of bringing together a divided state. I'm well aware my election to governor is only one step in our journey toward reconciliation, which in my view has really never ceased since the fratricidal Civil War. The misguided ideas Matthew Strong used to manipulate others remind us of the urgent need to educate our children about the ways hatred festers like a sore, and racism is a cancer in need of a cure.

To ensure this process of finding a cure moves forward immediately, I have established a commission of dedicated professionals tasked with providing recommendations for how best to root out the hate that continues to pulse through the veins of those who commit horrendous acts, as well as the philosophical systems that inform these acts.

As you know, a commission is only as valuable as its members. And those who come together to complete such a task must have a strong leader—one dedicated to truth and to the greater good. Truth must always take precedent over comfort. Furthermore, this leader must have an established reputation and understand the complexities of these ideas. Allie, on behalf of the people of Alabama, will you serve in this role?

I have been told that you have refused to speak to the media about all you have endured. And, thus, I realize this is a tremendous request. You have sacrificed enough already. Yet, your intimate knowledge of Matthew Strong's ideas will provide the commission with an immeasurable perspective. Allie, there is no one on earth better suited to tell this story.

Please consider my request not as your governor, but as your humble servant and friend.

Sincerely,
Thomas Turner
Governor-elect of Alabama

David tucked the letter back in the envelope and set it on the counter. I sipped my wine, then shook my head, gently. The last thing I intended to do was spend the next six months leading a commission of inquiry into Matthew Strong's mission. People often say *the truth will set you free* without ever acknowledging the cost of real truth. Some truths scratch the scabs covering our comfortable lies, and expose our moral failings. When the time came, I would tell my story.

EPILOGUE

We southerners have identified with the long sorrowful past on such deep levels of love and hate and guilt that we did not know how to break old bonds without pulling our lives down.

—Lillian Smith, *Killers of the Dream*

PRESENT DAY

So, there you have it.

Odessa was saved, Thomas Turner was elected the first black governor of Alabama, and Matthew Strong was locked away.

Since my ordeal, most people consider me a hero for finding Odessa and standing up to Matthew Strong. Yet, whenever someone says this, I remind them that my grandmother and the mothers' group—not to mention all the people across the South who came together—deserve the adulation. They were the ones who never gave up faith they would find us.

Even now, a year later, as I recount this story to you, I feel frustrated about how infrequently the media acknowledges the way the community came together in defiance of Matthew Strong's movement. Instead, they write about Matthew Strong as if he is some crazed monster who used his evil powers to manipulate those who joined his movement. I don't deny Matthew Strong was delusional. Paranoid, for sure. Schizophrenic, perhaps, and certainly a fanatic. But was his insanity the root cause of his campaign of terror? When I'm asked this, I usually reframe the question. Whether he is insane or not is less important than why so many young white men carried out his devilish acts. Could all of them *also* be insane?

Besides, Matthew Strong's movement was only possible because so many people looked the other way rather than stop his poisonous ideas from embedding in the souls of those seeking someone to save them from their unfulfilled lives. He is another man in a long line of men from every race, ethnicity, religion, and class who prey on the vulnerable by promising something better than what they have. For this reason, I don't believe our society benefits from focusing on individuals who orchestrate these campaigns. We should concern ourselves instead with those who stay silent to save themselves rather than speak the truth regardless of the personal cost.

When Barack Obama won the 2008 presidential election, I recall watching on TV Barack and Michelle Obama hold their daughters' hands, waving to a crowd of more than two hundred thousand people gathered in Grant Park in Chicago, and feeling a sense of dread that some racist would run up to the stage and assassinate the first black First Family. I know this is a dark thought, but often when I tell someone this, they admit to having felt a similar fear.

Although we were spared such a horrifying spectacle, the morning after the election a white man crept over to a newly constructed black church in Springfield, Massachusetts, about twenty miles from where I live, and poured gasoline all over the church and burned it down. The hatred that motivated this white man to burn down a church was the same hatred I feared would compel some racist to shoot President Obama. As Dylann Roof's assassination of black State Senator Clementa Pinckney in Charleston, South Carolina, in 2015 illustrates, black success represents to white supremacists an existential threat to their "way of life," to what defines them and provides them a sense of respect and power in U.S. society. However, the events in this novel testify to black people's willingness to do all in their power to stop those who would shoot the first black president, burn a black church, or kidnap black children to gratify their base desires.

Although the main drama of the novel takes place in the South—specifically, Alabama, where my paternal grandmother was born—I agree with Malcolm X's conclusion that as long as you are south of Canada, you are in the South. The geography of hate in the United States is certainly not an exclusively Southern phenomenon. For proof, one need only consider the success of Ku Klux Klan organizing in New York, Connecticut, and Michigan since the 1970s, or listen to the voices of New York state troopers shouting "White Power" after raiding Attica Correctional Facility and massacring unarmed inmates. More recently, consider the neo-Nazi from Ohio who weaponized his car to murder Heather Heyer and injure over three dozen others during the Unite the Right rally in Charlottesville, Virginia, in 2017. And, like some

sick racist ritual, another white supremacist—this
one from Maine—reacted to Donald Trump's 2020
election defeat by attempting to burn down the Martin
Luther King Jr. Community Presbyterian Church,
a black church in Springfield, Massachusetts, that
sits adjacent to the community center where I teach
US history to adults enrolled in the Clemente Course
for the Humanities. Certainly, there are men like
Matthew Strong in every state in the US. White
supremacists respect neither borders nor boundaries,
sacred or secular. Therefore, those who seek to preserve
democracy and stop fascism and racism must be
vigilant in every hamlet, town, suburb, or city.

Unfortunately, such vigilance has to be part of a
global movement against anti-black, anti-immigrant, and
anti-Semitic violence. The spirit of fascism and racism
has reawakened abroad. After all, the January 6, 2021,
insurrection in Washington D.C. was preceded by the
attempt by Germany's far-right to storm the Reichstag
in Berlin in August 2020. Even more horrifying,
something akin to Matthew Strong's fictional conspiracy
was attempted by a former German military official
known as "Franco A" and other members of the neo-
Nazi National Socialist Underground in Germany. They
targeted and murdered Syrian immigrants, robbed bank
trucks, and in 2019 assassinated the German politician
Walter Lübcke. As these efforts to foment racist,
xenophobic, and anti-Semitic violence continue, openly

fascist politicians win votes despite, or even because of, their hateful rhetoric.

Of course, the current resurgence of white supremacy fits within a long tradition, which I first researched as a graduate student in John Higginson's course on collective violence in South Africa and the American South. This novel is based on my twenty years of research on the racial violence in South Carolina and Alabama from Reconstruction to the present, including black resistance. Through this research, I uncovered many stories from the 1870s, such as that of Samuel M. Moore, the son of prominent slaveholder in Alabama, who led a group of young men of the former slaveholding aristocracy in a campaign of violence meant to terrorize black people who participated in politics or challenged employers, as well as those whites who dared stand in their way. While the characters, organizations, and events mentioned in this book are fictional, they represent the ideas and actions of actual people. In fact, I trace my family's Alabama roots back to slavery, and thus, this research and writing has always been personal. The intergenerational trauma I and other black people live with—only five generations since enslavement, and one generation away from segregation—continues to haunt no matter how high we climb, no matter how much money we earn, no matter how many degrees we claim. For my ancestors, and because of them, I wrote this novel.

When in 1972 Angela Davis warned that the United States was on the verge of a fascist takeover, some in the media accused her of using inflammatory rhetoric. But, as Davis explained to an audience at California State University, Fullerton, "Fascism grows and develops. It's something like a cancer. It starts attacking one group of people but like a cancer it begins to spread out with a fatal rapidity and eventually like a cancer it destroys everything around it." Davis's observation is as true today as it was then. If we are to prevent fascism and racism from metastasizing throughout the United States and killing our democratic society, we must join Angela Davis and others by calling it out and intervening early.

Fighting white supremacy has been a central feature of being black in America long before the appearance of the hashtag #blacklivesmatter. Black women activists— from Harriet Jacobs and Sojourner Truth, to Ida B. Wells and Rosa Parks—fought openly and defiantly on behalf of black women who were raped, lynched, and beaten and received no state or federal recompense. In the face of evil, they stood strong, they endured, they spoke out and inspired. Like Angela Davis, these women have inspired the writing of this novel.

There's more. As the late PBS news anchor and pioneering black female journalist Gwen Ifill pointed out in 2004, the mainstream media continues to show an obsession with missing white women, which she dubbed, "missing white woman syndrome." Far too long, the media have ignored black women who disappear, despite black families' efforts to pressure politicians, law enforcement officials, and reporters to give their daughters and sisters the attention they deserve. Meanwhile, these families have knocked on doors and plastered "Have you seen me?" posters on telephone poles and brick walls in their crusade to find out what happened to their daughters, sisters, and friends. Be it the Combahee River Collective's campaign to "Take Back the Night" in Boston in the late 1970s, or the Black and Missing Foundation's decade-long campaign to raise awareness about black women who have disappeared, these and other black female-led organizations continue the tradition of self-reliance pioneered by black women in the nineteenth century.

As Toni Morrison declared in her Nobel lecture in December 1993, "The vitality of language lies in its ability to limn the actual, imagined, and possible lives of its speakers, readers, writers. Although its poise is sometimes in displacing experience, it is not a substitute for it. It arcs toward the place where meaning may lie."

Again and again, as I wrote and rewrote this story, Morrison's words provided me with a North Star. Let this novel serve as a tribute to my literary predecessors and contemporaries, as well as the fathers, mothers, sisters, and sons who live everyday with the pain of losing a loved one.

ACKNOWLEDGMENTS

When you work on a novel for fifteen years, you rack up many debts to those who inspired you or helped you along the way. This novel would never have been finished without the unwavering love and support of so many family members, friends, colleagues, and mentors.

My formative creative writing experiences took place under the careful eye of the author-activist-intellectual Michael Thelwell. Mike's lessons on the elements of storytelling and, at times, harsh criticism has made me a stronger writer. John Higginson's lessons about how to research and write about the history of violence are central to the ideas in this novel. John's mentorship and parenting advice continue to inspire me to thrive in all that I do. Thank you.

My other professors in the W. E. B. Du Bois Department of Afro-American Studies at the University of Massachusetts Amherst, some of whom are not even aware I write fiction—Ernie Allen, John Bracey, Manisha Sinha, Jim Smethurst, Bill Strickland, Esther Terry, and Steven Tracy—have taught me how to think and write in sophisticated ways about the intersections between black art, politics, and activism. I'm blessed to have you all as my teachers and mentors. As for Allia, Chris, Cristy, Dan, David, DeRoy, Karla, Lindsey, Mike, Shawn, Stephanie, Stephanie, Tkweme, Trimiko, Zahra, and Zeb, I'm immensely grateful for your support over the last twenty years. Dan, thanks for your keen eye in all things creative and your wise counsel when knuckleheads need to be kept in check.

I have grown as a writer and thinker because of professors and the students in Columbia's creative writing program. To all of you, I owe a deep debt of gratitude. Victor LaValle generously offered me encouragement and immeasurable advice about the publishing industry. His suggestions for how to structure a story have been central to my evolution as a writer. Paul Beatty is one the best teachers I have ever had. Not only did he teach me specific techniques to improve my prose, but he also showed me new ways to read fiction. Sam Lipsyte's suggestions about how to deliver backstory and dense historical content came at the right time and made this novel immensely better.

After a semester of reading William Faulkner alongside Toni Morrison, Gabriel García Márquez, and Édouard Glissant, my professor Erroll McDonald taught me how to glean insights about experimentation from these challenging, if brilliant, authors. Likewise, Erroll's seminar on international literary figures, who some in the US consider "peripheral," enhanced my appreciation for the innovation of non-Western writers. Ira Silverberg's advice about the publishing industry and lessons about writing fearlessly were indispensable as I completed this novel. The other brilliant author-educators at Columbia, specifically Keri Bertino, Nicholas Christopher, Monica Ferrell, Rachel Sherman, Lynn Strong, and Monica Youn, have shaped my ideas about literature and craft in both subtle and substantial ways. Paul LaFarge's lessons on the elements of "horror" had a big influence on how I revised this novel. A big thank-you goes to my "COVID cohort," who spent less than a year at Columbia before the pandemic forced us behind our computers. I am appreciative of all of those who have been supportive and generous in their suggestions about my writing. There are too many of them to name, but I'm especially thankful for the wisdom of Anna, Cam, Cerys, Howard, James, Jinwoo, Kam, Kim,

Liza, Mariam, Marie, Nicole, Raad, Robert, Rona, Sam, Sean, Sofia, Sonia, and Sooji.

I am fortunate to have a former editor as my agent. Thank you, Sarah Bedingfield, for your patience and perseverance over the course of many, many drafts, as well as many long emails. Your suggestions have made this a stronger novel. My publisher, Judith Gurewich, stopped everything when I needed her advice and support. Not only did she read every word of this novel—several times, actually—but she also helped me trust my voice and vision. To Judith, I'm immensely grateful. I am also grateful to have such a brilliant and patient editorial team at Other Press. Thanks to Alexandra Poreda, Yvonne Cárdenas, and Lisa Silverman, who forced me to stand behind all of my decisions to violate the rules of grammar and style. Thank you to Gage Desser, Jessica Greer, and Terrie Akers, who have worked tirelessly to ensure my book finds an audience among those who seek stories about black women heroines like Allie Douglass.

I thank my colleagues in the History Department, Africana Studies, and the Center for Gender, Race, and Area Studies at Clark University for inspiring me to be the scholar-teacher I am. Stephen Levin deserves special mention for teaching me so much about postcolonial literature and for his well-timed, enthusiastic support of this project. Thank you to all my students, especially Ahiela, Belianish, Cesca,

Cheyenne, Chineme, Demetry, Florcy, Kadijha, Kam, Karleen, Lamarre, Linda, Michelle, Nia, and Savia, who have inspired me. Thank you to my Clemente students as well as my colleagues Barbara, Dan, Gina, Guy, Jim, Liz, and Ruth.

I owe a huge debt of gratitude to Geoff Sanborn for his encouragement throughout many versions and drafts of this novel. Geoff, you have been a steadfast friend, especially whenever I worried that this novel would never be published. Trent Masiki, my friend and colleague, a fiction writer and academic himself, was one of the first people to read portions of this novel and offer crucial insights. Thanks, Trent, for your friendship and support. And thank you for introducing me to the brilliant scholar Nadine Knight. Nadine, I'm so thankful for your encouragement when this novel was in its infancy. Raphael Rogers, from Amherst to Clark, thanks for always believing in me and being an early reader of this novel. Raphael (*aka* Whatif), I'm constantly appreciative of your eyes, your ideas, and your suggestions. Brandyn, thank you for always supporting me and my ideas. To my FAF family, Akara, Anna, Craig, Dan, Holly, Jonathan, Kshinte, Leah, Mark, Megan, Pat, Shay, Sumie, Terna, Tom, Yemi, and hundreds of others, thank you!

Much thanks to my dear friend Sarah Towers, who is the only person who has read *all* of my work! Your support, since I dropped off a crate of manuscripts in your kitchen six years ago, has meant more to me than you might realize. Thank you also for introducing me to your brilliant mother, Pat, who in one evening taught me more about publishing than I ever even thought to ask. Pat, thanks for your advice and always being eager to talk shop.

This novel is immensely better because of the wisdom and comradery of two brilliant writer-activists, Ernie Brill and the late Dan Georgakas. Once a month for four years, we'd come together at Dan's kitchen table and spend hours reading, discussing, and arguing each other's poetry and prose. Thank you, Ernie, for setting me straight and your unwavering support for my fiction, and Dan for pushing me to stay true to my vision.

To Samuel, Nick, Dan, Kyle, and others who I first told the story of Matthew Strong around a campfire in Samuel's backyard, and who continue to ask when this novel will be out, thank you. Peace and immeasurable gratitude go to Jake Grinsted, who housed me in New York every week for a year and offered valuable suggestions on an early draft. Thank you, Rosaly German, for always offering me insights about art and life that inspire. My Y-town friends, Adam, Andy, Chris, Hank, Hap, John, Lisa, Matty, Mike, Rocco, Roy, Stephanie, and TL deserve mention. Though Jimmy passed away before ever having a chance to read this, I'm forever in his debt for offering me an ear whenever I needed someone to run my ideas by. And to my Northampton friends—too numerous to name—I'm so thankful I live in a community with so many passionate social justice educators. Chief among them is my comrade in arms in the fight against white supremacy and ignorance, Michael Lawrence-Riddell of Self-Evident Education. Thanks for listening and continuing to inspire me. Liz and Liz, thank you for your consistent support for over twenty-five years! Much respect goes to my colleagues at the David Ruggles Center in Florence, Massachusetts, for their continual efforts to teach our community about the incredible legacy of David Ruggles, Sojourner Truth, and the other black and white abolitionists who established a utopian community more than a hundred and fifty years ago. Thank you to Chris, Emikan, Kim, Sarah, Stephanie, Steve, Suzanne, Tara, Tom, and Tris. And I owe much love and appreciation to Linda. Your advocacy and activism continue to inspire me.

Special thanks to my "reading group" (rather than "book club"): Chris, Dan, Jan, and Tom. Each time we discuss a book, I feel like I'm in graduate school again. Thank you for your trenchant, at times ribald and raw, critiques of a dozen or so novels over the past three years. Many thanks to Hun Ohm, my fierce fiction-writing attorney friend! Much appreciation and respect are owed to intellectual heavyweight professors Ruth Smith, Tamsin Jones, and Sara Lennox, who generously offered scholarly advice and encouraged me to stretch conventional boundaries of philosophical and religious thought.

My greatest debt, of course, is to my family, who remain my chief inspiration and who keep me grounded throughout all my creative and scholarly adventures. You have sacrificed everything in order for me to make real all of my dreams. I thank my Grandfather Greene for his organic intellectualism and wise counsel, which continues to inspire me. A titanic thank you to my mother, Gwendolyn Greene, who is always willing to drop everything to sit at her kitchen table and read my work. Your faith in people, despite their faults, inspires all of us. Melissa, despite my inability to slow down, you continue to support me in every possible way. I love you. Phil and Diana, thank you for your constant love and support. Jodi, thanks for continuing to encourage my artistic side. Thank you, Steve, for your eternal optimism and fierce criticism of selfish people. Thank you to my children, Kyla, Coletrane, and Imanni, for listening to my ideas and putting on your headphones whenever my stories began to bore you. Speaking of ideas, thank you to my niece Naomi for your artistic and literary companionship. We will make the Black Minds Matter Tour work! As for my nephew Savaughn, thank you for your encouragement when uncertainty got the best of me. Nicole, thank you for your humor and positivity. Amare, your smile. I'm so appreciative of my brilliant/creative/grounded sister-in-law Charlotte, for supporting this and all my projects.

I owe my brother, Maurice (*aka* M. Sayyid), special recognition for showing me how to be vulnerable and constantly reminding me to focus on the process rather than the outcome. Much love to my nephews Max and Bazile. Much love to Aunt Tam and Aunt Fatima, Uncle Jesse, Uncle Frank and Aunt Carole, and Aunt Elaine. Much love to my cousins Al, Aswad, Chelsie, Daisy, Dawn, JT, Nahlia, Raish, Rydell, and Shara. Finally, to my father, William T. Greene Jr., who passed away in 2017, and taught me by example the crucial dictate, "writers write," I love you. Dad, your spirit lives on in all that I do.

While this journey has forced me to reckon with my past, I have drawn inspiration from novelists and poets who have trekked similar trails. Chief among them were Chinua Achebe, James Baldwin, Toni Cade Bambara, Melba Boyd, David Bradley, Gwendolyn Brooks, Assia Djebar, Gayle Jones, June Jordan, Alex La Guma, Audre Lorde, Toni Morrison, Sonia Sanchez, Ngũgĩ wa Thiong'o, Alice Walker, John Edgar Wideman, Shirley Anne Williams, and Richard Wright. As well as my contemporaries Chimamanda Ngozi Adichie, Paul Beatty, Edwidge Danticat, Esi Edugyan, Ravi Howard, Mat Johnson, Tayari Jones, Victor LaValle, Danzy Senna, Jesmyn Ward, Colson Whitehead, and others. All of them have left me a literary road map of sorts for engaging history and memory with a love of language and life, and with the courage to write honestly about heroes as well as villains, the beautiful and the ugly, the comic and the tragic, and the fearful and the fearless.

I dedicate this novel to my grandmothers, two Southern women who made many sacrifices to ensure my brother and I could pursue our creative dreams. My deepest gratitude to my Grandmother Allen, who inspired me as a kid by completing her high school degree in her sixties, and my Grandmother Greene, for never backing down from a fight.

Ousmane K. Power-Greene is the Program Director of Africana Studies and an Associate Professor of History at Clark University. He is the author of *Against Wind and Tide: The African American Struggle Against the Colonization Movement*, and his writing appears in *The Harlem Renaissance Revisited: Politics, Arts, and Letters*. He has been featured on *All Things Considered*, C-SPAN Book TV, and NPR's history podcast *Throughline*.